TIGER

WWII COLLECTION

Books by James Rouch

The Zone Series
#1: Hard Target
#2: Blind Fire
#3: Hunter Killer
#4: Sky Strike
#5: Overkill
#6: Plague Bomb
#7: Killing Ground
#8: Civilian Slaughter
#9: Body Count
#10: Death March

World War II Collection
Gateway To Hell
Tiger
The War Machines

TIGER

WWII COLLECTION

James Rouch

SPEAKING VOLUMES, LLC

NAPLES, FLORIDA

2013

TIGER

ISBN 978-1-61232-923-9

CONTENTS

THE PATROL

19.10 TO 20.45 HOURS

Behind the German lines, a few miles to the west of the area of woodland, a battery commander began to worry about his dwindling reserves of ammunition and called an early halt to the barrage.

With a screeching crash, followed by the creak and snap of falling trees and boughs, the last shell plunged down beside the rutted track that snaked through the woods. The lashing rain penetrated the straggling cover of the leafless branches and extinguished the last sparks which flitted, wind-driven, among the splintered stumps.

After a pause, when it was clear there was no more to come, the side door of an AEC armoured command vehicle opened and Sergeant Bill Ellis stepped out into the ankle-deep mixture of rotting leaves and churned soil. The major's black Labrador puppy came hurtling out after him, making a snap at his leg as it sailed past.

The sergeant felt tempted to help it on its way but out of the corner of his eye he saw that the major was still watching. He decided against it.

'Be quick with that door.'

Ellis felt like slamming it, but contented himself with closing it firmly. He hunched himself into his upturned coat collar and plodded off through the mud, not bothering to avoid the water-filled ruts.

The twenty-minute shelling seemed to have done little damage among the mass of soft and armoured transport spaced out along the edge of the track, and in among the trees. In one place an erratic fountain of white tracer showed between the trunks as an ammunition truck burned. Further down the lane a group of signallers were trying frantically with axes and bare hands to break open the buckled rear doors of a blazing radio van. Even as Ellis looked, the vehicle's petrol tank exploded, the pounding and screaming from within it ceased, and the would-be rescuers had to throw themselves in the mud to quench the flames that flared over their sleeves and coat fronts.

He turned off the track, passing the Labrador as it cocked its leg at a bush. This time Ellis was unable to resist the temptation.

7

After a furtive look round, he lashed out at it. His heavy boot connected and the animal was bowled over. It picked itself up and ran howling, tail between its legs, back to the command vehicle. The sergeant dived into the undergrowth before the door opened to let it in.

Corporal Morris and Private Donald 'Dicky' Bird had rigged up a canvas sheet among some saplings and were preparing a brew on the tiny spirit stove Ellis had looted from an abandoned Hitler Youth camp.

As the sergeant crawled in to join them, he disturbed the sagging canvas, sending an icy stream of water down his neck. He shuddered, feeling the warmth his body had absorbed in the truck melting from him and being replaced with the numbing chill he had lived with for a week now.

'Won't this bloody rain ever stop? How long is it since we've seen the sun?' Morris addressed his remark to no one in particular. The absence of an answer didn't bother him. He watched as Ellis held out his hands to gather what warmth he could from the small stove and the oversized kettle perched precariously atop it. Water running off the sergeant's fingers dripped with gentle hisses on to the hot metal.

The water boiled. Dicky took from his pocket a brightly embroidered oven glove and lifted the kettle off, filling each of three mugs before him. He added to them a pinch of the mouldy leaves their tea ration had become and, with the edge of an apostle spoon, shaved into each can some sugar from the lump that the dampness had reduced it to.

Kettle, spoon and oven glove had been funny at first, welcome relief in a seemingly endless, ghastly existence. Now the humour was forgotten, their use was just habit.

Corporal Morris had to grab at the edge of the sheet to stop it falling as two latecomers joined them. 'Careful, you nearly had the whole lot down.'

Sappers Eric Church and Alex Pitt did not look contrite and they caused further havoc as they squeezed in and took off their bulky packs.

'Well, is he coming?' It was Alex Pitt who asked the question.

'Is who coming?' Morris looked up sharply, peering suspiciously at Ellis.

The sergeant didn't answer for a moment. He picked up his mug of tea, savouring the sudden warmth it brought to frozen fingers. He felt all eyes on him, took a sip of the scalding liquid and then, with his head down, mumbled a quick reply. 'The Frenchman, Barras. The major says he's going out with us,' he added, hoping to quell in advance the inevitable objections. It didn't work.

Eric Church said something under his breath. Pitt just shrugged and busied himself with the ritual of tea making. Morris expressed his feelings more openly.

'What do we want that murdering madman along for? We can take care of ourselves. Better without him along to stir up trouble.' The corporal shook out the layer of grouts from the bottom of his mug. 'Why doesn't the major get rid of him, send him back wherever he came from – the nut house or the funny farm?'

Dicky tried to get warm and hide from the world by ducking into his coat. His helmet seemed to rest on the turned-up collar, making him look like a khaki-coloured toadstool. His voice floated out to them. 'I think I'll try hibernating until the war's over.'

Eric displayed a rare flash of humour. 'I thought birds flew south when things got bad.'

The rain continued to lash the woods. A fierce gust of wind drove a spattering into the shelter, stinging faces and putting out the stove.

Alex tried to relight the contraption. 'Do you know what Barras did yesterday? There was a knocked-out Tiger by a bridge a couple of miles from here. No one wanted to shift the bugger because what was left of the crew was still inside. Even the hygiene squads were putting off doing it, and you know what a load of hard cases they are. Anyway, Frenchy cadges a stack of demolition charges, climbs into the bloody thing and spends an hour in there setting them. You could smell it fifty feet away, and he spent a whole hour in there. Then he got out and set the ruddy lot off. The turret went sixty feet in the air and there were chunks of plate flying everywhere, a stick of bombs couldn't have done a better job. Barras just laughed his bloody head off. Oh, I give up with this thing.'

Morris took the matches and had a go at getting the stove to ignite, also without success. 'Where is he now?'

'He's here.' With ill grace Dicky moved over to allow the Frenchman room to sit down.

None of the men offered any word or sign of greeting. Barras expected none, would not have replied anyway. He was used to it, and it didn't bother him. He turned to Ellis. 'The major has told me I am going out with you tonight. He said where, but not why.'

Reluctantly, with as few words as possible, Ellis explained. 'The major wants us to do a vehicle count at a crossroads behind the Jerry front lines.' He looked hard at Barras. 'And that's all, just a straightforward road watch, not start a private war. I do the spotting, Corporal Morris here logs the details and Private Bird has the radio. We take that out just in case we come across an irresistibly juicy target. If we do, we call down artillery fire. Otherwise we maintain silence.'

'And these two?' The Frenchman indicated Alex and Eric.

'They cart along some mines. If we get the chance they'll be planted just before we pull out. With a bit of luck they'll block the road and cause a nice little traffic jam for our fighter-bombers to hit at first light.' He looked up at the leaden sky. 'If they're able to operate. If not, the artillery will plaster the area an hour after we leave. It's all nice and simple and safe.'

Morris pushed his finger into Barras's chest. 'This is our fourth little jaunt in six days. We've not had any bother so far, we'd like it to stay that way. Do you understand?' He emphasized the last word with a hard jab.

Barras slapped the finger away. 'We are fighting a war, do you want me to forget that? We have to kill Germans, however, whenever we can.'

The corporal wasn't prepared to let it drop. 'Well, so far you've caused a few deaths on both sides. Sometimes it's hard to tell which you're on. Do you know?'

Barras lunged forward but Ellis's big hands clamped down on the Frenchman's wrists. 'Pack it in, the pair of you. Morris, you stop stirring. Frenchy, you just better do as you're told. You put us at risk and you might have to start watching for bullets coming from behind as well.'

Reluctantly, with pent-up fury writ large on his dark features, Barras resumed his seat. 'If you do not want me with you, go and tell the major. See what he has to say.'

'I already have. He says you know that bit of country and, as it's a deeper penetration than we've done before, we've got to take you.' The sergeant's tone hardened. 'But you hear this – we may be stuck with you but if you try any of your tricks, like that stunt last week when you opened up on that Storch, then God help you.'

Barras slipped the MP40 machine-pistol from his shoulder and shook it at the sergeant. 'I brought it down, with just one magazine.'

'Oh yes, very clever.' Dicky didn't spare his sarcasm. 'Very clever, firing on a rocket battery's spotter plane. Before that Kraut went down he told his mates where we were. The stonk they put down on us caused more bloody casualties in thirty minutes than combat had done in the previous month. And all because you're trigger-happy.'

'Shut up, will you?' Ellis felt his guts churn as the tension built up inside him. He looked at his watch, then at the sky, and decided to forestall any further argument. 'This lot's not going to ease. It'll be getting dark soon, we might as well make a start. Clear this stuff away and stow it in the Bedford.'

He was sweating despite the cold. The small of his back prickled and itched. As he stretched and tried to reach the spot, his coat pulled tight across him and he felt the hard outline of the flask. With an effort he forced the thought it prompted from his mind. He had problems enough already.

To take his mind off it he drew the French guide to one side, took out his map and, with a grubby finger, stabbed at a point beneath its clouded waterproof cover where two faint black lines met. 'You know this stretch of road?'

Barras nodded. 'I know it. On this side of the junction there is an embankment. At the top of it is good cover. Nice and safe, if all we are to do is hide and watch the Germans go by.'

Ellis ignored the sneer. The Frenchman looked at the map again. 'There may be military police at a crossroad so near the front.'

Alex looked over their shoulders. 'I doubt it. We've seen them patrolling, but they don't like staying in one place for long.'

'Well, if there are some stationed there, then we'll just have to find another location to set up a watch.'

Paul Barras snorted at the sergeant's suggestion. 'We can deal with two or three of their head-hunters. Perhaps we will get a medal from the Germans for doing it. There is no love lost between German soldiers and their field police – their chain dogs, as they call them.'

'No.' Ellis rounded on him. 'Get it through your skull, we're after information, not scalps. If, after we pull out, the little presents we leave behind make a balls-up of their convoy system then that's a bonus. But while we're there we keep our heads down. That junction is at least a mile inside Kraut territory. If we stir up trouble, our chances of getting back are buggered.'

Barras adopted a resigned expression and sighed deeply. He seemed not to notice the hard look the sergeant gave him.

The clouds piled up, ever thicker, ever blacker. The rain, which for a short while had slackened and almost stopped, now fell in sullen drops, cratering the mud and heralding the approach of yet another downpour.

They assembled beneath the partial cover of a gigantic elm. Each man checked his weapons and ammunition. Alex and Eric checked each others. The two men were inseparable. They shared the same bale-out box on the platoon truck, shared their food and, speculation had it, the same women when they went on leave. Most of their time together in the Royal Engineers had been spent on mine laying or clearance and the reason for their survival in such a notoriously dangerous job was well demonstrated by the meticulous checks they carried out on the carefully packed anti-tank mines they carried. There was little conversation among the men. They knew their job and worked quickly and quietly through the well-rehearsed routines.

Ellis tried to scrape some of the cloying load from his boots, only to find it instantly replaced with more when he put a foot back on the ground.

'Right, if you're ready. It should be dark by the time we reach the Jerry outposts. Keep the talking down, watch for my signals. We may have to close right up to avoid getting separated. Try not to trip over the bloke in front. If you walk into a trip-wire don't just stand there wetting yourself, we'll never hear you in this weather, warn the others. There's supposed to be a moon tonight, but I don't think we'll be seeing it. Okay, let's go.'

As they passed in single file between the furthest forward positions, the crews of the big Vickers machine-guns barely acknowledged them. They were too busy baling out their soggy, sandbag-surrounded hollows.

The sergeant led, cradling his sten gun and moving with surprisingly little noise for all his bulk. Immediately behind him, where an eye could be kept on him, was Paul Barras. Next was Morris with the bren, then the two sappers and finally Bird with the radio. The last three were armed with sten guns in addition to their hefty loads.

Several well-trodden paths led away from the track, ample

evidence of the aggressive patrolling that had been carried out continuously since the advance had been halted by the need to let supplies of petrol and ammunition catch up. Ellis struck off to the right on a path that showed only faintly. Grass and weeds that had been trodden down the previous night were almost restored to their previous state. Temporary relief from the rain was afforded by a plantation of mature fir trees, then it was out once more into the full fury of the storm. The leafless branches of the oaks and elms offered little protection.

They were half a mile from their lines when Ellis signalled a stop to rearrange the travelling order. With obvious reluctance he put Barras in front, then himself, then the three men with loads and, bringing up the rear, Morris with the bren. From now on there was the chance of running into enemy patrols and they proceeded with greater caution. Even the Frenchman, laden with knives and grenades and carrying two German pistols besides his captured submachine-gun, moved silently.

A big field, offering no other concealment than a couple of inches of stubble, had to be skirted. It meant taking to a stagnant ditch part of the way. When the gaunt black outline of a ruined church tower showed above the trees, Barras made a sudden change of direction and they plunged into a miniature forest of young evergreens. The water-burdened branches whipped back into their faces, drenching them and stinging their bare flesh with a million tiny needle pricks.

In places where the drainage ditches were blocked by accumulated leaves, they had filled and overflowed, flooding dips and hollows to several feet. Getting round them, the men were spattered in mud and rotting vegetation. Without comment, other than the occasional muted swear word, the file kept moving.

Ellis signalled for the line to close up. What little light there had been was fast disappearing as the unseen sun set. They were forced to take to an overgrown lane when the passage through the flooded woods became impossibly slow. It was narrow, with deep ruts at the sides, ready to catch and twist an unwary ankle. Branches above it hoarded vast quantities of rain, seemingly for the sole purpose of dropping the accumulation on the men as they trudged by underneath. The cascades splashed noisily on to the steel helmets and sodden packs.

They passed a spot where a swathe had been cut through the trees by a crashing aircraft. It had come down on one side of

13

the track, skidded across it, breaking up as it went, and then plunged into the woods on the other side, cutting a dark and gloomy tunnel in the undergrowth. A fragment of wing panel propped against a holly bush bore a fragment of a white-outlined black cross. An engine lay half buried in the ploughed ground.

As he bypassed the obstruction, Ellis felt something brush his face. He jumped to one side as he recognized the broken fingers of a shattered body that was suspended among spike-tipped foliage. The others made a wide detour to avoid the gruesome pennant to the skill of some Allied fighter pilot or flak-gun crew.

Out of habit, without prompting, Corporal Morris took out his notebook and jotted down the plane's location and brief details.

Above the sound of the rain, from somewhere ahead of them, came the throaty growl of an engine. Ellis had to grab the guide's belt to restrain him as the Frenchman tried to spurt ahead.

'I said you take your bloody cue from me. Where the hell do you think you're racing off to?'

He signalled to the others to gather round. The six men crouched beneath a bank of brambles, listening to the noise. Ellis closed his eyes, willing the sound to go away. He reopened them as it continued. He whispered to Barras: 'Go and see what it is. That's all. Just have a look. You start anything and God help you.'

Paul Barras flashed his teeth in a travesty of a smile and crept forward and out of sight, dissolving in the darkness beneath the trees. It was a full ten minutes before he returned, the front of his leather jacket plastered in a light, clay-coloured mud. His smile was real this time.

'Germans, five of them, with a half-track. I could not read the unit signs but I think they are either engineers or pioneers. They are parked by a cottage and are unloading boxes of mines. The woods just forward of here are sown thick with them.'

Morris leant forward. 'Have they got look-outs, or are they all working at it?'

'Only two are working. There are two NCOs in the kitchen and at least one more at an upstairs window with a machine-gun. It is trained on the path.'

'Well that's blown it. Come on everyone, turn round. We're going back.' Private Bird matched his actions to his words.

'Shut up and come back here.' Ellis wished it was that simple.

Barras sensed his hesitation. 'There are only five, at most six of them. Three grenades and it will all be over.' He grinned at

Ellis, enjoying the sergeant's dilemma.

If Barras was enjoying the situation, Ellis was not. He found his mind reeling round the problem with which he had suddenly been confronted. He forced himself to be calm, tried to slow his pounding heart and consider the alternatives, hoping it would seem he was deep in thought. The act was wasted. To the men with him it just seemed like hesitation. 'Find a way round it.'

Barras threw his arms wide in a gesture of exasperation. 'I have told you, the woods are mined. There are trip-wires everywhere and some are connected to bombs set high in the trees. I tell you, there is no way round. Only the track is clear. Why not take them? They are only a few. They are tired and cold and wet, they have been out here all day and want only to get back for a hot meal and a dry bed. It would be so easy.' Barras threw in every argument he could muster. He was putting a strong case, and Ellis into an impossible situation.

The others listened, though they feigned interest elsewhere.

'If we're going on, Sarge, I'd rather tackle the Krauts than try and get through the woods and have me knackers blown off by tree bursts.'

Alex's sentiment was echoed by the others.

Bill Ellis rounded on him. 'I'm running this patrol. We're not here to start a battle, just to slip in, get some information and slip out again.' An inspiration struck him. 'Besides, there may be civilians in that house. We've got orders to avoid civilian casualties.' He said it as though declaring a winning hand.

Barras was ready with a counter to that. 'I had a look in, there are only the Germans. Can you think of any other excuses?'

The sergeant felt like smashing the Frenchman in the face, but he didn't and kept control of his voice as he answered, though he wanted to scream the words. 'I told you just to have a look, not go taking silly arse chances like that. What if one of them had spotted you.'

'Then I would have killed him.'

Ellis felt trapped. If he aborted the patrol he would have to go back with a first-class reason for doing so. The major didn't like NCOs who didn't pull their weight or shirked their duty. He thought it reflected on him. His way with cases he discovered was fast and ruthlessly efficient. The process started with a field court-martial and ended with reduction to the ranks and a long detention sentence. Ellis had no wish to have that happen to him. He realized suddenly that the engine noises had ceased and drew confidence from the hope that the Germans had gone. 'Wait here. I'll go and have a look for myself.'

'Okay if we drop our packs, Sarge?' Alex was slipping the straps from his shoulders as he asked.

'It looks like you already have. Just stay here and keep quiet.'

As he crept away, taking the same route Barras had, Eric and Dicky loosed their loads and slipped them to the ground. Alex took out a bar of chocolate and offered half to his mate.

Through a gap in a thicket Ellis examined the cottage. It was small, probably two up and two down, with a wash house in a single-storey extension on the back. At some time the walls had been whitewashed but now, and in the poor light, they looked a dingy grey. Large patches had flaked off, exposing the rough brickwork. The remains of a paling fence surrounded the garden. In places it sagged, and at one point had been crushed into the earth where the half-track had been driven over it to park in the lee of an end wall.

Two German soldiers were stacking boxes they had dragged from the armoured vehicle. A slight movement at an upstairs window drew Ellis's attention. It had been thrown wide open and the barrel of a light machine-gun rested on the sill. Above and behind it showed the faintly glowing tip of a cigarette. At regular intervals whisps of exhaled smoke would come wafting out to be accelerated up into the night sky.

From his vantage point Ellis stared at the scene, mesmerized into a trance-like state, as his brain refused to come to grips with the situation. He moved slightly to get off an uncomfortable lump on which he lay; as he realized it was the flask he lost the mental battle he had been fighting for a week.

He had been so careful to avoid such situations and had so far been blessed with incredible luck, much more than he'd ever dared hope for. Even now that luck might have held. If Barras hadn't been with them they could have turned back. The major would have accepted whatever story he concocted. It was his policy never to undermine the authority of his NCOs by seeming to check up on them. But Barras altered everything. He had the major's ear and if, by dropping a hint of two, he could put Ellis in it, then he certainly would. So they had to go on, and for the sergeant there was only one way he could do that.

Ellis reached down into his coat pocket and slowly pulled out the flask. He could hardly see it but he was familiar with the feel of its pigskin cover, worn smooth at the sides where it rubbed on the coarse material of his pocket lining. He didn't have to see it to know that its marked and grubby appearance revealed considerable usage in the last couple of years. He hated the sight of the thing but, like some deformity, he had no choice as to whether it was with him or not. It had become almost a part of him. On waking in the morning it was the first thing he looked for, the way that other men look for their watch. He shook it just as often, too. Even when he felt sure he wouldn't need it, it was always there, always full, at first.

His mouth felt dry, his teeth clenched and the skin of cheeks and jaw were suddenly tight. He felt he had the will to throw it away, but it stayed there in his hand. The thought had been no more than a pathetic rearguard action against an enemy who had him beat. A dim, distant corner of his mind was screaming at him, pleading with him, but it went unheard or unheeded. His whole world was a flask, a furred tongue, a distant glowing red dot and an enemy he couldn't fight alone.

The hinged cap was flicked back in token of surrender. Ellis raised the flask and put the cool metal to his lips. Rum burnt into the back of his throat and the world became instantly different, his private world at least. It was wider, bigger, bolder. A second swig and the trance was lifted, tiredness flowed from him and his mind felt sharp and alert. A third gulp and he was warm, content and confident.

He returned to the others. 'Right, we're going to take them. Morris, give me the bren. You take my sten gun. We'll hit them from three sides at once. Keep it brief and avoid a shooting match. Barras, take Bird with you. Get as close to the kitchen as you can. When you hear the bren, break the window with a burst then shove a couple of grenades in. Pitt, Church, work your way round the side of the cottage and get a clear view of the pair by the half-track. Take it easy, there's not a lot of cover for your approach. On the same signal hit them with everything you've got, and make sure first time. We can't hang about while you lay siege to that armoured bus of theirs. Morris, you back them up and keep an eye on the woods, just in case there's any more of them out there and they come running to see what the noise is about.'

Bill Ellis felt good. He was thinking clearly. He wished he could have another quick drink but he didn't want to while the others were around.

17

'What are you going to do, Sarge?' Morris was double-checking the sten Ellis had swapped for his light machine-gun.

'I'll take out the Kraut at the window. That'll be your signal.' He looked at his watch. 'You've got fifteen minutes to get into position. Leave your packs here. We'll pick them up after, if nothing goes wrong.'

'What? On a belt and braces job like this, Sarge? What could go wrong?' Dicky remained unmelted by the look Ellis gave him.

The sergeant waited a minute after the others had left, listening to the faint sounds of their passage through the undergrowth, then he moved forward to the thicket he had lain in before. He poked the tip of the bren's barrel through the screen of thorns and settled down to wait. The German at the upstairs window was still smoking. Ellis squinted down the dull tube of the barrel and sighted on the glowing red dot.

Eric unclipped a fragmentation grenade from his webbing and waited patiently for the signal. The ugly, angular front of the half-track was only twenty yards away from the crumbling wall of the well he was sheltered behind. He watched as the two Germans worked on, methodically stacking and checking off on a list the long wooden packing cases with their stencilled skulls and crossbones.

Alex tapped his friend on the shoulder. 'You better use the sten. If you chuck that, you might set the whole bloody lot off. I don't fancy going with them.' He looked over his shoulder to where Corporal Morris crouched behind a weed-sprouting compost heap several yards to their rear. 'I reckon the rim of the crater would be about where he is.'

'It's all right, I'll pitch it short. The frags won't punch through those crates. Here, did you get a whiff of Ellis when he came back?'

Alex wriggled into a more comfortable position. 'He's all right. So long as he stays on the cautious side he can booze as much as he likes. In the *bocage* most of the armoured-car crews were stoned every time they went out. They managed okay. Anyway, don't worry, you've got me to look after you.'

'That's funny,' Eric whispered back, 'I thought I was looking after you.'

Ellis knew a moment's panic. He had forgotten what time the others had left. Had he said ten minutes, or fifteen? It seemed, ages ago; it must be about time. He squeezed the trigger. The bren kicked back five fast times. There was a shower of red sparks at the window and the machine-gun barrel fell back out of sight into the room.

From the back of the cottage came a burst of automatic fire, blending with the sounds of breaking glass and screams of alarm and fear. A small black object rebounded from the side of the half-track, bounced off a pile of boxes and was lost in the mud. A face, starkly white, turned to look in the direction from which it had come and was dissolved in a welter of blood as a burst from Alex's sten hit it.

An explosion beside the half-track came at the same moment as two inside the building. The second German in the open was scythed down by fragments and thrown against the end wall. He lay slumped against it, looking uncomprehendingly at the shattered ruins of his legs, until a short burst from Morris caused his head to flop forward and rest at an odd angle on his chest.

Slates clattered as they settled back on the roof, echoes boomed through the woods and from inside the cottage came unintelligible shouts. A sten punched out four rapid single shots, blending with a ripping blur of fire from Barras's MP40, and the gabble of German was cut short.

It was over. Silence – after the violence, the stark contrast of complete silence, save for the steady applause of rain clapping leaves. A figure appeared at the back of the cottage and gave a thumbs-up sign.

The kitchen was a shambles. Flour and powdered plaster made the room look full of snow. Every window was shattered, the back door hung by one hinge and what was left of the curtains smouldered gently. The old pine furniture was gouged and splintered; broken crockery littered the floor, scrunching underfoot as the men entered. The dusting of white powder hid the worst details of a body beneath a table in the centre of the room. Another sprawled in a corner, its blood combining with the red wine that trickled from a cracked bottle clasped in the corpse's hand.

Ellis looked at the spilt flour, the crockery, and the steel ploughed but recently scrubbed table and sink tops. 'Where's Barras. He said this place wasn't lived in.'

'He's gone upstairs.' Morris picked up a chair, set it on its

19

legs and sat down. 'You were a bit sharp off the mark, weren't you, Sarge? I'm sure you said fifteen minutes, seemed more like ten to me.'

The sergeant was saved from having to give an answer. Everyone ducked as a grenade detonated overhead, bringing down great chunks of the ceiling and smothering them all in dust.

'What the hell was that?'

No one stopped to answer Bird's question. There was a stampede for the stairs. Morris was the first to reach the landing. Barras stood at the entrance to a room, flapping his hand back and forth in an effort to disperse the smoke that swirled out and obscured the interior.

'I heard a movement in there,' the Frenchman offered by way of explanation as Morris pushed past him.

The corporal had to kick aside part of a door frame that blocked the entrance. Then he stood still for a moment, waiting for the last of the smoke to be sucked out of the open window. It cleared to reveal a dead German sprawled on a tattered bed, his throat and lower jaw smashed.

At a faint noise Morris turned and looked at some material heaped against the bottom of a crushed wardrobe. Something about the arrangement of the stained rags made him look again.

'Oh God, no.' He clamped his hand over his mouth and rushed from the room, barged through the others who crowded the door and tiny landing, and hurled himself down the stairs and out into the garden.

The sounds of his being violently sick rose to the others. Cautiously, Ellis stepped inside and looked. Prepared as he was, the sight wrenched at his stomach. The blood-soaked bundle was all that remained of two elderly women. As he looked, a mutilated hand came out from the heap and clawed the air imploringly.

Alex was behind him . 'What the hell do we do?'

'I don't know. Barras said the place was empty – no civilians, he said. You heard him. Where is he? He did this. Where is the bloody madman?'

Barras entered and stared down at the spectacle. His face was flushed but in no other way did he display any emotion, not even when pitiful whimperings began to come from the two women.

'Don't you care?' Alex grabbed hold of the Frenchman's shoulders and whirled him round to look into his face. 'Don't you care? They're your people.' He searched Barras's expression but found in it no feeling, saw no regret.

'What do we do with them? We can't just leave them here, they might hang on for hours.' Ellis tried to lift one of the women on to the bed but she began to screech a protest and held on tight to the other, so he left them on the floor. His efforts did nothing but increase their distress and reveal the full extent of the savage injuries the grenade had inflicted in the small room.

From his belt, Barras drew out a Walther P38 and proffered it to Ellis. 'There is only one thing you can do. We cannot take them back, we cannot stay here with them. They will die soon anyway.'

Ellis pushed the pistol back at him. 'You commit your own war crimes. Don't involve me. I don't even want to watch.' He went out of the room and his boots could be heard clattering down the stairs and into the kitchen.

Paul Barras offered the pistol to Alex Pitt. Alex glanced a last time at the dying pair, fought down an urge to retch, then followed the sergeant.

Barras found he was perspiring. He sat on the edge of the bed and watched the old women on the floor. A single, lidless eye peered back at him, unseeing. He stretched out a hand as though to touch a withered buttock, exposed and blood-flecked where a garment had been ripped open by the blast, but he stopped short and instead raised the pistol and, with the tip of the barrel only inches from the nearest body, fired twice.

There was no transition from life to death. One moment the form was gently writhing, the next it was still; life fled so easily from it. He had to stand to get a clear shot at the other woman. Save for the slow rise and fall of a flabby-breasted chest there was no sign of life and the state she had been reduced to by the explosion suggested that even that would not long continue. A single shot rang out as, with great deliberation, Barras fired at and hit the matted mass of blood and hair that was the woman's temple. The shallow breathing stopped, a single large pink bubble rose from the black hole where the mouth had been and it was all over.

The executioner turned away from the bodies, already stripping the magazine from the pistol and pushing in three fresh rounds that he took from his pocket. He stopped suddenly on seeing

Eric standing in the doorway. For a fleeting fraction of time his face registered surprise and fear, then he was under control again.

Eric barred his path, standing in the narrow doorway. 'You enjoyed doing that, didn't you? Have you killed many women?'

There was a momentary spark of animation in the Frenchman's eyes, then the lids drooped to hood them once more. Without answering he pushed past and went down to the kitchen.

Eric crossed to the bed and with the toe of his boot shoved the German off and stripped one of the blankets from it. Then he draped it over the women and went down to join the others.

Sergeant Ellis was slumped in a chair, heedless of the body on the floor only inches from his leg. The first flush of well-being and confidence induced by the rum had gone. Now he was left only with the nightmare he was living.

'Don't you think we'd better be moving, Sarge?' Morris stood looking out of the back door towards the woods. 'In case any Kraut patrols heard the racket and come nosing around.'

'Okay. Have Bird and Barras go back for the packs. Is there anything on the half-track we can make use of?'

Morris shook his head. 'Nothing much. We could use some of it to booby-trap these bodies, but that's about all.'

It took an effort but Ellis managed to clear some of the fog from his brain. He wished he could find a quiet corner to have another drink. 'We can't spare the time. It'd take too long. We can use that stuff to cover our tracks, though. Pitt, can you rig up something that will go off a minute or two after we pull out?'

'I suppose so, but it won't be anything clever.'

'Doesn't have to be, just so long as it works. I want it to cover our tracks. If the Krauts come along before morning and find this lot they might just get the idea of hanging around and catching us on the way home. If the whole lot goes up, with a bit of luck any one poking about will just think this bunch got careless and had a nasty accident.'

'Some hopes.' Alex went out to do the job.

'Well, if you can think of something better,' Ellis called out after him, 'then let me bloody know, otherwise keep your trap shut.'

In the same marching order as before, they left the cottage, striking away from the track as soon as they were through the belt of mines. Behind them shone the ghostly flicker of a growing

22

fire as the crude incendiaries they had left in the half-track ignited. Even as they put more trees between themselves and the cottage the light rapidly grew, making the beads of water suspended from the branches flash rainbow colours. When they had gone a quarter of a mile the light flared from the white glare of phosphorus to the orange glow of burning petrol. Seconds afterwards, the vehicle's cargo detonated.

The tree tops bowed beneath the surge of air created by the blast. For a while it rained pine needles and cones, and for several more minutes the low cloud bases reflected the light of a fierce fire, then gradually it diminished until the only evidence of the destruction they had wrought was the distant sound of an occasional small-arms round going off in the house. When even that ceased, the sight and sound, but not the memory, of the cottage was gone.

Ellis tried to shut from his mind the image of the attic bedroom, with its cheap furniture and soiled sheets, but it wouldn't leave him. It prompted, unbidden, thoughts of another attic. They crowded upon him and he longed to reach for the flask and drown them.

SERGEANT ELLIS

THE UNEQUAL BATTLE

The couple turned the corner and the uniform-crowded bustle of Shaftesbury Avenue was lost from sight. The woman staggered occasionally under the weight of her companion whose arm was over her shoulder. The big sergeant wasn't drunk, but his step was uneven and walking straight required concentration.

They turned another corner into Old Compton Street. The buildings were drab and ugly, the rows gapped with bomb sites. Despite the blackout, Piccadilly and Leicester Square maintained much of their peace-time atmosphere. Here, only yards away, it was like another world. Apart from one or two small groups of young sailors trying hard to look sober and uninterested, the street was near empty.

A few girls, women – it was difficult to determine beneath thick make-up in the poor light – loitered in doorways. They were the ones too ugly, old or expensive to have found clients yet. They would start to do business when the pubs closed.

The buildings either side of the heaps of rubble were braced with carelessly positioned beams, their footings lost in the deep shadows of the cordoned-off areas. From some bomb sites came the grunt and rustle of hasty transactions, as couples risked the unsafe ruins for the sake of speed or cheapness. Darkness hid the details but now and again would come the rattle of a small fall of debris and a muttered curse, as someone's concentration was disturbed.

'Steady, Bill.' The woman used the sergeant's name with the familiarity of a lifetime companion, rather than the casual aquaintanceship of ten minutes that was actually the case. The sudden loss of balance had nearly propelled them both into the road.

They stopped before a door. The woman pushed it open and led him into the unlit building. As his free hand brushed the wall, the sergeant felt the peeling streamers of damp wallpaper. The smell of mould was strong and glass scrunched beneath their feet. He staggered as he was led to a flight of uncarpeted stairs, nearly slipping on the third unseen step when a bottle rolled out from under his foot. The couple paused at a landing while the woman shook from her shoe the pages of the newspaper caught in the buckle. From behind a door came a harsh, forced, female laugh, sounding very artificial. Another flight of rickety stairs, then the woman was fumbling in the handbag she clutched. At the third attempt the much worn lock gave up resistance and let them in.

The short walk from the bar had started to clear the sergeant's head, but it would be a while longer before recovery was complete. He closed the door and leant against it, blearily trying to take in the small attic room that clearly served as kitchen, sitting-room and bedroom, as well as place of work.

The woman put her purse in a drawer and turned to look at him, very slowly unbuttoning her ill-cut jacket as she did. 'You're a quiet one, aren't you? I've never met a quiet sergeant before.' She hung her jacket on the back of a chair, sat on the rumpled double bed that dominated one side of the room and patted the covers beside her, in invitation. 'I hope you don't think I'm trying to rush you, dear, but I'm ready if you are.'

Sergeant Bill Ellis turned and looked at her for the first time. It certainly seemed like the first time. Until that moment she had barely registered in his mind. He had wanted to pick up a woman, she had been looking for a customer. Short of some outrageous deformity neither had been particularly bothered what the other looked like. Now Ellis had a good look at what he was buying.

Her age wasn't easy to determine, about thirty perhaps, maybe a bit more. He had always been hopeless about women's ages. He was rather glad she wasn't too young. He hadn't wanted a young one tonight. It was nice to have one sometimes, but this was the last night of his leave and, for some reason that he didn't understand himself, he knew he needed more than the surly rudeness of the young ones who so often mistook it for maturity, and for which their bodies so barely compensated.

Yes, about thirty, he thought. Her body was well rounded, tending even to plumpness. The white breasts that bulged at him over the top of the low cut blouse bounced with her every movement, appearing to live a life of their own. She was shorter than him, about five foot four, he guessed. He smiled inwardly. What did height matter when you were lying down? Her legs were rather on the full side, tending to confirm the impression her body had created, but she was well proportioned. The overall effect was very female. Ellis reckoned that, all things considered, he had been lucky in getting just about what he had wanted.

'Finished looking, love?' the woman stared at him in return.

'Are we going to do anything, or are you the sort who just likes to watch?'

'How much do you make a night?'

The question surprised the woman. Her mind flicked to the soiled bundle of notes beneath the floorboard the sergeant was almost standing on. Her mind raced. She had always counted herself as lucky that she had never, as yet, run into any of the bad trouble some of the other girls had. She had never been robbed or badly hurt. She had even managed to talk her way out of a nasty situation a month before when a little runt of an American had made threats as to what would happen to her if she didn't go to work for him. Now, suddenly, she wondered if she might have to tell this big sergeant a lie about having the pox. Hoping this was not about to be a break in her career long-run of luck, the woman tried to sound casual. After all, some of them did ask funny questions. Perhaps this one was harmless.

'Three, sometimes four pounds a night. Why?'

Bill Ellis put his hand in his pocket. For a moment the woman thought he was going to get out a knife. He didn't. Instead he brought out a thin wad of bank notes that matched her own for their filthy condition. He took a folded fiver from the roll and pushed three crumpled ten shilling notes back into his pocket. He shoved the large white note at the woman.

'Here's five pounds. My train goes at six in the morning. I want to stay here till then.'

She got up and took the money, opened the drawer and crushed it into her purse. 'I'm all yours. Did you want something special? I'm good with me hands.'

Ellis shook his head. 'I'll let you know if I think of something.' He stood in front of her and cupped his hands beneath her breasts, testing the weighty warmth of them.

The woman started to undress him, pushing him to the bed and making him sit down so she could pull off his boots and trousers. 'You're a funny one. Most of them have me on my back by now.'

For the first time Ellis showed a spark of animation. 'I don't want to hear about the others.' His voice was loud and hard. 'Sorry, I didn't mean to shout.'

The feeling with which he had spoken was not lost on her. She avoided his eyes and tugged at his remaining boot. It came off and she reached for the fastening of his trousers.

'That's all right. You won't disturb the neighbours here. It's

26

just that some of the blokes – well, most of them – like me to talk about it, so long as I tell them they've got the biggest cock.'

The trousers came undone and she pulled them down. He caught her hand as it went to the waist band of his underpants.

'Have you got a drink?'

Without saying anything she got up and went to a small wall cupboard, part hidden behind the curtain that partitioned the room from the tiny alcove that served as a kitchen area. Ellis watched without emotion the expanse of thigh that was revealed as she reached up to take a bottle from the top shelf. He looked down at himself. Even before he did, he knew there was no reaction from his body.

Bill Ellis hated himself. It seemed he always had to have a drink before he could stir his mind or his body to any sort of action – even this, that should have been so easy. It hadn't always been this way. He could remember managing all right before he had started drinking. Now, though, he had it in his mind that he couldn't do without it. There had to be that one surrender to the bottle, that first drink that became two, then three.

The woman came back to the bed. She carried a quarter-full bottle of whisky and two tumblers, one of which a moment earlier had been holding a toothbrush. He watched it poured and took the offered glass. Mechanically he lifted it, wishing desperately that he could find the will, the courage, to hurl it away, but he knew he was going to drink it. He always did. It had been that way the day he was wounded.

*   *   *

An occasional incoming shell would cause the waiting infantry to duck and shelter against the comforting bulk of the armoured half-tracks beside which they stood. The engines had warmed up now, and in the early-morning chill the flood of warm grey exhaust fumes was a comfort as it gusted about their legs. Two troops of Cromwell tanks clanked and squealed their way past to take position at the head of the column. For the third time the regimental sergeant-major stalked past Ellis and his section. The captain had given him a hard look as well and the sergeant had the distinct impression he was being watched.

Experience, though, had made Sergeant Ellis careful. A half hour before the others had risen he had sneaked down to the vehicle park, selected a half-track and concealed a flask on it. When the time came, it had been surprisingly easy to make sure he got his section to the right carrier. As they waited for the order to board he could actually smile at the thought of the pint of rum that nestled in the ammunition locker on the other side of the steel plate against which he leant.

Everyone dived for cover as a shell closer than the rest plunged into the hedgerow towards the rear of the file. A call went up for stretcher-bearers. Ellis found himself thinking not about the man or men who had just been struck down, perhaps killed, not even about the dangers that the day might bring. He found he was trying to work out how long it would be before they climbed into their transport. Would the shell-fire bring the moment nearer? Visions of the flask, thoughts of its contents, filled his mental horizon.

When the order came, Ellis got his men aboard so fast that the RSM watched with deep suspicion, but he said nothing. Let them think what they like, was the thought that passed through Ellis's mind. He felt almost gleeful, anticipating the taste of the contents of the flask in the locker beneath his feet. A momentary fear flashed through his thoughts: what if someone had discovered the flask and taken it, or what if he's picked the wrong half-track? He dived down to rummage among the grenades and boxes of cartridges and his fingers closed around the familiar shape. The temptation was too great. He took a swig. His eyes watered, as the burning liquid bit into the back of his throat.

* * *

The generous measure the woman had poured was downed in almost frantic haste. Ellis instantly felt some great weight had been lifted from him. His back straightened, his vision seemed to clear and his brain appeared vigorously alert. He felt the warmth of the woman beside him and his body began to stir. Then her hand was seeking something among the white folds in his lap. The questing fingers fastened on his rapidly hardening core.

'I shan't have to tell you any fibs, shall I?' She gave his rock hard body a fierce squeeze. 'I thought at first you must have something to hide. If it keeps on growing like that you won't be able to hide it, will you? Would you like to undress me?' She was smiling at him, not the artificial smile you usually got from such women when they were trying to attract you, which then disappeared rarely to return until the moment the money was handed over. No, it was a genuine smile. 'You're going to ask me if I like doing this, aren't you?'

'No.'

She looked surprised. 'Everyone else does.'

'Are you sure it's not you who likes talking about it?'

She hastily changed the subject. 'Are you stationed in England, or are you just on leave?'

'I'm off to France in the morning.'

She had been easing his pants down as he spoke and had seen the long crevasse of the scar that ran from mid-thigh to waist. 'Is that why you came home?'

'Home? It's the reason I came back to England. Home was Coventry.'

They sat on the bed looking at each other, he hoping she would say nothing, she wondering if she should say anything. Despite the number of times she had been in this situation, she still didn't know what was the best thing to do. She wondered with professional detachment what was coming next. Often in the past it had been a long, rambling and embarrassed account of the loss suffered, sometimes with photos being shown, and she had feigned interest and sympathy. And all the time she would be preparing herself for the stumbling request that would force her to submerge her own identity and for a while take on that of another. She had played the part of a hundred different wives and lovers for as many different men. The part was never difficult, calling for nothing more than a response to a name that wasn't her own, and perhaps in the dark to perform some part of the love act in a special way. Passion would soon take over from pretence, though, and then she became just a human machine, helping sad and lonely men forget for a while. The climax of the act was always followed by a hurried departure, and usually 'something extra' was left on the table.

A second drink was poured and drunk in silence and then, as her companion still took no initiative, she started to undress. She pulled back her skirt to unfasten her stockings and, as she began to unbutton her blouse, the sergeant stood up and allowed his pants to fall to the floor. He stepped out of them and kicked them away. He just stood there then, looking down at her. He held out his hands, took hers and pulled her gently but firmly to her feet. He undid the last button and pushed her blouse back. As she shook it free and let it drop he slipped the straps of her underwear from her shoulders and pushed the light material to her waist.

The woman tried to tighten her arms to her side, to support and hide the perceptible sag of her heavy breasts. But he didn't look at her body, just pulled her into his arms and held her close. She found herself responding. They stood in the centre of the room, locked together, not speaking, not moving, both by the human contact alone fulfilling a need they had neither of them realized they had.

Ellis buried his face in the woman's hair. She smelt feminine and soft, warm and yielding. He clung tighter to her, willing the moment to last. She made no protest but he sensed he was hurting her and slackened his grip. They sat on the bed again and for the first time he kissed her. It was not the kiss of a whore and a stranger. It was the kiss of two people who had been alone and had found something they needed.

*   *   *

The column started up, some twenty vehicles. The Cromwells led, ripping the surface of the French country road to shreds. Behind them the pounding half-tracks flattened it again.

Sergeant Ellis stood in the machine-gun turret, aft of the co-driver. The rum had warmed him and now kept out the creeping damp cold of the Normandy dawn. They moved fast, within minutes passing the furthest forward anti-tank gun pits and machine-gun nests. The rapid pace was forcing Ellis to hang on tight to the bren to keep his balance. He felt, well, almost contented. He wondered whether he should risk ducking down to take another swig and decided to chance it. When he came up again RSM Hyde was watching from the vehicle in front. Somehow Ellis didn't care any more.

There was a pause while one of the Cromwells and two of the half-tracks were detached to deal with a persistently bothersome artillery observation post that the Germans had set up in a copse on top of a knoll. A short, one-sided engagement quickly over, the column reformed and was off again.

The familiar feel of the bren and the steady growl of the GMC engine combined to give Ellis a feeling of security. He knew where he stood with such things. They were his link with reality. As the rum sought to filch his mind and his reason from him he needed something to anchor his understanding on. His knuckles whitened as he gripped the armour tighter and tighter. He ran his hands over the bren. It was a thing he understood. It was uncomplicated. It made no demands of him. He slackened his hold but didn't let go as the file of armour-plated machines raced towards the climax of their existence.

*   *   *

30

Pulling herself gently free of his arms, the woman hastily removed the last of her clothes and went to put out the light.

'No, leave it for a moment.'

His words stopped her, even as she reached for the switch. She went back to the bed and slid in beneath the cover that Ellis had pulled over himself, one full breast nearly touching his face as she did.

He briefly glimpsed the wrinkles of fat that formed and bulged about her waist as she swung her legs up and in, then everything else was forgotten as they once more locked together. He made no move to commence intercourse. He always felt that was a final act. No matter if they coupled a second or third time, beyond the first climax was only anti-climax. So they lay full length against each other, kissing, touching, exploring.

'Could you do it soon, this is getting me going.' She grasped his organ and tried to pull it into her.

'Perhaps you should be paying me.'

The words hurt her, lightly as they were meant. For a moment she had managed to forget that he was still the customer; for a while there had been no need to put on a show. She had been enjoying real, not simulated emotions.

Ellis saw the look that came into her eyes, and knew he had said too much. He sensed, too, that their being together was not the usual sort of thing, not the sordid act such unions were as a matter of course. By some incredible chance their needs were for the same tenderness and care. It was no lasting thing: afterwards, their lives would revert to what they had been, but now, just for a short, precious while, they had something special and his clumsy words could have ripped the moment from them.

'I talk too much, got to learn to keep my big gob shut.' He leaned over the side of the bed, took up the bottle and drank from it.

'Do you really need that stuff?'

He shrugged. 'It makes me more lovable and improves the performance.'

The answer was hollow. He didn't like to probe deeper in case he found the real reason. He couldn't use Betty and the kids as an excuse. The drinking had started long before that. Then, with sudden, startling clarity, he realized how long ago it was he had began to lose the long drawn out battle against his own weakness. But he couldn't accept that. It had to be more than just weakness. All right, it wasn't the death of his family, but it had

31

to be something. The war? Well, if it was, not in the way that he could put a name to it.

He pulled the woman on top of him to try and swamp his mind with other, more immediate things. For a while they lay still, then the cover began to move rhythmically and their eyes closed in concentration. The straining bodies glistened with sweat that made transparent the thin sheet over them.

In a scruffy little room, lost in the seedy back streets of London's theatreland, two bodies lay woven together, intent to the exclusion of all else on the action they shared and fought to keep up. Outside, the world went on. In that room under the harsh glare of the unshaded bulb, two human beings struggled to forget everything save the physical needs of their bodies.

* * *

The thunder of the engines and the tracks drowned out the noise that would have told Ellis the exact moment they came under attack. As it was, the first indication he had that they had run into trouble was when the lead tank stopped and its crew did a fast bale out with flames chasing them from the hatches. Immediately the other Cromwells opened a furious fire on a thick hedgerow six hundred yards away, across ploughed fields bristling with the green sprouts of young barley.

Explosive and armour-piercing shells tore into the dark green foliage. The burning remnants of leaves and branches were crushed into the scorched soil as the towering bulk of a Tiger tank lumbered into view. It made no attempt at concealment, coming right out into the open and advancing fifty yards before stopping and firing twice. It repeated the process three times, with every shot finding a mark among the close-packed British column. With cool deliberation it put an end to any hope of escape for the trapped vehicles by destroying a half-track at the rear of the file. The wreck blazed fiercely, the fire spreading to the hedges flanking the road.

Another Cromwell disintegrated under the impact of a direct hit. Chunks of steel rained down, a jagged section of gun-barrel lanced down past Ellis and killed the co-driver just in front of him. At that their driver panicked, trying to skid the half-track off the road in the hope of escaping across the fields.

The big front wheels thudded into the steep-sided waist-high bank. The tracks smoked as they threshed at the surface of the lane, seeking to propel the ten tons of steel up and away to safety. Cursing as the vehicle failed to lift, the driver raced through the gearbox. The only effect was to dig the winch on the front deeper into the earth wall. In places the tracks wore through to their steel reinforcing cable which squealed and screamed as it whipped at the rubber-smeared road.

In the back the section of men were hurled about, given no chance to bale out as frantic attempt followed each short, mad charge in the little width of the lane there was. Then, without warning, the front wheels rose up as a section of the bank collapsed beneath the unrelenting assault. The gunner of the Tiger chose that moment to turn his attention to them.

Over-reacting to the sudden surge forward, Ellis's driver applied the brakes, leaving the front wheels canted high in the air and the vehicle a sitting target. An eighty-eight millimetre shell clipped the top of the rear superstructure and ripped a path through the tangle of struggling men on the floor, went on through the metal of the floor itself and detonated the fuel tank. Ellis felt the scorching heat on his back as he tumbled over the side.

He landed in the hedge, already beginning to burn about him. Blazing figures crawled and squirmed to get clear. Half the column was already destroyed, two of the Cromwells had succeeded in climbing out of the sunken road and were trying to work their way unnoticed to a position where they could get in a shot at the massive panzer's thinner side armour.

The Tiger went on ignoring the torrent of shot and shell that bounced in cascades of sparks from its thick frontal plates. At times it was hidden by the smoke and dust and flying fragments of rounds that shattered against it. While its main gun dealt out savage destruction to the opposing armour, its bow machine-gun chopped down the crews and infantry who escaped the burning vehicles.

Ellis still had the flask in his hand. As he crouched in the shelter of the bank beneath the shattered stump of an elm, he drank deeply from it without thinking. He looked about him. The scene was horrific. Burned and hideously wounded men lay scattered in heaps and ones and twos among the wrecked transport for a hundred yards in either direction. Some screamed, some tried to staunch with bare hands alone the gush of blood from severed limbs, others with folded arms tried to contain the intestines that pulsed in a tide from gashed bellies. Many more lay still.

A gust of wind and Ellis had to slap at his sleeves as wind-driven sparks set them smouldering.

T.–B   33

A group of infantry began to work their way towards the Tiger, carrying Piat bomb launchers. Machine-gun fire swept through their ranks, cutting down several men. One did loose a shot but was hit as he fired. The special tank-killing hollow charge bomb flew wild, to expend its lethal force against a distant oak. The Tiger turned its full attention on them and none moved after a cannister shell exploded overhead.

Twin plumes of exhaust announced another move forward. When it halted, it was to deal with two British tanks trying to move in behind it. Four seventy-five millimetre rounds shattered on the Tiger's turret and side armour before it could swing the long tube of its cannon to bear.

One of the Cromwells dissolved inside a boiling cloud of smoke and flame as a hit set off its ammunition racks. Lumps of raw meat were hurled from its centre to festoon the trees and land with squelching thumps amid the fresh green shoots in the fields. The second of the British tanks lurched down on one side as several of its road wheels were ripped off by a shot that sent lengths of track and tool boxes flailing across the meadow. Two more shots in swift succession set it alight and it burned with its crew still inside.

For Ellis the scene through his rapidly growing alcoholic daze took on all the dimensions of a nightmare. He watched as the Tiger singled out and destroyed the few half-tracks that remained intact. Even individual men were picked out and mown down by the panzer's bow machine-gun. It moved again and was now barely a hundred yards from where the sergeant cowered in the lee of the bank. When he risked a look, Ellis could see every detail of the tank's construction.

A handful of infantry, in a futile attempt at retaliation, opened up with small arms fire and a mortar. Though they presented no danger to the big German tank, still it sought them out and shredded them with cannister shot.

Ellis fought to get a grip on his growing anger and frustration as he witnessed the butchery that continued. In some measure he succeeded. He cast about for something with which he might harm the panzer, but he knew there was little chance of his killing it. Twenty yards off he saw the overturned half-track of his company's heavy weapons section. The men were tumbled in a heap among their smashed weapons and equipment.

Slithering across the road on his belly, Ellis could not avoid the spilled guts of several dead who barred his path. The sight

34

and smell of the mangled bodies in the carrier was nearly over-powering. He had to keep one hand clamped over his mouth and nose as he tugged at the firing trough of a Piat protruding from the messy heap. He said a silent prayer as he yanked at it. A body flopped off the pile and the Piat came free. It was undamaged. He said a quiet 'thank you', before extracting two rounds from a broken ammunition case.

Now he had a weapon. In the befuddled, angry brain of Sergeant Bill Ellis there was only one thought. He risked running back to the bank. Bullets chewed the road behind him, but he made it. He spared a moment to nurse a torn shin, caught by the ill-finished end of the unwieldy bomb thrower. Cleaning off the worst of the clinging filth that adhered to the sights and trigger guard he had to close his mind to thoughts of what those grisly scraps had been a part of.

With relief he saw that it was already prepared to fire. There was no way he could have survived long enough, standing up, to cock the powerful spring. Nor was he sure he would have had the strength to do it. He picked up a round and slotted it on to the spigot. Then, crouching behind the bank, he rested the end of the heavy tube on the top of it and prepared to fire.

The metal was cool against his cheek as he sighted on the target, but the rum was still at work on his body and he felt as if he were swaying. The movement seemed to be getting more exaggerated. Something told him it wasn't real but the delusion persisted. There rose the thought that he needed a drink, just one little one to help him think straight. All that was going on about him merged into a dim background, became unreal as he floated in a trance-like state. He was sweating and his clothes were soaked. He was trying so hard to do a good job but, God, how he needed that drink.

Before him was the slab side of the Tiger, disappearing from his field of vision either side of the sight through which he poured all the concentration he could muster. For him, that was all that there was in the world. There was a reason for what he was doing. He was proving something. Something . . . but he couldn't recall what. The thought was only half formed on the verge of his understanding. He could not bring it fully into focus, any more than he could his vision. But there was the Tiger. If the other thing wouldn't come, there was still the Tiger that grew in his mind to dominate everything.

* * *

35

The bed creaked its protests as the couple bounced. The woman moaned and clasped at the man for a long instant as her body reacted to the climax she had achieved. Beneath the cover the movement diminished, but didn't stop: the man was still trying to reach the same conclusion but failing. The gritted teeth, the veins standing out on the temple between the strands of damp, matted hair showed the effort being made, but it couldn't be sustained. The sliding, rising movement slowed and stopped.

'I must be getting old. Maybe I need another drink.'

He looked over the side of the bed to see that the flapping cover had knocked the bottle over. It was almost empty. It slipped from his sweaty grasp as he lifted it and the last dregs ran out as it fell.

The woman was doing something to herself under the cover with a corner of the sheet. She looked at him. 'Never mind, Bill. Have another go in a minute.'

He swung his legs over the side of the bed and sat on its edge, looking down at himself. His shoulders were bowed and his back hunched. It wasn't possible, he thought. He had never failed before and even now he couldn't transfer the blame to that part of his anatomy. The fault must be elsewhere. It couldn't be the drink. It must be that he was tired. That must be it – he was tired.

'I could do with another drink.'

'That was all there was, love. Too late to go out and get any more.' She leant over, curled her arm around him, put her hand in his lap and toyed with his erection. 'You don't need that stuff. Look, a lot of the blokes who come here have had a few. None of them are much good at it. It's the drink, you see. You think it helps but it doesn't, not really.'

The words were lost on Bill Ellis. All that was going through his brain was the thought that he had failed. Yet somehow an integral part of that thought was the fixed idea that he could do with another drink. Without enthusiasm he climbed back under the cover.

She lay with her large breasts exposed above the edge of the sheet. The large dark nipples stood firm but the mounds of flesh slumped across her body. Between them and the top of her arm showed dark tufts of hair. Ellis played with one of the erect nipples, twiddling it like a radio tuner. He pulled the cover back to expose all of her. The fleshy thighs were together but, when she saw where he was looking, she parted them slightly.

Ellis tried to picture her as he would doubtless describe her one day in the sergeant's mess of the unit he was going to join. The memory of her would change and he would start to believe his embroidered recollection of her. Doubtless she would become slimmer, but keep the big breasts. Perhaps she would be blonde instead of brunette and the one room would become a suite, infinitely more luxurious. He smiled at how quickly and glibly the false picture was built up.

'That's a good sign. Are you cheering up a bit now?' She ran her fingers through her pubic hair and rubbed herself with the heels of her palms as she stretched. 'Come on, love. Have another go.' In invitation she opened her legs wide and arched her back.

The action melted the folds of fat from her middle. Ellis felt blood pumping his body to new hardness. He wanted her. More than that, he had to have her, had to achieve the climax his body had failed to attain earlier. He hurled himself on her, squashing the breath from her, and began to couple frantically.

'Here, steady, Bill. Not so hard. You're not in properly. That's it . . . that's better. That's nice.'

The light bulb began to emit a tinny, buzzing sound and flickered from shining white to a dirty yellow, making the room look more dingy than it was. The change went unnoticed by the pair on the bed. Then the flickering became more frequent and violent.

'The bulb's going.'

For Ellis, for a moment, it was almost like being with Betty again. She had always noticed fresh cracks in the ceiling or some other trivia when they were making love. With her it had annoyed him, but not put him off. Now, though, it seemed to and he stopped. He would have had to anyway.

'It's no bloody good. I can't do it. My God, I want to though.'

She held him tight and tried to stimulate him, encourage him to try once more. Briefly he did, but it was no use. He rolled from her. He felt bitter and tired but, above all, he felt angry – with himself, with the whole world, with his drinking, everything.

The woman was sympathetic. 'There's lots of time yet. Have a bit of a sleep, let some of the drink wear off. It'll be all right after you've had a rest, you'll see.' She reached down and stroked his shrinking core. 'And if you can't . . . well, I told you, I'm good with me hands.'

Ellis felt as if he wanted to cry with the utter frustration that was building up inside of him. A metallic 'ping' from the bulb as it failed and plunged the room into darkness summed up the whole mess for him. The woman giggled. He slept.

The room was pitch black when he woke from a fitful sleep. He lay still, trying to identify what it was that had awoken him. The bed was moving slowly up and down. Carefully, he turned his head to look at the woman. She lay on her back and he could just make out her outline as his eyes grew accustomed to the dark. Her arms were beneath the cover; stretched out down her body towards where her knees made twin mountains with the sheet. Ellis stayed quiet, listening to her laboured, regular breathing, realizing that this was the ultimate humiliation.

The woman had achieved satisfaction during his first attempt but not the second, now she was taking care of that for herself. At intervals her body went taut and then relaxed as she strove to reach a climax. With a gasp and long-drawn sigh the orgasm came and she squirmed in the pleasure of the sensation, then turned on her side away from him and fell immediately to sleep.

Bill Ellis lay still and very quiet. There was no greater misery he could feel, nothing that could add further to his utter dejection. When he was sure she was asleep he eased himself out of bed and groped about for his clothes. Carrying his boots he opened the door to leave. He paused, then turned back into the room and went to the tiny dressing-table in a far corner. Questing fingers found a lipstick and, as best he could in the dark, he scrawled a message on the mirror.

It was brief and brutally crude. He tried to inject into the words the loathing and hatred he felt for himself. A faint grey light was beginning to filter through the thick curtains. By its pale illumination he read the ill-spaced writing. 'Hope you had a good one' it said.

'Even that's no bleeding good,' he muttered to himself as he clumsily obliterated the legend. Instead he wrote on top of the mess, going over some of the letters three times before they stood out above the smears. 'For the drink'. He took out the three crumpled ten shilling notes, hesitated, then put all of them on the dresser.

As he went down the stairs he tried not to hear the sounds coming from other rooms. He remembered the glass in the hallway just in time and sat on the bottom stairs to put his boots on. Then he went out into the rain that had begun to fall.

As he trudged through the puddles towards the station his mind was numb, dulled and filled to overflowing with self

38

pity. He had failed again. Before it had been in battle, now it was even in bed. Failure. If only he had not had that extra drink. He swore to himself that he wouldn't the next time.

Ellis was quite sure there would be a next time. He knew it and he felt fear. He wasn't afraid of what form the test might take; his terror was of his own doubts and weakness. But if he could just manage for once without the drink, then it would all be different. The next time would be different, it just had to be.

* * *

The hull of the Tiger swam before him. Ellis shook his head, tried to recall all the drills, the tedious hours of practice and instruction on the weapon. He lined up the sights, let his breath out, held it and ever so gently squeezed the trigger. At least he meant to do it gently, but it seemed to snatch. The recoil kicked back painfully and when he looked up he clearly saw the projectile describing a lazy arc towards the panzer. Its low velocity made it seem to move so slowly that it looked as if at any moment it must stall and flop to the ground. The gap between it and its target closed to a last few yards until it was skimming the engine deck. It had missed. The bomb went sailing on to expend itself in the middle of the meadow.

He let go of the weapon, sat down in the road and held his head in his hands as the Tiger went on dealing out death. Ellis was completely exhausted. It was as though a tap had been turned on and all his strength and energy drained away. The crack of a detonating anti-personnel round, accompanied by volumes of hysterical and agonized screams, made him look up.

The Tiger had flushed from hiding a dozen or more British infantry who had taken to the shelter of a hollow. Whirling fragments from the airburst had sliced the men open, clothing and webbing had been slit like tissue paper. Now, one after another, the sufferers reeled out into the open, displaying the full horror of their mutilation. A handful not lucky enough to succumb quickly to the butchery they had suffered staggered about until, one by one, with aimed single shots, the Tiger's ranging machine-gun tumbled them into the dust and blood of their companions.

Taking up the remaining round, Ellis tried again to put an end to the slaughter. When he sighted on the Tiger it felt and looked as if the whole countryside were see-sawing up and down. In wild desperation he fired. A great fountain of earth several yards short of his target smothered its turret and hull top in clods of soil.

39

A hefty shove sent Ellis stumbling sideways. He lost his grip on the Piat and it was caught by RSM Hyde before it fell. The sergeant-major was covered in blood and his face looked strange. Ellis had to look again before he realized Hyde had lost the end of his nose and his facial hair.

'Get out of my way, you useless turd.' Hyde threw an ammunition case at him. 'See if you can unpack these.'

Ellis half caught the case, righted it and fumbled with the catch as if he'd never seen one before. Hyde snatched it from him.

'For fuck's sake, give it here.'

The RSM slotted a round into the trough, positioned himself, sighted and fired in one fluid motion. It was a hit, striking the Tiger dead centre. When the cloud of smoke drifted clear it revealed a neat round hole in one of the tank's road wheels and the track above it twisted and broken.

'Too bloody low. God those tough bastards. Give me another round.' Hyde grabbed the bomb from Ellis. 'Well, they'll not be going anywhere in a hurry. Let's see if we can keep the buggers here permanently.'

This time he took longer over the sighting. Even as he lined up on the panzer's turret, it began slowly to turn. The long tube of its cannon depressed to bear on the bank behind which the NCOs sheltered. Ellis found he was staring straight into the black mouth of the eighty-eight, imagined for a wild moment he could see right into the panzer. He thought of them there, dark garbed men, angry at the insolent fools who had tried to kill them when they were demonstrating so terrifyingly that it was they who were the killers.

'For Christ's sake, fire now. Fire now!' Ellis grabbed at Hyde's sleeve.

Hyde had to let go of the weapon to flap him away. 'Let go, you bloody fool. You're pissed out of your mind.'

Ellis made to snatch the Piat. 'Give it to me. I'll do it, I've got to do it.'

The RSM turned on him, livid with rage. He struck out at Ellis but missed, almost losing his balance and sprawling backwards. 'What are you fucking playing at? If I ever get you back . . .' As he shouted he threw himself at the bank and aimed the Piat.

The German gunner fired first. Five feet of compacted soil are no impediment to a high velocity shell fired at point blank range. The round skimmed the field and plunged into the far side of the bank to explode in its centre. The burnt remains of the hedge went straight up into the air; the packed earth, bound together by an elaborate root system, held for a fraction of time against the forces unleashed beneath it, then sprayed out before the propulsive fury of the explosion. Several cubic yards of flame-laced soil and ruined plants hurled outwards, liberally seeded with red hot, razor sharp fragments of shell casing.

Hyde and the Piat took the full blast. The stove-pipe-like weapon was bent double and whirled from sight. The RSM had both arms ripped off at the shoulder and was thrown back the width of the lane to land on a burning tyre. Blood sprayed from the great rents in his upper torso until they were crudely cauterized by the flames.

Ellis too was caught and thrown by the blast. His short flight ended painfully on a jagged, soot-stained lump of steel. A generous portion of the bank came down on top of him, driving in deeper the metal that impaled his side.

Swimming back out of the darkness that had engulfed his mind with the shock of his injury, Ellis twisted with the pain of his wound. The involuntary movement made him roll from the spit that held him. The sensation of the metal withdrawing was agony, but this time unconsciousness didn't come. Even through his own suffering he knew the stench of roasting flesh and the sight of Hyde rapidly frying to a crisp made him retch, then vomit.

He began to drag himself back down the road, the way the column had come. Past the broken and burning vehicles, past and over the dead and dying. He caught a last glimpse of the Tiger through a wide gap torn in the bank. It still sat like a metal fort in the middle of the field, brooding over the battle ground. The damage Hyde had inflicted on its track and suspension had done nothing to detract from its massively powerful and menacing appearance. It just sat there, waiting for the repair crews who would soon be along to recover so valuable a vehicle.

He tried to get up, but the pain the effort caused brought waves of blackness that washed over him and receded only when he began crawling again. Hardly noticed against the sensations in his side, was a hot throbbing in his shoulder and cheek. His progress was slow. It took thirty minutes for him to get clear of the rear of the file and out of the smoke. That was longer than the whole action had taken.

Shock, pain, the residual effect of the drink, all combined to induce in him a total confusion that, with weakness engendered

41

by loss of blood, quickly became delirium. As he inched along, leaving a trail of blood behind him, he talked to himself, sometimes shouting as he became aware by degrees that he couldn't hear, not even his own voice.

'I would have got it. I would have . . . damn you, Hyde. It was mine . . . it was my Tiger. Stretcher-bearers, over here . . . I'm hit, I'm hit.'

Now his last reserves of strength were exhausted and he moved only occasionally, dragging himself with elbows stripped of flesh by the gravel surface. He shouted again, watching red drops from his face dripping down to glisten and dry in the dust.

'It was my Tiger, mine. I was just too tired. Another drink . . . I would have done it . . . It was my Tiger.' He could go no further, and collapsed with his face in the dirt, arms outstretched. He jerked awake as sounds burst upon him with the sudden return of his hearing.

There was the sound of bird song, drowning out the distant, ugly noises of conflict. Ellis flopped over on to his back and, through the white mist that clouded his eyes and dimmed the bright sun, looked up into the overhanging branches. A breeze was rustling the trees and hedges, producing a sound like gentle surf on a sandy shore. A fluid sound, like lots and lots of water. He needed a drink.

'But not the next time, not the next time, not the next time.'

Sergeant William Ellis was picked up an hour later by the crew of a bren gun carrier belonging to the scout platoon of a motorized infantry battalion.

He was ferried back to a regimental aid post where a dressing was applied, and from there to an advanced dressing station where he was given a shot of morphia and a pint of plasma. From there he was transferred by field ambulance to a casualty clearing station where he was given one pint of whole blood and then operated on. It was just four hours since he had been wounded.

After twenty-four hours he was considered strong enough to travel and was moved to a field hospital near the beach-head where he underwent further surgery, during the course of which fifteen small fragments were removed from his cheek, jaw and shoulder muscles. At that time the gash in his side was sutured after minor work on the arteries that had been tied at the CCS. It required twenty-six stitches to close the wound.

Three weeks to the day after being wounded he was transferred to a convalescent depot in southern England and fourteen days later to an infantry base depot near Guildford in Surrey.

He managed to worm his way into a cushy little job in the administration block and there he might have seen the war out, had he not had a drink too many in the sergeant's mess one night and gone over the mark in some friendly ribbing of a sergeant-major who had that day become a father. Violence was prevented by Ellis falling down drunk.

A version of the affair came to the ears of the camp's CO. That was how Ellis suddenly found himself with an unexpected two-day leave in London, preparatory to a trip across the channel and ultimately across France to the front.

He spent the leave, drunk, in London; and the long journey by train, boat and truck, cursing and drinking in equal, substantial amounts.

THE PATROL

20.45 TO 22.15 HOURS

'I thought France was supposed to be a warm country.' Dicky felt the cold water, that had worked through his many layers of clothing, trickling down against his skin.

'You're thinking of the South of France,' whispered Alex.

'Too bloody true,' was all Dicky added.

Ellis's voice hissed back at them. 'Cut the cackle, you two. You're like a pair of old women, always gabbing.'

Private Bird was quick to answer the accusation. 'Don't say that, Sarge. With Frenchy around that's the last thing I'd like to be.'

Again the sergeant's disembodied voice floated out of the darkness. 'I said shut it. We'll be coming on to the Jerry outposts any time now.'

The line of men closed right up, stepping almost on one another's heels. If Barras in the lead stood on a mine or snagged a booby-trapped trip-wire, then he wouldn't be the only one to suffer.

The first German defences consisted of well-spaced machine-gun nests and dug-in anti-tank guns, positioned so as to give interlocking and mutually supporting fire: but the nature of the ground, its many dips and sunken stream beds and, in places, the very density of the belts of trees, meant that at one or two points it was possible for a small group to slip through. The foul weather also ensured that any sentries posted would be less likely to do a thorough job. The same incessant rain that would drive them to seek shelter would also mask any noise the infiltraters might inadvertently make.

It seemed for a moment as if they had been detected. From a concealed position in front and slightly to the left of them came a rippling burst of machine-gun fire. Green tracer flashed out and away among the stiffly standing trunks. As a single man, the file dropped, clawing at the ground to offer as small a target as possible. The fire was joined by other guns further off and the woods were filled with bobbing, ricochetting tracer of every hue.

Ellis dispatched Barras to investigate when he realized the fire was random and not directed at them. Indistinctly he heard a gabble of irate German being shouted somewhere in front. Gradually the fire slackened and eventually, after more shouting, it petered out. The woods became quiet again.

'For God's sake, don't go creeping about like that.' Barras had reappeared like a wraith out of the darkness, making Dicky jump.

'It's a bloody good job we *have* got someone who can move quietly. You sound like a ruddy travelling tinker. Can't you secure that damned radio properly?' Ellis was in a bad mood; he had been about to take a swig from his flask when their guide had returned.

Dicky offered what defence he could. 'It's not my bloody fault. The extending aerial keeps extending itself.'

'Well, wedge it with a bit of rag. Anything. It's rattling like a set of castenets.' Ellis turned to Barras. 'Well?'

With a long, wicked-looking knife, the Frenchman tried ineffectually to scrape some of the mud from his clothes. He put it back down the side of his boot after wiping it on a clump of grass. 'It was nothing. A sentry saw something that was not there. He set the others off. The shouting was an oberleutnant who did not like his sleep being disturbed. They will not, I think, be in a hurry to do it again this night.'

'How much further to this road junction?'

'A little more than a kilometre, about one of your miles.'

'What's the going like?'

'The going?' The phrase puzzled Barras.

'The going, the going. What is the ground like?'

'Oh, the going. It is good, like this. There is a stream to cross and on the far side a track which the Germans might patrol. But nothing we cannot deal with.' His teeth flashed white.

Led by Barras they passed between two machine-gun positions, without even catching a glimpse of a German. Still crouched low and moving with extreme caution they slipped past a hastily prepared anti-tank gun emplacement, and further on had to skirt a well-camouflaged flak gun mounted on a half-track chassis. As they crept by they could see the glow of a cooking-fire from the far side, and smelt pork and garlic. Then they were through the defence belt and were in an area where the only danger would be the occasional patrol, or the very real possibility of stumbling into a German encampment in the dark.

When they reached it, the stream Barras had mentioned was much swollen by the rains. What was normally a clear trickle

45

running between shallow banks was now a deep-gouged water-course, three yards wide, filled with a mud-coloured, tumbling torrent. It bore with it all manner of debris torn from its bed and sides.

By chance the men struck it at a place where some German, unwilling to get his feet wet, had thrown across a rude bridge of three dead tree trunks. For the men with the heavy packs it was a nerve-wracking business crossing the crumbling, slippery logs; made worse by the knowledge that if they slipped into the several feet of water their hefty loads would drag them straight under. The force of the flow would swiftly sweep them beyond hope of rescue.

It was with relief that they gathered on the far side, standing on a well-used track that ran alongside it as they checked equipment and weapons. For an instant they froze, then hurled themselves into the mud beside the ruts as the needle beams of a Kubelwagen's headlamps cut towards them. The silver filaments, their light dimmed to a dirty yellow by the mud that part filled the horizontal slits in the lamps' masks, threw twin bars of light ahead of the car.

On bulbous, balloon-like tyres the angular little vehicle skidded towards them, the faces of its occupants pale orbs behind the broad arcing smears on its windscreen left by the wipers.

As the car drew near, Ellis heard the snick of a safety-catch being eased off beside him. He reached out and pushed the barrel of Paul Barras's machine-pistol into the dirt. Despite the force exerted to try and raise it, the sergeant maintained his iron grip.

The spluttering of the Kubelwagen's VW air-cooled engine came nearer. Twenty yards, fifteen. The men buried their faces in the liquid soil and became a part of the landscape. Ten yards, and they could hear the splashing of the wide tyres, pushing walls of water before them. Five yards, then the Kubelwagen was alongside and showers of the surface mud were being thrown over them. There was a moment's sudden surprising warmth as the exhaust burbled past, and then the corrugated panels of the car were disappearing from sight. It was gone, and they dared to breath once more.

'Hell's bloody teeth.' Dicky raised himself, water pouring from his clothes. 'I can just see the bloody headline: British Soldier Drowns Inside Greatcoat. If a Jerry bullet doesn't get me I stand a fair chance of going down with double pneumonia.'

Barras at last managed to wrench his machine-pistol from the sergeant's vice-like grip. He shook with barely suppressed anger, but it was Ellis who got in the first word.

'Just once more, you French loony, just one more try at a stunt like that . . .' He didn't finish the sentence. The after effects of the drink, the crying need he felt for more, and his anger at himself for needing it, plus – and above all – his intense dislike of Barras, all bubbled just below a dangerously thin veneer of control. He almost felt regret when he heard the safety-catch click back. 'I told you, I run this show. It's not a bloody hunting trip. We've other work to do. Do you understand me? Do you?'

Barras spat mud and curled his lip in a sneer, but made no reply and turned away. Ellis let it go at that. He couldn't trust himself to push the matter further and still retain self-control. He realized that he was just putting off what seemed like an inevitable show-down between them.

Over the last three hundred yards to the road junction the woods grew even thicker, with many of the trees bearing the marks of recent shell or bomb damage. Water-filled craters of various sizes were dotted about. They passed a gigantic oak and then almost immediately Barras signalled a halt. They were on the top of the embankment overlooking the road.

They lay in the cover of the close-spaced trees that grew right up to the edge, and examined the whole area slowly and minutely. The embankment was overgrown with weeds and fell steeply some fifteen feet to the large levelled clearing in which the junction was situated.

The road itself stood out starkly before them, like a giant inverted T, the lighter-coloured mud that smothered its surface contrasting with the darker churned soil of the ground about it. From the foot of the bank it was about thirty feet to the edge of the road, which ran away to right and left to lose itself among the trees, while facing them they could see a hundred yards up the third arm of the junction before it was swallowed by the darkness beneath the canopy of trees.

Patches in the road surface, circles of scorched undergrowth and flattened pines about the clearing gave ample evidence of the effectiveness of the Allied fighter-bombers and artillery. As did the gutted shell of a Bussing-Nag radio location van resting on its axles in a far corner.

A hide was quickly constructed by slinging a camouflage-painted canvas sheet above a swiftly scooped-out hollow amid a tight-packed clump of firs.

'Get down.' Alex on look-out had heard a truck approaching.

A lone six-wheeled Matador machinery lorry with German markings growled down the road opposite, straight towards the hide. It stopped at the crossroads and its three-man crew could be seen pouring over a map, then it swung slowly to the left and went grumbling on its way. The men immediately resumed work on improving the hide.

Two lengths of rotting wood were laid in front of the position and arranged to look as natural as possible. They dug through the inches-thick layer of pine needles and found the ground beneath warm by comparison, dry and well drained.

Dicky got carried away, throwing handfuls of spoil on to the sheet for extra concealment. When it started to sag alarmingly and showed every indication of imminent collapse, he had to stop while everyone got out and frantically scraped the surplus away.

The moment the space was large enough to accomodate them all, they crammed into it. They were wedged in so tight there was hardly room to move, but after the wind and rain outside it was sheer luxury.

Alex took his boots off, performing incredible contortions in the confined space to manage it, so that he could wring some of the water from his socks.

'I can see this is going to be a real fun night.'

'I don't know what you're complaining about,' Dicky grumbled. 'Only this morning you were saying how you could do with a night out. Some people are never bloody satisfied.'

The sapper was not in a receptive mood for Bird's humour. 'Do me a favour. Go and tell your rotten jokes to the first Jerry troop convoy that passes.'

Taking the gentle hint, Bird turned his full attention to the radio. So far it had stubbornly refused to function. It was not the only thing that had succumbed to the cold and damp. The sergeant's bladder was playing him up, and he had to keep diving out to relieve himself. After Ellis had upset the arrangements for the fifth time, Morris began to get a bit irritable.

Corporal Morris was cold and wet. He was squashed in beside Barras and the Frenchman stank of garlic. Neither his comfort nor his peace of mind were improved by the fact that the pack he leant on contained four anti-tank mines. Morris watched the two sappers as they shared another bar of chocolate. He envied them their comradeship. He was a loner; somehow it just wasn't in him to strike up a close relationship with anyone. He didn't even have a regular girlfriend. There was only his parents, and he rarely saw them.

Even now, close to these men on whose mutual support perhaps all of their lives might depend before the night was over, he still felt alone, isolated. He took out his notebook, chewed the damp stub end of his pencil to expose more of the lead, headed a fresh page with the date and time and entered details of the Matador's route and unit signs. It gave him something to do.

'Well, why can't you get the bloody thing to work? You're the one who went on the course. Stop buggering about and get it working, damn you.'

Ellis immediately regretted his over-reaction to the news from Dicky that the radio couldn't be made to operate.

'What is wrong, Sergeant?' Barras sounded amused. 'Did you want to ask the major if you could go home now?'

He couldn't see, but Ellis knew the Frenchman would be grinning. 'You damned well know why we need that radio. With the weather closed in like it is, air reconnaissance is out, so if we see something we've got to be able to call down artillery fire on it. The major said Jerry might be moving armour through here. If they are, that's when we'll need the radio.'

Dicky was not happy at the sudden revelation that enemy tanks might be in the area. 'You never said anything about armour. I'll tell you this, if I see so much as one turret I'll be back behind our own lines so fast you won't need the set – I'll be there before the radio waves.'

The rain stopped at last, but the bitingly cold wind shifted direction and began whistling in beneath the roof of their shelter. A hastily pushed-up low wall of soil and decomposing pine needles did little to break its force. The grumbling and bickering went on, ceasing briefly while four Opel supply trucks drove past, then restarting immediately the ragged exhaust note of the last vehicle had faded from hearing.

The moon put in a brief appearance between fast-moving bands of cloud, and only showed the size of the next storm on the way. A straight black line, like a blind drawn across the sky, caught and engulfed the moon and, with a precision that would have been the envy of any master bomber, it dropped its load of water with unerring accuracy on to the woods below. Rain slashed at the trees and clearing, washing the road clear of mud and forming small lakes at its edges. For half an hour there was no other noise save the sounds of the storm. The road remained empty.

In the hide, conversation and argument alike petered out as each man conserved his energy. The incessant drumming of the rain and the absence of any distraction had a soporific effect. Each man retreated into his own little world, pulling his clothes about him, and closing eyes and thoughts to the unpleasantness of their situation.

'What is that?'

It was Paul Barras who was first to sense some change. He crawled to the front of the shelter and peered out over the logs. There was nothing to be heard or seen, but some animal instinct told him there was a change in the patterns his brain had grown used to in the last half hour.

Alex felt something too. He watched as Barras pressed his ear to the ground. Out of curiosity Alex copied the Frenchman's strange action and, when he did, realized the barely detectable difference his subconscious had registered. A definite vibration was running through the forest floor.

Morris was alert. 'What is it?'

Eric put his hand out to feel the amplified resonance in the trunk of one of the trees. 'There aren't any elephants in France, are there? What the hell can it be?'

The question remained unanswered as the trembling of the ground grew stronger. Then their ears picked up the bellow of diesel exhausts and into sight down the road opposite came the twin beams of high-set headlamps. As they drew nearer the men made out the huge slab front of a Krupp tank transporter and, towering over its high cab roof, the massive turret of the panzer on its semi-trailer. The heavy outline, the long snout of the cannon, could only belong to one vehicle: a Tiger tank.

Struggling with its huge burden, the transporter crawled almost to the junction. Then, with its driver crashing down through its gears, the giant truck turned off the road to park beside the trees at the edge of the clearing. Behind it at two-minute intervals came five more, each similarly laden. They too pulled off the metalled road and parked around the perimeter of the clearing.

Morris watched in amazement as the rigs wallowed through the mud, which came only an inch or two up their tyres. 'Those damned great things should have sunk from sight in that soft ground. With the Tiger and all they must weigh over eighty tons apiece.'

'I was just thinking that. They must have paved the whole area with a thick slab of concrete. Nothing else would support that load.'

Ellis took out his spyglass and softly read out to the corporal the tactical and unit numbers and emblems he could make out on the tanks and their tractors.

'What are they doing out here, in the middle of nowhere.' Dicky squeezed in between the others to take a look.

Some of the Krupp drivers and their tank crew passengers jumped down from the high cabs and stretched, like men who have been travelling a long time. Ignoring the rain they gathered in small groups to talk, a few set up small spirit stoves beneath the trailers and put water on to boil. Several went off to relieve themselves. One fat German in tanker overalls squatted near the bottom of the embankment, not twenty feet from the hide.

'What a target for our gunners.' Ellis turned to Bird. 'Get that set working, but keep the volume right down. I don't want a sudden blast of static attracting attention to us. They've got more fire-power than we have.'

Dicky was not optimistic. 'It's no good, Sarge. The set's soaked. Water must have got in through that aerial socket. I've had the back off trying to dry it out, but there's not a chance here.'

'Looks like that Kraut's going to finish his shit in peace, not pieces then.'

Ellis ignored Morris's remark. He could feel the tension building up inside again. Without thinking he took out his flask and swigged from it. They'll be gone from here before first light, be dug in and camouflaged by then.'

'Yeah, waiting for our advance to restart,' Morris added gloomily.

'Six Tigers can do a hell of a lot of damage, Sarge, if our lot run into them.'

'Do you think I don't know that. Listen, Bird, I've seen what one of those sods can do. I don't like to think what two troops of them could manage.'

The sound of more engines approaching brought all eyes back to the junction. A convoy of assorted vehicles, led by two motor-cycle combinations, came down the road from the right. Twelve vehicles in all, including two half-track mounted light anti-aircraft guns and two articulated fuel tankers, joined the transporters.

A platoon of pioneers jumped from two Skoda trucks and

immediately began unloading shells, cases of flares and boxes of machine-gun ammunition. Human chains passed the stores up to the tank crews who had climbed on to the Tigers and handed them in through the hatches. Hoses were unreeled from the bowsers and with the aid of small auxiliary motors petrol was pumped to each of the panzers in turn.

'Now you know why they're here.'

Morris didn't bother to look up at Dicky as he spoke. By the dim light of a heavily masked torch, he was too busy dashing down into his note book the details Ellis was giving him about the new arrivals.

'A few rounds of tracer in the ammunition lorries and the fuellers and we could start a lovely fire. We have six machine-guns, we could do a lot of damage before they could know what was happening. Perhaps we could cook one or two of the Tigers, yes?'

As he spoke, Barras sighted down the barrel of his machine-pistol at the nearest tank, wishing as he did that he had a weapon capable of blasting it to pieces. How he would have liked to do that; rampage about the clearing, destroying, killing. The fantasy filled his mind while his eyes stayed locked on the Tiger, examining every inch of its thickly armoured construction, missing no detail.

Ellis found an opportunity to get his own back, his voice was full of sarcasm. 'Even you aren't that bloody stupid, Frenchy. The only way doing that could make sense would be if we could be certain of killing every one of the hundred and fifty-odd Krauts down there, first go. If you really reckon we can do it, then maybe we'll have a go. If not, then shut up.'

Barras breathed hard, but gradually lowered the barrel of his weapon. 'Well then, Sergeant, what shall we do? Would you like us to sit here, nice and safe, and just watch them work. When we go back you can say to the major: "Guess what we saw in the night." I do not think that will please him very much. So, is that what we do, just sit and watch?'

Alex finished a whispered consultation with Eric. 'We could nip down the road a way and set the mines, Sarge. We might get one of them that way.'

Ellis felt them all looking at him and he suddenly realized he had the flask in his hand. He couldn't recall taking it out. His mind raced as he tried to remember if he'd taken a drink from it in front of them. There was a strong taste of rum in his mouth.

He slipped the container back in his pocket.

'No, that's no good. Chances are we'll pick the wrong road and, if we do choose the right one, maybe the supply trucks will pull out first and set them off instead. That'll warn the tank and flak gun crews. I don't fancy being around if they start hosing fire into the woods.'

Barras sought some other way and he didn't hide his feelings. Though he had to reduce his voice to a hissing whisper, his determination to have a go at the Tigers and their crews came over clearly. But his voice conveyed more than that; an inner, bitter, twisted dedication to destruction. 'Then let me have the mines. I can put them under the wheels of the transporters. When they move we will send some of the pigs to hell.'

'Shut up and let me think. I'll tell you one thing, though, the last thing I'll do is turn you loose on your own down there while we're still around.'

Barras pushed his face into the sergeant's. 'So what do we do then? Come on, let us hear. You are so good at destroying ideas, turn your genius to those panzers.'

'Well, if we can't use the radio, we could get back as fast as possible, and hope the buggers are still here when we report.' It wasn't much, but it was all Ellis could think of on the spur of the moment.

'You're forgetting, Sarge,' Morris reminded him, 'we've already stirred up a hornets' nest back there. It might be hours before they stop sniffing round what's left of that cottage and settle down again.'

Dicky made a suggestion. 'How about sending just one bloke back? He could move fast, slip through where a group might run into trouble. We could pull back into the woods and when the artillery have finished make our own way back.'

It was Corporal Morris who raised muted but strenuous objection to the idea. 'I don't fancy that. What if the bloke gets caught, or even seen? It'll stir them up even more. Then we could be tiddle-arsing about in these bloody woods for days, trying to elude their patrols. I don't fancy staying out here till we starve, get bagged or shot.'

Sergeant Ellis knew there was another, unvoiced objection to Bird's scheme. Logically there was only one person who could travel fast through this country. The very thought of Barras out on his own, creating God only knows what sort of havoc and storing up trouble for those staying behind . . . well, it didn't

53

promote a feeling of confidence in the night's outcome. Much as Ellis would dearly have loved to get rid of their guide, by any means, that was one way he dare not try. It would add an unacceptably high element of additional risk to an already hazardous situation.

'Okay, so that leaves only one alternative. Somehow Bird has got to make that radio work.'

'Sarge, I've told you. I need somewhere dry, and a decent light.'

Help came from an unlikely source. Barras chipped in. 'There is a farm, perhaps ten minutes from here. I think it will be abandoned, but it will be dry, and we can use a light.'

Ellis grabbed at the chance. 'Right, we'll do that then.'

He jumped as one of the Skoda's backfired. The steady throbbing of its engine underlined the need for urgency.

The work in the clearing was already half done, with one or two of the now empty supply trucks preparing to pull out. The sergeant watched as a hose was coiled and stowed on one of the bowsers.

'We'll split up. Barras can guide me and Bird to this place he knows. Morris, you stay here with Church and Pitt. Keep a note of any new arrivals or anything passing through, and watch which direction this lot go if they take off before we're back. Give us an hour. If we're not back by then, make your own way home. If you get the chance, plant the mines. If you can't do it here, then on that track by the stream. With a bit of luck though we'll be back soon, then we can pull out and let our gunners do the work on those bloody Tigers.'

Barras was already slithering backwards from the hide. He stood, and at a steady lope made off through the trees. Not once did he look round to see if the other two were keeping up with him.

Corporal Morris and the two sappers spread cramped limbs, taking advantage of the extra room. They settled down to watch the antics of the Germans in the clearing. No blackout precautions were being taken. Torches were being used freely and a mobile, lorry-mounted generator had been started up so that welding could be carried out on the driver's hatch of one of the panzers. Showers of sparks cascaded down the textured, drab surface, lighting every intricate detail of the Zimmerit anti-magnetic mine paste with which the armour was coated.

54

The cannon barrels of some of the tanks bore white hoops of paint, each hoop denoting the tank's 'kills'. One sported more than twenty, those nearest the muzzle brake faded and scorched.

The big Mercedes fuel carriers manoeuvred to service each rig and its load in turn. Cab lights burned in most of the lorries and tractor units. All the clearing was filled with light and noise and movement, but dominating the whole scene, aloof from the bustle, oblivious to the coming and going of their attendants, sat the Tigers.

'Is that it?' Dicky wrestled with the straps of the radio pack, trying to stop them from biting into his shoulders.

'There's a light.' Sergeant Ellis leant over Bird's shoulder and he in turn leant over the Frenchman's, as they looked out from behind a tree at the farmhouse.

The building was dark except for a pale yellow glow from one downstairs window. Sheds and outbuildings about the house were ramshackle and decayed. With the background of a forbidding copse of gnarled oaks, it looked eerie. The impression was intensified by the distant baying of a dog. To complete the picture of slumbering evil the place presented, the horizon was lit by a single jagged streak of lightning and shortly after there came the echoing rumble of thunder.

Ellis swore under his breath, cursing the complication that the faint illumination in the house brought. Bird was the radio man, he couldn't be risked. Either he would have to check the place himself or he'd have to send Barras. Ellis knew he wasn't up to the job himself. It had to be the Frenchman.

'Frenchy, circle the house, check for sentries. If there are none have a look in, and this time I want the truth, otherwise, so help me when we get back I'll find a way to queer things for you with the major. There's a number of blokes will want to have a crack at you, and they'll all be standing in line behind me.'

Barras threw a mock salute. 'I hear you, Sergeant, sir.'

With a snort of derision Barras turned and left. His outline was briefly visible a few minutes later as he made his way round the back of the house. It was a full fifteen minutes before he returned.

'No Germans, but at the back there are sandbags, shovels, picks, and coils of barbed wire.'

Dicky threw his hands in the air. 'Wouldn't you bloody know it. I suppose there's a battalion of pioneers in the house just waiting for the rain to stop so they can start work again.'

'Shut up, Bird.' Ellis was irritable. 'Let's hear what he's got to say. Who's in there?'

'An old man, the farmer I think, and his wife. They are packing. It looks like the Germans are going to turn it into a strong point and are turning them out.'

'If that's the case, where the hell are the Krauts then?'

'Belt up.' Ellis leant back against a tree.

He knew it was only the presence of Barras that had induced him to carry on this far. He fervently wished the Frenchman a thousand miles away or, better still, dead, but it did no good. When he opened his eyes after the silent prayer Barras was still there.

'The major will not be happy if we do not get those Tigers.'

Paul Barras enjoyed digging at Ellis, prompting him to make decisions he would never have normally reached.

'How long will it take to fix that thing?' Ellis prodded the radio.

'I can't be sure I can fix it, not till we get inside and I can get the back off. That's if we're going in. Are we?' Dicky shivered. 'It's worth taking the risk just to get out of this freezing rain for a while. How about it, Sarge?'

Ellis was cold as well. He looked again at that distant light and tried to picture what the room would be like. Perhaps there would be a fire. He screwed up his eyes, but he couldn't be certain that what he'd thought he'd seen really was a wisp of smoke from the leaning stack that rose above the sagging roof.

'All right, we'll try the house. I can't see the Krauts coming back at this time, in this weather, to do a bit of digging. But we'll take it slow and easy anyway. First sign of trouble and we run. If there are any Krauts in there, there's no way the three of us can winkle them out. We'll go in the front way. Bird, you hang back a bit . . .'

'Thanks for your concern, Sarge.'

'. . . I don't want a bullet going through that matchstick body of yours and buggering the radio.'

On the whispered count of 'three' the farmhouse door gave way beneath an assault by boots and gun butts. It opened straight into the main room. An elderly, weather-beaten couple jumped back with startled expressions from the battered suitcase on the floor, into which they had been cramming possessions. The woman gave a scream and every sign of intending to do more. Ellis

56

leapt forward and clamped his hand over her mouth.

The woman's husband, slow to comprehend who his unexpected visitors were and conscious only of what he saw as an attack on his wife, jumped at the sergeant's back. He never made it. Barras felled him with a swipe from the butt of his machine-pistol. The farmer crumpled and fell soundlessly to lay at full length on the worn square of carpet between the fire and sofa. Blood trickled from a cut above his ear.

'You didn't need to do that.' Ellis let go of the woman. She had ceased trying to bite his hand and now struggled only to reach the unconscious man. The moment she was released she threw herself down beside him, shielding his body from further blows with her own.

'Frenchy, tell her who we are. Tell her we're sorry. Say we'll not hurt them. Say it.'

Barras uttered a few gruff words in French. Ellis had no way of knowing what he had said, whether it was what he had wanted, but the woman was too distraught to pay attention anyway. She was using a corner of her apron to wipe blood from her husband's face.

'Well, don't just bloody stand there, Bird. Put the radio on the table. Get to work.'

While Ellis watched the woman and Barras poked the contents of the case and then looked out through the broken door at the rain, Dicky unslung the set and laid it on the polished table. He took off his helmet that dripped water and dried his hands on a dress hung over the back of a chair. He glanced round the room. It was spartan but clean. The four ladder-back chairs matched the shine of the table top, as did the old-fashioned china cabinet and long-case clock that faced each other across the room. Faded tinplate photographs on the cabinet and a gilt-edged mirror flanked by two simple framed prints of wild orchids above it completed the room. The illumination came from two burnished oil lamps supported from wrought-iron brackets either side of the fireplace.

The back came off the radio and Dicky set to work, taking out the components one at a time, checking and rough drying them, then blowing the last moisture from them and placing each carefully to one side.

'I'll check the house. Barras, keep a look-out, but see if you can fix that door and put something over the window first. No point in advertising our presence.' Ellis opened the door to the darkened kitchen. It was small, and the briefest of glances revealed nothing of interest. He crossed the room and looked out of the back door. A compacted shale path led to a collection of tumbledown sheds and beyond were the outlines of a couple of barns. He stood a moment, letting his eyes grow accustomed to the dark. An animal snorted and shuffled in one of the out-buildings, but there was no other noise or movement. Ellis closed the door and secured it, then went back into the front room.

As he went to the stairs the woman began crooning over the body of her husband as though he were dead. The treads groaned as he took them two at a time, echoing the woman's lament.

There were only two rooms at the top of the house, and one of those served only as a lumber room. Perhaps at some time it had held children; crude, hand-made toys were piled in a far corner. In places the dust of years had been recently disturbed where some cherished memento had been removed, taken away to go with the old couple.

The other room held a four-poster bed, a wardrobe and a wide six-drawer chest. On the drawers stood a china wash-basin and jug. The four-poster was strangely out of place in that room. It was in a dark, almost black, wood. Every detail of its intricately carved, exuberantly decorated form was polished to a brilliant shine. It reflected at a thousand points the beams of light from the candle Ellis found and lit. On the bed the covers had been pulled back and neatly folded, ready for packing.

It was very quiet in the room. Although its ceiling was the roof of the house the noise of the storm barely intruded. The windows were tiny, cowering under the eaves as lightning flashed closer than before. The sergeant sat on the edge of the bed, heedless of his wet muddy clothes soiling the worn but spotless mattress. Seemingly of its own volition the flask came out. Ellis drank deeply.

A call from downstairs roused him and he blinked to sudden wakefulness. The flask was still in his hand and his first concern was that he hadn't spilt any when he dozed off. As far as he could tell he had not.

He went down to find the woman more composed and struggling to lift her husband on to the sofa. She made no protest when Ellis helped her, nor offered any sign or word of thanks when he thrust at her his pack of field dressings.

The farmer was pale and blood still flowed from the cut to stain the flower-patterned upholstery, but his pulse and his breathing were strong. In a few hours he would have nothing worse than a bad headache and a very large bump. Though the drink had dulled Ellis's concern, still he was pleased.

It was one small weight lifted from the accumulated load on his conscience.

'Any luck with the radio yet?'

'That's why I called. The bugger's come to life, but we'd better wait till the cover's on before giving it a try. These are temperamental sods at the best of times.'

There was the sound of shattering glass from the kitchen. Ellis whirled to face the door, bringing his sten to the ready.

'It is all right, Sergeant, sir. It is only me.' Barras stepped in, carrying two bottles in each hand. He grinned, showing off his teeth. 'I have brought you reinforcements.'

'You're supposed to be on look-out.'

'Oh, Sergeant. There is no one in these woods but us and it is so cold out there.' He nodded towards the couple. 'Besides, I knew they would have something hidden, and here it is.'

He put the bottles down and rummaged in a drawer in the table. He produced a corkscrew and opened two of the bottles. The wine was a deep-velvet red, giving off a heady, fruity aroma. Barras offered one to Ellis, and when he didn't immediately take it, lifted the other and drank three great mouthfuls from it.

'It is fit only for these peasants, but it is the best they can afford. Go on, try it.' He drank again.

'Tell her we'll pay for it.' Ellis grasped the thin cool neck of the bottle.

'Save your money. When they leave here they are as good as dead. If they survive the fighting they will not live through the winter. They are peasants. This is all they know. They will pine for their home and when the spring comes, when this place will be a pile of rubble, their bodies will be rotting in a ditch or mass grave somewhere.'

Dicky spoke, but he didn't look up from his work. 'Do you know, you're such a nice chap it's difficult to decide which side of your nature I like best. Why don't you piss off? Go and play with a live grenade.'

'Oh, so the young funny man speaks. Wait until you have been fighting as long as me, then you can talk.'

'Give it a rest for a while.' Ellis had half finished the big litre bottle. He turned to Dicky. 'You've had half an hour, how much longer?'

'Any moment now, just these two to put back.' He held up the two valves and again there was the sound of breaking glass as one of them slipped through his fingers and imploded on the floor. 'Don't panic, Sarge.' Dicky had seen the look on Ellis's face. 'I've got a spare for that one.' He plugged the last components in place, loosely secured the back of the radio and turned it on. 'Nothing yet." He reached in and pushed the battery terminals down tighter. 'Ah, there it is. I said there was life in it yet. Just give it a moment longer to warm up, then you can call the major and arrange for some of our heavy guns to gut those Tigers.'

The sound of breaking glass was much louder this time. The rug Barras had rigged across the window bulged in, and amid a shower of bright shards a large stick grenade thumped to the floor . . .

PAUL BARRAS

HIS STORY

Clack clack clack. Another short burst from the light cannons on the flak tower sought targets among the bomb-damaged buildings at the edge of the marshalling yard. Spotlights glared down, their roving beams picking out the dancing bright motes of dust raised by previous rounds. Now the flak guns on some of the railway flat-cars joined in, multiple machine-gun mounts adding their ripping blur of rapid fire to the punching crack of the twenty and thirty-seven millimetre cannons.

Paul Barras shook powdered brick and mortar from his untidy black hair, now turned grey by the debris showered from the battered wall behind which he crouched. More stonework nearby was pulverised by an explosive shell and a length of charred timber flipped into the air to tumble from sight among the ruins. He hugged tighter to him the captured German MP40 machine-pistol that was his favourite weapon and waited for the spotlight and the gunners' attention to move elsewhere. Faintly, between the bursts of fire, there came to him from the far side of the complex of sidings the bark of a dog and the light crackle of distant rifle shots, interspersed with loud, unintelligible shouting in German.

The resistance leader whirled round to see a great dark shape looming up behind him. A split second before his finger tightened on the trigger he recognized the bulky outline of his bearded second in command. He was supporting another man, whose face was so covered in dirt and blood it was a moment before Barras recognized the face of a youngster who had joined them that night for his first taste of action. Barras reached out for a limply dangling arm and dropped it carelessly when he found no pulse.

'Put him down. There is no point in carrying him any further.'

The big man gently eased the corpse to the ground, then squatted beside it. He took out a grimy scrap of cloth and scrubbed it back and forth across his forehead. 'It's a mess. They're cutting us to shreds.'

Barras was quick to sense the implied criticism in the comment. 'It had to happen sooner or later. The Allies have been ashore eight days now. All the Germans are alert. There are no more lax sentries.'

The bearded giant said nothing. He knew his leader too well to risk incurring his anger. Though he dwarfed Barras's slight frame, and at forty was fifteen years his senior, still he treated the younger man with a respect that bordered on fear. Barras had shown his hardness towards his own men as well as the enemy. He allowed no mistakes, admitted no criticism, and dealt swiftly and savagely with either.

'Did all the look-outs get clear?' Barras forced his voice to sound normal, unstrained. He fought down the temptation to add to the sentence the words which in his thoughts had prompted it. He knew he wanted to say her name, ask if she had got clear, but he left it at that and waited for the answer.

A searchlight beam flashed above their hiding place. Fifty metres to their right it hesitated, stopped and flicked back to light a section of pock-marked wall behind them. It lingered a moment, turning night into day, then it was gone again.

The big man let out the breath he had been holding. 'I thought they'd seen us. I'm not sure about the look-outs. Most of them got away. I couldn't check the old jute warehouse, some Germans were setting up a machine-gun nest in the doorway.'

Barras felt cold. He forced out the question he didn't want to ask, even though he knew the answer. 'Who did we have there?'

There was a hesitation of several seconds before the reply came back out of the dark. 'Stefan was there, on the top floor, with Nicole.'

Barras felt his stomach go cold, and a clammy sweat broke out on his forehead. He had sworn to himself to treat her like one of the men, had made himself push to the back of his mind the memories of what there had been between them. Or would have been, or should have been if things had been normal, if he had been normal. They had been lovers, almost, during his last few months at the university just before the outbreak of war. And now, in the middle of an operation that had gone all wrong, right at the moment he needed to concentrate all his thoughts on salvaging whatever he could in the way of men and materials, he found himself trying to sort out his feelings towards her.

He recalled their first time alone together, in his room. The memory of her softly rounded body came back to him with startling clarity. He remembered her high-cheeked, bright-eyed face, the jet fringe of hair that didn't quite come down far enough to hide the tip of the little white childhood scar, about which she was so conscious. And above all that, fighting to the surface of his mind, through all the years of suppression, came the recollection of his total failure as a lover.

His mind raced back to the incident with the old man in the park, when he was twelve, and how the old pervert had made fun of him, saying over and over again: 'Look, I can make mine stand up.'

The resistance leader wrenched his thoughts back to reality, and found it no clearer. Everyone had been given their instructions. When things got bad it was every man for himself. Better to cut and run, accept such losses as were inevitable and conserve what was left for another time. But this was Nicole, Nicole Duval who once had meant something to him, as much as anyone could ever mean to Barras. He made a decision.

'You get going. The Germans will start a thorough search soon. Get out while you can, before they cordon the area off.'

'And you?'

'I'll . . . I'll check the jute warehouse. Stefan has the bren. We can't afford to lose it.' It was a lie, Barras knew it was a lie, knew it sounded a lie.

'I'll come with you.'

The voice that cracked back at the bearded man was like a whiplash and he recoiled from it as thought it were one.

'No.' Barras lowered his voice. 'I'll go alone. I can move quicker that way. Now get going. I'll join you as soon as I can. Now go.'

The big man offered no further argument. With a last look at the body beside him, he rose and left the way he had come.

Paul Barras was alone. He looked out across the converging lines at the throat of the yard to where the huge building that was his objective stood gaunt and isolated from the surrounding property. The cannon fire had stopped and from the shouts and barking coming from somewhere among the lines of wagons he knew that a thorough search had been started. It was time to move.

The British bombers had hit the goods yard several times in the last three weeks and the surrounding buildings nearly as often. The piles of brick and jumbled, twisted girders gave good cover, but it was impossible to move in silence. Every few paces he would dislodge some precariously balanced pile and it would slide to the ground, creating a cloud of pale dust. Once a light played over him but, by freezing amid the blackened tangle of beams through which he was threading, he avoided detection.

Thirty yards from the only doorway into the warehouse he ran out of cover. Protruding from the shadow of the opening, laid atop a hastily thrown-up barricade, was the snout of a machine-gun. Showing ghostly behind it, its two man crew.

Barras looked at his watch, took out a grenade and settled to wait. While he did, he examined the face of the building. There were four floors above the ground, the windows to the first three being heavily barred. Apart from the machine-gun crew there was no sign of life about the building. He watched the glowing, luminous minute hand creep to the half hour and clutched the grenade tighter as it approached. The thin bar of pale light edged up to the six, and past it.

There was a short burst of machine-gun fire behind him and some shouted oaths as the trigger-happy soldier among the steadily nearing line of searchers was berated by a nervous officer.

The first explosion when it came was bigger than the Frenchman expected, causing spikes of white light to fly out from its centre, even above the flak tower. It was accompanied by a heavy movement of air and the rumble of wagons toppling over. Barras leapt forward and hurled the warm grenade at the doorway even as a series of secondary detonations blasted apart the massed rolling stock.

There was a shout from behind the barricade as the oval of grooved steel bounced off the stonework to fall behind the stacked bales and timber. The opening filled with smoke and flame as the grenade destroyed the position. Fire and explosion were racing through the yard as Paul Barras hurled himself the short distance to the doorway, in through the acrid mist that still filled it, and over the mess that littered its floor.

Heart pounding, he paused at an angle of the wall at the foot of the stairs. No one came and he started up them three at a time. A bullet blasted plaster from the wall by his head, the particles stinging his face, almost blinding him.

'Nicole, Stefan. It's me, Paul.'

There was a pause, and then he heard the girl's voice. 'Stefan is hurt. I can't stop the bleeding.'

Barras leapt the last few steps to the landing where Nicole knelt beside the wounded man. By the poor light of the orange glare coming in through the dirt-clouded windows he examined the wound. It was massive. There was a fist-sized hole in Stefan's right side and blood was pulsing from it.

'How did it happen?'

'He tried to silence the guns on the flak tower, but they saw him. I got him down this far, then I heard the Germans in the entrance. How is he? Can we get him out?'

Paul took the man's wrist. It took him a moment to find it, but there was a pulse, weak but regular. Stefan was Nicole's half-brother. Barras knew he would never get her to leave while the wounded man lingered on. The steady throbbing in the vein beneath his fingers persisted.

There was so little time. If he was to get the girl to safety they had to start now. Soon the Germans would recover from the shock and confusion caused by the delayed-action charges his men had set, then they would reform and continue their sweep of the area. It would not be long before they found the bodies downstairs, then they would search the warehouse. The building was a shell, offering no cover or concealment. Barras entertained no delusions about their chances of eluding death or capture if they stayed there. He made a decision.

'He's gone.' Barras laid the arm he had been holding across the chest of the still living man. He pulled Nicole away. 'We must go now. There is nothing we can do for him. He's dead.'

She looked at the body. Blood still oozed from it. 'Are you sure . . .'

'Yes. Yes, I'm sure.'

He pushed her towards the stairs, glancing back at Stefan as he did, willing him to make no sound. He had condemned the man to death, either from his injuries, or at the hands of a vengeful enemy who would find him before long. Hardened as he was, even Barras couldn't immediately wipe from his mind the thought of what he had done. He only half understood his reasons, but even that didn't stop him.

They raced down the stairs, pausing a moment amid the litter and broken bodies in the doorway, then they were sprinting at lung-bursting speed for the shelter of the winding streets of the commercial district adjoining the shunting yard. As they ran, Nicole stumbled. Paul put out his hand to catch her. Her clothing was sticky with blood.

A wave of excitement passed through him as it occurred to him that she might have killed that night. The thought aroused him. As they entered the twisting, cobbled lanes he tried to dwell on it, explore the sensation it gave rise to, but the unlit way was difficult and needed too much of his attention for him to concentrate.

As dawn broke they collapsed exhausted on to the dusty floor of an attic in a disused grain store. The Germans had sealed the area very thoroughly. Twice the couple had been fired on as they investigated potential escape routes. Both times they had eluded their pursuers. Several times in the night they had heard automatic fire coming from other parts of the quarter. Apparently they were not the only ones experiencing trouble.

Barras sat propped against a beam as he looked out at the road through a gap he had made in the slates. Nicole lay curled in the middle of the floor. She was trying to sleep but it wouldn't come.

'Will we find a way through, Paul?' Her eyes were dark ringed and her face streaked with dirt.

He answered honestly. 'There is a good chance. I think we will. And if we can't slip through, well, there are a hundred large buildings in the area they've cordoned off. It would take an army months to search them all. We may go hungry for a while but, if we have to, we can hide until they call off the search or grow careless. It's light now. We'll wait till night before trying again.'

They took it in turns to sleep while the other kept watch. It was midday when Nicole wakened Paul to watch the first signs of activity outside. A squat, cannon-armed Panhard armoured car turned into the street. The angular four-wheeled vehicle bore the white ringed eagle emblem of the Wehrmacht police. It stopped in the middle of the road, the bell-shaped muzzle of its Hotchkiss twenty-five millimetre gun slowly traversed as the commander in the turret sighted on each building in turn.

Round the corner behind it came a platoon of infantry. They set up a light machine-gun in the first doorway and deployed themselves about the car. An ancient Citroen lorry growled into view and disgorged a section of pioneers, who immediately began unloading and setting up a barbed-wire barricade across the full width of the road behind the Panhard. The procedure looked well rehearsed, and was completed with few shouted orders.

After the barricade was finished there was a brief pause, and then, at a single shouted command, the soldiers moved off by sections and began entering the buildings. More pioneers and

66

some assault engineers arrived. They stood in the rivetted shelter of the car, ready if their specialist help was required. Most carried bulky satchels, others were armed with flame-throwers.

'Thorough, very thorough.' Though he had spoken the words out loud, Barras had meant them for himself. He had not noticed Nicole beside him, watching the German troops as they kicked their way into one building after another. When one particularly stout door resisted the united efforts of several burly soldiers the pioneers were called up and a small demolition charge used.

'Time to be moving,' said Paul, as dust showered down on them. 'No, not that way. They'll have sharpshooters covering the back alleys. Here, give me a hand.'

Nicole came back from the trap-door and joined him in hacking with her knife at the mortar joining the bricks of the end wall. Under their combined efforts a hole appeared through to the roof space of the next building, just as they heard, three floors below, the street door collapse under a hefty shoulder charge.

The wall was old, the cement crumbled at a touch and the pair had passed through two more like it before the searchers reached the attic they had left. By the time the first German was discovering the start of their escape route they were safely in the back streets of an as yet unsearched area.

Barras led the girl through the stench of a tannery yard to put any tracker dogs off, and then to a huge stone-built, five-storey structure. The few small windows in its thick blank walls were right at the top of the building, and heavily barred.

Nicole hung back as he led the way in. 'What is this place?'

He took her firmly by the arm and led her inside, across the great cold slabs of stone that paved the ground floor, to a narrow iron staircase that hugged the wall. Barras said nothing until they paused on the third landing.

'It's a fireproof depository. Look at this door. It's steel.'

He threw his weight against the rusted metal. It resisted for a moment, then with a squeal of protest slammed into place, wedging itself tightly into the grooves that assisted it in retarding the spread of fire. He braced it with some baulks of timber that lay about, then took Nicole's hand and led her to the top of the building.

'It's like a fortress, isn't it?'

'Or a prison.' She rubbed some of the accumulated grime from a small pane and peered out.

*   *   *

Several times during the course of the afternoon they heard the distant crump of small charges and once, far off, the hissing, roaring wail of a flame-thrower. Black smoke had drifted for a while over the rooftops.

It was late afternoon when the Germans entered the street, following exactly the same pattern as they had before. First an armoured car to provide cover, a Horch this time; then the troops, followed by the pioneers with their barricades and demolition charges, and the engineers with their flame-throwers. The shouted exchange of orders and the thudding of metal-shod boots moved nearer. Then they were in the building and the crash of many feet on the metal stairs made the vast structure echo. Paul and Nicole exchanged looks and waited.

The searchers below reached the great door. More orders were shouted and there was the sound of much movement as the pioneers were called. Nicole looked out through the small patch of clean glass, then turned back to Paul Barras.

'They've got us now, haven't they? I don't want them to take me, Paul.'

Barras stretched out his hand to her. She didn't move nearer, he didn't reach further. The hollow gesture seemed for him to sum up what their relationship had been. He looked at her. She had aged. In one night and a day she had become years older, but it made no difference. For them there was no more time for growing old. Perhaps she would have been better off on her own. He knew that her presence had made him more cautious, knew that there had been moments during the last eighteen hours when either of them, on their own, might have tried blasting a way through the ring the Germans had put round the district. His concern had restrained them, and brought them to this. He realized that his body had reacted to the thought of Nicole killing; started to concentrate on the thought.

The building trembled and dust fell like a fine mist as a small demolition charge was fired. There was a pause, and then, from the irate shouts and oaths, he gathered that the attempt had failed and the door still held. There was more scuffling and movement, a brief interlude of silence as the men below retreated to a safe distance. A bigger bang this time, followed by more dust, more shouting, but apparently no greater success.

Somewhere in the street a German officer was raising his voice in anger. The stoutly constructed depository was defying their efforts and holding up the search. They were working to a pattern and a time-table and the officer had been made personally responsible for this street.

Nicole watched out of the window. 'Perhaps they will leave this building, if it is too much trouble.'

It was a plea, rather than an expression of faint hope, which was all it could be. He couldn't think of anything to say that might offer a ray of hope or crumb of comfort – at least, nothing he could make sound truthful.

'I don't think they will give up. We must just be prepared for whatever they do next.'

Though he felt bitterness that his own life was probably soon to come to an abrupt and painful end, he still couldn't fathom what his true feelings were towards Nicole, not even the reason he had gone back for her. He felt in a way guilty that he couldn't sense any emotion within himself at having brought her to this. He felt nothing identifiable to which he could attach a label and say: this is regret, or love or even hatred. Their affair had been like that. She had been patient, tried hard to help. Perhaps part of the problem had been that he had never even been sure he really wanted her. And now, so very close to the end, there was still nothing.

'They're leaving the building. Paul, they're leaving.'

He joined her at the window. It was true. The Germans were all hurrying back down the road. It didn't seem possible that a single steel door should have deterred them when everything so far had indicated their determination to do a thorough job.

'Get down!' His shouted warning came just in time.

The Germans had good reason for quitting the building. They had left a much larger charge behind. It detonated and the concussion thundered through the warehouse. The whole structure swayed and, had they still been on their feet, their ankles would have been broken as the floor heaved and fell. A section in the centre of the room suddenly sagged and collapsed to the floor below, setting in motion a chain reaction that gutted the building.

Noise, dust and fumes filled the air. As it slowly began to settle, Paul and Nicole could see the gaping void where the boards had been. Broad cracks radiated out from it to the corners of the room. Peering carefully over the ragged edges Barras could see right down to the ground floor. Even as he looked the metal staircase, deprived of much of its support and unable to sustain its own weight, buckled. With a grinding, rending crash and shower of sparks it settled in a tangle of twisted angle-iron on to the rubble below.

A barely audible ranting from the street gave an indication that the results of the explosion had exceeded the requirements of the officer in charge.

The ruined floor creaked and shed a few more sections as it tried to adjust to its new configuration. Barras lay at full length to distribute his weight and watched to see what the next development would be.

A small group of ultra-cautious Germans entered, gingerly picking their way among the scrap iron that had been the staircase. Expecting to find no one alive they were searching the debris for bodies.

Another piece fell away from the floor, bouncing all the way down to land among the men probing the wreckage. Barras saw his danger too late and began to shuffle back from the edge. The slight movement caused the cracks to spread, and the section he was on began to tilt. Frantically he scrabbled to push himself back but the slope of the floor steepened and he began to slide forward. A ragged burst of fire swept past his nose, a single pistol shot thumped into the floor. The thickness of its construction saved him.

'Paul!' Nicole shouted and held out to him the butt of her rifle.

As the angle of the disintegrating floor became acute, Barras put all his remaining strength into a twisting turn that enabled him to get one finger through the trigger guard. Another fusillade of shots from below flew through the space that an instant before his head and neck had occupied.

The metal of the Mauser's guard bit into his finger as he flailed about with his free hand in search of some additional hold. More of the floor fell away and, for a moment, the Germans were kept busy avoiding the splintered planks and joists that showered down. Questing fingers found a crack wide enough to wedge into for a decent grip and he began to haul himself out of the line of fire. A long burst from an automatic punched into the underside of the floor. With a final effort he pulled himself to safety just as the very last bullet tore into his shoe and he felt his toes smash.

It was the first time he had been wounded. The first real pain he had ever known. It made him feel sick and giddy. He would have slipped back had the girl not grabbed hold of him and heaved him to the edge of the room.

The bullet had entered through the toe-cap and gone out through the sole, leaving two neat round holes. To Barras's intense relief the initial agony fast subsided to a painful but bearable throb. Blood squelched in the shoe. When, with assistance, he stood and tried to apply weight to the foot waves of pain washed through him and he had to gasp for air to stop from crying out.

Nicole tried to help, easing him down to sit with his back to the wall.

'You must take the shoe off. We should try to stop the bleeding.'

He pushed away her attempt to unlace it. 'It's all right. The bleeding will stop.' There was a rushing noise in his ears and he despised himself for his weakness, especially displayed in front of the girl. He won his fight against fainting, but a feeling of sickness persisted. 'Just let me rest, for a moment. What are they doing now?'

Nicole worked her way to the window, sidling along the wall. Even with her slight weight every step she took brought fresh protests from the ill-supported boards and caused further falls.

'Some of the pioneers are going into the building across the street.'

'How tall is it?'

She looked back at him. 'One floor less than this.'

She screamed and recoiled from the window clutching her face as cannon shells exploded beside it and on the bars.

The firing went on, blasting at each window in turn, but Barras ignored it. He watched Nicole where she knelt on the floor, covering her face with her hands. He felt sure she must have been blinded at least. Again the cannon shells smashed back as a fresh magazine was emptied at the face of the building. Most of the small square panes were broken but none of the twenty-millimetre rounds found their way in. Slowly Nicole moved her hands and looked up at him. Her fringe now sparkled with pieces of trapped glass but apart from some scratches she was unhurt. Her eyes were open wide with fear but she fought to regain control.

'What are they doing?'

'They know that these walls will withstand that light calibre gun, so they must have done it to break the windows.'

He eased himself to a standing position, pushing himself up

71

with his palms against the wall, using the MP40 as a crutch until its shortness gave him no more leverage.

'The flame-throwers?' Nicole went pale, put her clenched fist to her mouth. She hurried back to him. 'Can they reach this far? You said this building was fireproof.'

Barras tried to remember what the street was like, how wide it was, trying to find some fact he might offer to her as reassurance.

'I think they will reach this building, but not this far in.' He saw the relief that came into her eyes, but he knew he had to prepare her for what was coming. 'It's not the flame we have to worry about at this range. It will exhaust the oxygen, that is the danger. When the flame hits, hold your breath for as long as you can.' He pointed to the great hole in the floor. 'The Germans have kindly installed air-conditioning for us. The smoke and foul air will quickly disperse.'

Nicole was quite calm now. She knew she had been told the truth and she was prepared for what might happen. They sat quietly for a while. There was more shouting in the street, and from across the way the sound of breaking glass. Then the cannon fired once more, the shells pock-marking the dressed stone of the exterior. One of them found its way in between the bars and buried itself in a rafter.

The echoes had hardly died away when the first screaming, belching wailing, roasting tongue of fire mushroomed on the outside wall. Flame licked in at a window. A wave of hot air and black smoke gusted across the room, pushing a wall of dust before it. A second attempt followed and this time the aim was better, hitting the window dead centre. Some unbroken panes burst inwards. Streamers of boiling fire roared between the bars and the air surged from them as it was drawn to feed the flames. Then it was hurled back as a roasting gas, leeched of its life-giving element.

The flames receded, the dust flew thick, whipped up by violent currents of air. Black-tipped guttering fire played over the window bars and frame as the last of the paint burnt off. More dust fountained from the floors below, drawn by the rush of air coming to replace that consumed by the fuel-fed flames.

He had not noticed the moment at which it happened but as the last of the smoke cleared Paul Barras realized the girl was in his arms.

'I'm sorry.' She pushed herself away, straightening her hair as best she could.

It had been a similar action and the same words that had brought their affair to an end, some five years before. Barras recalled the last afternoon in her apartment. He had known even before they undressed that it would be the last time. Now once again it marked the last time, for everything.

Her firm, warm body nestling against him then had aroused no more passion or emotion than it did now. He felt no loss at her moving away from him. He realized that her action had been no more than that of a frightened animal seeking comfort in the herd.

He examined his machine-pistol, counted his spare magazines.

'They'll be coming in again now, to count the bodies. We could give them a surprise.'

Nicole just nodded dumbly. There was no animation in her eyes as she picked up her rifle and helped him hobble to the side of the hole. They got down on their hands and knees and crawled the last bit, choosing a section that seemed more stable than the rest. It dipped a little beneath their weight, but it held. It was possible to aim down to the ground floor through the cracks, without having to hang over the edge and give their ambush away.

'I'll hold my fire until a few are in.' Barras sighted on the broken doorway sixty feet below. 'Wait for my signal.'

This time the Germans were even more cautious than they had been before. The first thing they did was to sling in a stick grenade. It landed on the piled brick and stone, and suddenly a rapidly expanding ball of fire was racing to the top of the building. Fragments flew and rebounded like steel hail among the lower floors and before the last had rattled to a halt the first Germans were rushing in, wildly spraying automatic fire as they came.

Now a dozen men were in, and still the couple held their fire, waiting for the right moment. The search party became bolder as their conviction grew that the flame-throwers had finished the job for them.

Using first the pile of scrap and then ropes and grapnels, they began to climb to the upper floors. On the third, two of the group set up a light machine-gun to give cover to the men preparing to mount to the top two floors. As they climbed higher without meeting resistance their manner became more casual, their precautions less thorough. The men on the ropes exchanged banter with those still on the ground and manning the MG-42.

The barbed prongs of a grapnel lodged on the torn edge of the fourth floor, immediately below where Paul and Nicole lay concealed. An unteroffizier pushed aside the soldier who had hurled it, took hold of the dangling rope, gave it a hard tug to check it was firmly anchored and started to climb.

'Now.' Barras's shout filled the structure and for an instant all action stopped and everyone looked up.

A short burst from his MP40 and the two machine-gunners collapsed writhing beside their weapon. Nicole shot the unteroffizier who hung on the rope. The German's hand flew to his side as, at point blank range, the heavy bullet smashed his pelvis. He lost his grip and fell, to bounce screaming from floor to floor until his body was impaled on the broken ironwork below.

The others broke and ran. Three more were cut down before the building was once again empty of the enemy. Nicole scrambled up and ran to the window, where she stood and snapped off shots at the fleeing men as they rushed out into the evening sunlight. The first of five retaliatory shells from the Horch was a fraction low, giving her ample time to duck before the others pounded at the bars, wrenching two from their sockets. There was a pause and then another magazine was emptied at the smoke-stained opening. Two rounds came in through the gap, to expend themselves harmlessly against the underside of the roof, with only a few cracked and dislodged slates to show for it.

Paul dragged himself to the window. He refused her offer of assistance and struggled to stand, leaning against the wall to take the weight from his injured foot. Standing to one side, so as not to offer a target to any snipers who might have taken up positions, he looked out.

Through the pain, through the exhaustion and giddiness brought on by loss of blood, he felt his body reacting as he saw two dark shapes sprawled on the cobbles. Irregular tentacles of dark liquid zig-zagged away from them. Nicole was close, and he felt he wanted to reach out, touch her, do anything in an attempt to explore, maintain and intensify the longed-for reaction. The moment was snatched frustratingly from him. The armoured car was driven forward and under cover of it the two corpses were dragged off.

'They are not going to give up now.' Nicole was no longer asking questions. That was a statement.

'No.'

He could think of nothing else to say, but then his mind was not on the immediate conflict. The thought, the knowledge and

74

the sight of Nicole killing had caused a reaction that had been beyond him in the bedroom. Now his thoughts ranged back through time, seeking some clue as to why it had taken this to rouse him. He picked and sifted through the incidents he could recall.

He was fifteen and, passing the kitchen door, had seen his father lifting the skirts of their middle-aged and matronly domestic as she stood rinsing cups at the sink. From the ease and familiarity with which it was done it had been clear even to a young boy that it was not the first, nor an isolated incident.

He remembered being surprised at the bright pink bloomers the woman wore, and how she had cooed and simpered as greedy hands had rummaged in her underwear. How for a moment she had feigned protest as one hand was withdrawn to unfasten the coarse worsted trousers that pressed against her. The ample folds of the bunched up skirt had hidden detail but the two sweating figures had stayed locked together for a long time until, with a last convulsive shudder, his father had pulled clear. The woman's skirt had dropped and she had resumed the washing-up. Something that crinkled had been pushed into her waistband. He had heard his parents bed creaking a lot that night.

He thought of the games his elder sister had made him play when their parents were out, and how she had told him she preferred to play mothers and fathers with the boy down the road because he made it more real.

The incident in the park sprang back to the fore. The old man's leer, the offer of money and the furtive looking round before they had gone into the bushes, and then his growing revulsion, and the wizened old degenerate making fun of him.

Nicole's hand brushing against his arm brought him back to reality. The Horch had backed from sight. Only ribbon-like stains marked where the dead had lain for a while. He clipped a fresh thirty-two-round magazine into place on his machine-pistol.

A movement on the roof of the building opposite caught his eye. Slates were shifting. One slid down the roof to shatter in the street. Barras thrust the snout of his gun out through the twisted steel rods, sighted carefully and fired the whole magazine. The last shot jammed but the rest smashed into the roof, snapping thick slates in half and sending more to the road. There was no further movement.

Nicole tensed, straining to hear something. 'What is it?'

They stood poised, trying to anticipate the next development.

The sound came again, clearer and nearer now. It was unmistakable: the grind and squeal of tank tracks, moving ever closer. They looked at each other.

The hauptmann looked anxiously at his watch for the tenth time in as many minutes. He was responsible for clearing the street, and he was a worried man. The oberst had already sent two messengers with urgent instructions for the job to be hurried up. All the other companies were ready to move to the next sector, his alone was delaying them.

The hauptmann feared at any moment to see the arrival of the oberst's staff car. What for three years had been a comfortable and undemanding garrison post was fast becoming a nightmare. He had thrown everything he had against the maquisards who held out in the big building. Now he had been forced, most reluctantly, to ask the oberst for heavier weapons with which to try more drastic measures. The oberst had asked the hauptmann how many he thought he had trapped. Hauptmann Reinberger had sweated on that one. If he said too few then he would be berated for not having already shifted so weak an opposition. If he gave too high an estimate the oberst would turn up to personally supervise the operation, and afterwards a body-count might prove most embarrassing. Sweating profusely, the hauptmann looked at his Tissot again.

Another drab-painted BMW roared up. The dispatch rider handed over yet another message. The hauptmann wished there was time to relieve himself. He crumpled the scrap of paper in his wet palm and looked up at sound the of approaching tank tracks. Hope surged through him as the bulk of a Tiger tank slewed round the corner. The giant war machine looked factory fresh save for one corrugated track-guard and a scattering of broken masonry on the front hull top, evidence of the difficulty the driver had experienced in negotiating the narrow roads. The panzer's dark-green paint was scarred in places. The white runic formation sign on its glacis plate was half obliterated by brick dust.

The Tiger slowed to ease past the Horch. Hauptmann Reinberger stepped behind it and, taking care to avoid the hot exhaust covers, hauled himself with some difficulty on to the tank's engine deck in order to talk with the commander who stood half out of the turret. Reinberger had to shout to be heard above the rumble of the V12 Maybach engine.

'It's the big building halfway down on the left-hand side. They're holding out on the top floor. We've tried everything. We've gutted the place with satchel charges, burnt it with flamethrowers and sent in storming parties. I've got seven men dead and four wounded, and we haven't even seen them yet.'

The tank's commander, a young oberleutnant, barely glanced at the building indicated. His manner was totally confident. The silver insignia of an SS regiment flashed on his shoulder as he lifted his hand to adjust his throat microphone.

'It doesn't matter where they are, how many they are, or what they have done to your puny attempts to dislodge them.' He patted the turret top. 'They are dead men already.'

His manner was insolent to the point of being insulting, but the hauptmann had to bear it. The oberleutnant knew that.

'Have your men seal the back alleys. They can manage that, can't they?' He grinned at the hauptmann. It was not a friendly expression, rather the look a superior might bestow out of compassion on a pathetic simpleton. 'Hauptmann, you are about to have your first lesson in total warfare. Heil Hitler.'

With that the oberleutnant turned away, not caring if the salute was answered or not. As far as he was concerned the hauptmann was a failure, fit only for cannon fodder. There was no place for his sort in the new German Socialist Europe that would be built after the Allies had been taught their final lesson in the fields of Normandy.

From their vantage point at the top of the depository, Nicole Duval and Paul Barras caught their first glimpse of a Tiger tank as the behemoth backed and manoeuvred to position itself in the centre of the road. The long barrel of the eighty-eight milli-metre cannon began to elevate as, very slowly, the turret traversed to bear on the building. The huge tank, lacking entirely the grace of the animal after which it was named, lumbered forward over the cobbles.

'Give me your rifle. Help me to stand.'

Ignoring the danger of snipers, Barras poked the rifle barrel through the bars. Nicole tried to support him as he sighted and fired twice at the black-uniformed figure leaning casually out of the turret.

The pain in his foot, the handicap of his unsteady position, proved too great a difficulty to overcome. Both shots missed their target and didn't even hit the tank. They were clearly heard by

77

the SS oberleutnant as he looked up sharply, straight at their window. The long tube of the barrel elevated a fraction more, and then the tank half turned on the spot to position itself so as to take advantage of the the few extra degrees that could be obtained by parking at an angle on the steep camber of the road. When it came to rest, the eighty-eight was pointing directly at their window.

'Here, let me try.' Nicole took the Mauser from him.

Close behind and slightly to one side of her as he leaned against the rough-textured wall for support, Barras could see her face, see her concentrating as she took aim. He felt his heart starting to thump and was filled with a wild excitement as he realized what was happening to him. This time there was no distraction, no check to his body's reaction. It was absurd, stupid, but it was real. The present pain, the past memories, they didn't matter. They were gone, forgotten. All that mattered was what he could feel his body doing.

Nicole drew in a deep breath and held it, making the thin material of her blouse go taut. Over her shoulder Barras saw the end sight of the rifle and the black-clad target. He couldn't help himself. He was exultant, couldn't and wouldn't have stopped himself if he'd had the power to. His free hand went to his trousers, ripped them open, releasing and exposing the damp-tipped rod of his erection.

The girl's head jerked back under the effect of the rifle's recoil. As the piece of racing steel passed through the oberleutnant's chest and came out below his left shoulder blade, the colour drained instantly from his face. He made one attempt to articulate and failed, even as he failed to maintain his grip on the sides of the cupola. Slowly, mouth gaping soundlessly, he slid from sight into the turret.

'Nicole. Nicole, look!'

Paul's clutching hand whirled her round. She read the wild excitement in his eyes, but didn't understand until he grabbed her hand and took it to his fluid-pulsing core.

The muzzle of the Tiger's eighty-eight belched flame and the top storey of the depository became a hell of steel and fire and blood. The roof lifted and then caved in. A second shell blasted away much of the front wall below the fourth floor and the whole of the top of the building collapsed in a dust-spewing cascade of splintered wood and broken brick. Again and again the high explosive projectiles thundered into and through the remains of the structure, each successive round finding less to destroy as the destruction became complete. The tank gun fell silent only when its shells began to tear holes in the warehouses behind the ruin.

That first shot which crashed through the wall beside the window at which Paul and Nicole stood, was deflected up into the roof and exploded against the thick beam supporting the ridge. Without that key timber, the weight of the slates crushed the remaining rafters. The pair were caught by the storm of metal slivers the fireball spawned. Then, as the second shell struck, they plummeted with the debris to the floors below.

Paul Barras lay curled in a tight ball on the edge of the second floor, part buried beneath rubble and smothered in dust. His hands were clenched tight on his groin as he tried to stem the flow of blood from a massive wound. He thought he was dying. He wanted to die. More than anything he had ever wanted, he wanted to die. The pain was bad. He held himself tighter in an attempt to ease it. The action brought more light debris down on him. But there was something else, more important than the pain, more important than the longing for death. Rising above them was a hatred and fury that life, that fate, should have saved up such a trick for him. Then his hate found a more tangible target as out of the billowing clouds of dust came the angular outline of the Tiger.

Unblinking, he concentrated every ounce of his will on it, silently begging some power to intercede and wipe it out of existence. The Tiger came on, the booming note of its exhaust causing fresh falls in the ruined building. The wide tracks crunched over the littered road. Everything near it vibrated in time with its twenty-three-litre engine. The turret hatch was closed down. It came on, slewing from side to side as though searching for something, or someone.

Barras watched as bricks were ground to powder, thick beams splintered to matchwood. Still it came on up the road. It was almost level with the Frenchman's vantage point when he spotted the body of Nicole. The blast had thrown her out into the road and the blood flowed slowly from her body, turning the dust into a red-grey sludge. Her clothes had been torn away, but one arm was unmarked, it lay across the body, as if in mock salute to the mutilated monstrosity to which it was attached.

The driver of the Tiger saw the corpse and the tank's engine howled as it launched itself, all fifty-six tons, straight at it. In a macabre dance of revenge the oberleutnant's panzer churned the remains of Nicole Duval. The pieces, few of them recognizable, were carried up and round by the tracks until there was nothing left to see. The dust hid from Paul Barras the shreds and stains that had been Nicole.

The exhaust roared a last time. When Barras blinked from his eyes the stinging cloud it raised, the Tiger was gone. He was alone with his pain and his thoughts.

Paul Barras lay undiscovered in the ruins for eighteen hours. When their sweep was completed the Germans reopened the area. Members of the maquis were among the first through the cordons. Barras was found and smuggled to the convent St Jeanne d'Arc where Doctor Bruno Soult carried out emergency surgery.

The operation was crude and fast. Crude due to the limited facilities, fast because the resistance leader was weak from shock and loss of blood and could not withstand the rigours of prolonged surgery.

Barras, too ill to be moved, carried on his fight for life for six days. At the end of that time Doctor Soult pronounced it just possible that he might live.

Extracts from the personal diary of Doctor Bruno Soult, taken from part of an entry made the day after the operation.
. . . massive wound to the groin and abdomen, though most essential organs, from a purely medical point of view, are intact or repairable. There are simple fractures of both ankles and the second and third toe of the left foot have had to be amputated. He has suffered a traumatic amputation of the scrotum and the penis. I have done my best; it is just possible he may survive. Only time will show whether or not he wishes to when he regains consciousness and discovers the extent of his injuries.

Taken from an entry made the day Barras left the convent.
. . . a truly remarkable recovery, physically. He has displayed no emotion; no bitterness, self pity, nothing. Some reaction was to be expected but I can't draw him on the subject. His mental facilities are unimpaired by the shock of the experience or the nature of the injury. On the rare occasions I can persuade him to play, he is quite capable of thrashing me at chess but rarely does, due to careless mistakes during his single-mindedly

aggressive play. He frightens me. I would be far happier if he would break down, begin smashing things even. It is dangerous to keep so much bottled up inside. I must admit I am glad he is leaving. The last few times I have seen him it has been like being with a time-bomb. The timing mechanism must be very unstable and some day an explosion must come, I am thankful I shall not be around when he 'blows up'.

Only seven and a half weeks after being wounded Barras was once more working behind the German lines. Just three days after rejoining, he butchered three women being held by the resistance as suspected informers and collaborators. Even by the standards of the Communist-dominated, fiercely anti-nazi resistance in that area, his zeal was excessive. When irrefutable proof.of the women's innocence suddenly came to light, his self-appointed act as executioner became an extreme embarrassment to the local leadership.

They were already involved in a mud-slinging match with their Gaullist rivals and had no wish to hand a propaganda gift to them on virtually the eve of the contest for the control of the civil administration. A thorough cover-up operation was put in hand, its first stage being the removal of Barras to a place where he could do no more harm. He was ordered to join a British infantry battalion as a guide. The unit was pushing into northern France, Barras's home territory.

Late August saw him attached as a scout and guide to a company of light infantry in the vanguard of the British Second Army's advance.

THE PATROL

22.15 TO 23.25 HOURS

The German grenade bounced once and rolled to a stop at
Barras's feet. As though it were the most ordinary occurrence
in the world he stooped, picked it up and, half turning with
hardly time to take aim, tossed it under-arm into the kitchen.
It exploded before it touched the floor. The detonation brought
down masses of soot from the chimney which flooded across the
main room. Before the black tide had even begun to settle a burst
of machine-gun fire came in through the closed front door. Dicky
had to throw himself to one side as the flying steel chewed at
the table top, prising up long splinters and going on to sew an
irregular line of holes in the far wall.

More shots came in through the makeshift blind, tearing it
down. A hand appeared at the window, clutching another
grenade. Barras's weapon chattered furiously and the grenade
fell from smashed fingers just outside. There was a panicking,
anguished scream, cut short by the bursting bomb, and the wall
below the window bowed in.

The dust from the pulverized plaster added its contribution
to the soot-laden air, with which was blended grey smoke from
the kitchen. From the same direction came the crackle of burning
wood. A halo of opal light surrounded the oil lamps, which had
begun to sputter and flicker in the particle-laden atmosphere.
More bullets found their way in, boring through the thick wood
of the door and going on to bury themselves in the walls and
furniture.

'Get those lamps. We can't do a bloody thing while it's so
light in here.'

'No.' Dicky's shout came just in time to stop Barras from
following Ellis's instruction by shooting them down. 'Not that
way, you'll fry us.'

An unseen German marksman unwittingly punctuated the end
of the sentence. A single bullet nicked the underside of the top
of the window frame and thudded into the floor behind Barras.

'They have put a sniper up in the trees. He is looking right
down on us.'

As the Frenchman shouted he rolled across the floor to crouch
beneath the window, heedless of the broken glass on which he

knelt. Bird and Ellis followed his example, but now the three of them were pinned down in the narrow strip of safe area immediately below the window. There came an incoherent mumbling from the sofa. A tousled head appeared. The farmer had chosen that moment to regain consciousness. He shook his head, dazed and confused, staring uncomprehendingly at Dicky who shouted an urgent warning to him. It was too late.

The sniper's aim was a fraction off centre, but it was good enough. The high-powered round whined in and cut a furrow down the side of the farmer's head as effectively as a blow from a cleaver. Red-flecked bone and brain sprayed out, his mouth gaped open and, with an idiot expression, the dying man slumped off the sofa on to the floor. He landed beside his wife.

She had lain there since the grenade exploded, eyes tight closed, hands over her ears, willing the destruction of her home to stop. The thump beside her made her look. She saw her husband's gaping wound and slack-mouthed, drooling expression and began to sob and howl as with her bare hands she tried to scoop up and push back the spongy white mass that flowed from his broken skull.

Ellis had to do something quickly, or it would end the same way for all of them. He was glad he had had the drink. It helped.

'Get those lights.'

As he shouted he raised himself on one knee and, without pretence of aiming, hosed the whole magazine of his sten out towards the woods. By a miracle it didn't jam.

Bird and Barras flung themselves across the room and grabbed at the lamps. The Frenchman got his and dropped quickly to the floor, scurrying back to shelter with it. The lamp Dicky's hands closed on had been broken at some time and was fastened to its bracket by some intricate windings of wire. As he frantically fumbled with the fitting a shot smacked into the wall between his unraised arms and then the lamp was free. As he dived for cover he dropped it.

Private Bird cringed, waiting to be enveloped by a ball of flame. The wick gave off a spurt of bright yellow flame, a couple of sparks, and went out.

The room was dark now, but there was a growing flicker of fire from the kitchen that would soon render their position just as dangerous as it had been before. More bullets smacked against the outside wall. Some found there way in. The china cabinet and its contents jumped and shattered into a thousand pieces.

Without a sound the woman pitched forward across the dead body of her husband, a neatly spaced row of ragged punctures running the length of her side.

'Come on, before it's us.' Ellis was up and running out the back way before the woman's blood had begun to stain her dress.

Dicky grabbed at the radio without breaking pace as he dashed after the sergeant. Barras put the MP40 to his shoulder and emptied it out the window at the trees before turning and following.

Ellis didn't stop to unbolt the back door. He shoulder charged it. The hinges burst apart and the three men trampled out over it to race for the cover of the sheds and barns. A figure stepped out from behind a machinery store, two sten guns and a machine-pistol barked and it jerked back out of sight, propelled by the several impacts.

Behind the fleeing trio a flurry of stick grenades detonated in the farmhouse. Flame leapt from the kitchen window and doorway. From their right came stabbing white tongues of rapid automatic fire. Near misses struck sparks from the stone wall beside which they ran. Then they were round a corner and no more shots came. Another nerve-racking hundred yards and they regained the safety of the woods.

'I'm cold.' Eric tried to tug the collar of his coat up higher about his ears.

'I don't care what you bloody are, just stop wriggling about. I'd just got comfy.'

The movement of his friend had disturbed the carefully piled pine needles under which Alex was hoping to generate a bit of warmth. Corporal Morris looked back from where he lay by the bren, keeping a watch on the clearing.

'Stop piddling about, you two, and keep the bleeding noise down. There's two troops of sodding Tigers and half a flak battery down there, so for Christ's sake put a sock in it.'

'If I had a dry sock I'd put me foot in it.' Alex gave up trying to rearrange the heap and crawled forward to join Morris. 'You were with one of the tank regiments once, weren't you, Corp?'

Morris stared more intently at the scene below the embankment.

'Well, you were, weren't you?'

'Yeah. So?'

Alex was not to be put off. 'Well, it's just that . . . I was wondering. Did you ever come up against a Tiger?'

'Yes.' While the answer was affirmative, the tone was positively negative.

About a mile off a German Nebelwerfer rocket battery was warming up for its night's work. Three of the big hundred and fifty millimetre projectiles screamed skywards, carrying their cargoes of high explosives to target areas among the British lines. Even from that distance away, the take-off was frightening. The ranging shots done, there was a pause. Then the noise started up again in earnest as several batteries opened fire together. They flashed into the night sky, the glow of their rocket exhausts lighting the base of the clouds for a moment before they climbed from sight.

'I'm glad I'm not on the receiving end of that lot.' Eric stuck his head out the side of the hide to watch the mass take off.

'We don't know what we're going to be on the receiving end of tonight, yet.' Alex opened his ammunition pouch and checked the number of spare magazines he had.

One of the articulated fuel tankers was threading its way through the mass of vehicles down below. It pulled on to the road and drove off, going back the way it had come. The other bowser was having its hoses reeled in. Distant thunder now blended with the almost continual roll of far-off artillery fire and barrage.

A strutting unteroffizier moved among the sweating lines of men from the supply trucks to the tanks. With his swagger stick and a loud voice he kept urging the soaked and slovenly pioneers to greater effort. His hectoring appeared to have small effect on the men, who continued to work at a leisurely pace. Their attitude clearly irked the NCO who resorted to even more violent action with the stick and his tongue.

From his vantage point Alex saw some of the expressions and gestures that followed the unteroffizier's retreating back as he stalked from one human chain to another.

'Change the language and the equipment and that could be some of our blokes down there.'

Eric pushed between them. 'You're right there, mate. Every army's the bloody same. They've all got their slackers and scroungers and jumped-up NCOs. Just a general observation, Corp, nothing personal. Honest.'

Morris snorted, but he let it go. 'Where's that coming from?'

85

He heard the unmistakable sound of German machine-gun fire, not more than half a mile off. The unique ripping sound of its ultra-fast rate of fire was sandwiched between the crump of exploding grenades.

'It's coming from the direction the others took. Do you reckon they might have run into a spot of bother?'

'How the hell should I know? It might be nothing to do with them. I'll tell you one thing·– it's stirred that lot to action.' Morris indicated the clearing.

The hidden trio's concern over the not-too-distant exchange of fire was mirrored by the sudden speed with which the pioneers were finishing their work. On the flak guns the crews closed up to action stations and the weapons were hurriedly traversed to face the direction of the disturbance. The muzzle sleeves were removed and spare ammunition cases taken from lockers and stacked by the loaders on the gun platform.

Several motors coughed into life and the now-empty supply trucks began to jockey into a rough line behind the two motor-cycle combinations. The pioneers were no less swift in boarding their transport, and came in for a good deal of banter from the tank and transporter crews. In the hurry to form the convoy there was much stalling of motors and crashing of gears. The panzer troops greeted each occurrence with a derisive cheer, with an especially loud howl for every minor collision that occurred.

Within five minutes of the first motor starting up, only the flak gun with their crews, the transporters and their loads, two of the supply vehicles and one of the big fuellers remained.

'If Ellis isn't back here soon, the whole lot will have gone.'

Eric looked up at the sky above the treetops in the direction from which the firing had come. The base of the clouds was reflecting the glow of a rapidly growing conflagration.

'Maybe they won't be coming back.'

The thunderstorm hovered on the horizon, coming no closer. The rumble following each distant flash of lightning was barely audible above the regular booming of some heavy guns that had begun firing two miles away. Then both were drowned out by the blare of a klaxon on one of the Krupps. At the signal, the transporters were started, one after the other adding their deep-throated roar to the unholy chorus of sounds.

'Isn't there a way that we could hold them up a bit, delay them till the sarge gets back with the radio?'

'Of course there is, Pitt. Nip down and ask that officer in the Krupp with the fancy hooter on the cab roof if he'd be so kind as to hold on a minute while you pop a few mines under the wheels of his wagons. While you're down there, ask him which way they'll be going, so Church can nip along and set his load where it'll catch those you miss.'

Morris spoke with irritation. He too would have liked to have seen the Tigers blasted, but between the three of them they had only two sten guns and the bren, plus a handful of grenades – not enough to take on a determinedly crewed scout car, let alone two flak wagons and six Tiger tanks; even though they were on trailers.

The fourth Krupp stuttered into life, then the fifth. On one of them a panel rattled, gradually going quieter as an engine warmed and ran at a more steady note.

Morris watched, concentrating all his attention on the panzers, unable to take his eyes from them. They brought back memories. He remembered pain and fear, and screams that weren't his own. He sighted down the bren at the nearest Tiger. It seemed to expand, grow even larger. He tried to imagine what one, what all of them would look like spurting fire from their hatches and engine covers, but the only image he could conjure was the one that was always with him, the flash of flame tipping a Tiger's machine guns and cannon.

Despite the cold wind and his soaking clothes, Morris perspired. He longed to see them torn apart, hear the screams of their crews. Into his mind unbidden came a picture of what it was probably like inside the Tigers' fighting compartment. He screwed up his eyes to blot out an image they had never seen. The thought of the cold bare metal, the smell of warm petrol and hot oil, the sound of the extractor fan sucking the stinking yellow cordite mist away, the clatter of spent shell casings falling to the turret floor and the alternate purr and rising bellow of the engine. All these things crowded into his imagination.

'Are you all right, Corp?'

'Of course I am.'

He didn't feel it. His throat felt harsh and his head spun, and for a moment he thought he was going to be sick. He wrenched his mind from his imaginings, as he had once pulled physically away from the prospect of climbing into the real thing.

The starter motor on the last of the Krupps whirred. The officer in charge of the convoy stood half out of one of the roof hatches, leaning on the twin tapered horns of the klaxon, and looked over his charges. He raised his arm to signal for them to pull out.

Ellis, Bird and Barras plunged through the woods with little regard for the amount of noise they were making. Distance was the only thing that mattered. They needed to put as much as possible between themselves and the farmhouse. A stop had to be made eventually for Ellis to catch up, and to relieve his bursting bladder when he did.

While they stood quietly and waited for him to finish, they heard a search party behind them entering the woods. They went on at a more cautious pace, having to make a wide circle before they felt safe in starting back to the hide. Ellis fought to subdue an attack of hiccups, ridiculously loud in the dead of night in their stark contrast to the distant blend of guns and storm. When precious time was spared for a snatched glance back the way they had come, there was an orange glow from the farmhouse. The Germans had left it to burn.

During a second brief stop to see if they could detect the sounds of pursuit, Dicky made the discovery that they had suffered one casualty during the attack. The radio had been drilled by three close spaced bullets.

'Right through the heart,' he said, and dropped the pack. 'Sorry, Sarge, it's been buggered good and proper.'

It fell over and emitted tinklings and clatterings as broken glass and components settled.

'Do you mean all that was for bloody nothing? All that effort and we still haven't got a radio.'

'Well we had one for a while, Sarge,' was the only consolation Dicky could offer.

'Do not let it worry you, Sergeant. After all, the journey was not a complete waste of time, was it?' Barras reached forward and plucked a bottle of wine out of Ellis's coat front. 'I am not surprised you could not keep up.'

Ellis snatched the wine back. 'Mind your own bloody business.' He jammed the bottle back into his greatcoat.

'Pardon me, Sergeant. I did not mean to snatch your crutch from you. Forgive me.'

Barras and Ellis stood toe to toe, Ellis glaring, Barras smirking. There was a gulf between them, of temperament, of intellect, of motivation, that only physical violence could temporarily bridge.

'Why do you not go back to your miserable little island, to

your bar-room fights? They are more your style, that is your own level. In those places in a fight everyone is drunk. You will never be noticed.'

Ellis balled his fists. 'I need to be bloody drunk around you. Why in hell did I have to end up with the only French pansy sadist in the whole bloody war?' He took the bottle out, waved it under the Frenchman's nose. 'You see this? See it? After the war I can put this down. What are you going to do?'

Paul Barras bristled, balancing on his toes to look Ellis in the face. 'You? Put that down? That and others like it are welded to your hand for life.'

The bottle shattered against a tree, leaving Ellis with just the jagged neck in his hand. He held it out towards his antagonist, his tormentor.

'We'll see.' He hurled the makeshift weapon from sight among the trees. 'Well, I've let go. When are you going to start having women, instead of killing them?'

Tracer zoomed by overhead and the argument was cut short. The three men ducked and raced from the spot, seeking to lose their pursuers in the dense undergrowth. After a minute, rasping lungs forced them to moderate their pace and allowed them to travel more carefully, with less noise and disturbance. More tracer made beads and dashes of green light off to their right, and they slowed down to a fast walking pace, to move as quietly as the press of saplings would allow. Shortly after, tracer flashed again, even further away. They had shaken the German patrol from their trail.

'Where the hell have you been? We've been hearing firing on and off for the last twenty minutes. Where's the radio?' Morris tucked in his legs to make more room as Ellis and Bird crept in.

Barras stayed outside, sitting hunched under a tree, looking back the way they had come. His finger was on the trigger of the machine-pistol.

Ellis was only partially successful in smothering a belch. 'To a farmhouse . . . Have you really? . . . It died of wounds. Any more questions? No? Then it's my turn. What's been going on down there?'

'They got the frights and began pulling out soon after the shooting started.'

The sergeant wriggled to the front and looked out at the clearing through the gap between the logs. An officer had climbed down from the cab of one of the Krupps and was crossing to another that seemed reluctant to start. The German major stepped on to the running-board of the recalcitrant transporter and held a heated discussion with its driver. The officer was not happy. Frequently letting go of his grip on the door handle to wave his arms about, he was in imminent danger of falling back into the mire. When he had done shouting he went back to his vehicle and reappeared a moment later out of its open roof hatch. He whirled an arm in violent circles as a signal to the other crews, then had to snatch at a hold on the cab roof to avoid being hurled over the back as his own driver engaged first gear at too high a rev and the huge rig lurched forward.

'There goes our sitting target.' Morris closed his notebook and buttoned it in his pocket. 'What do we do now, Sarge? Wait till it's time to go back?'

Under cover of the pitch-black corner of the hide where he had settled himself, Ellis took out his flask as quietly as he could and took several long pulls at it, fighting back the tears and the urge to cough that the stinging spirit brought. A warm glow spread right through his body. It seemed to him that his thoughts had a crystal clarity. It was an exhilarating feeling, like being set free after a long captivity. He breathed deeply, straightened his back. The scent of the forest came to him. He was conscious of the sound of the wind as it gusted between the trees and could feel the sting of the rain as it was driven in under the canvas. It was like coming back to life.

'The only waiting there will be, is while the sergeant thinks of the best excuse he can. Is that not right, Sergeant?'

Barras poked his head in; he might have been looking else-where, but he'd been listening.

Before the Frenchman's interruption Ellis had been about to hand the flask round. The brief distraction gave him a moment to reconsider. After a gentle trial shake to determine how much of the contents were left he decided against it. Until Barras had spoken, Ellis had been working hard to convince himself that the right course of action was to report back as soon as possible, with due regard for caution on the return journey, but now he hesitated.

Five of the Krupp transporters and the two flak wagons were pulling out, leaving behind the one that had failed to start. The whine and whir of its fruitless attempts to get the motor to fire were clearly audible. Another, more prolonged attempt failed to elicit even a cough from the engine, but produced some ugly crunching noises from the starter motor.

The rig's driver and his mate climbed out and the engine inspection panels were thrown noisily open. They looked up from their scrutiny of the electrics as one of the Tiger's crew, sat in the back of the capacious cab, stuck his head out of the window to offer what sounded like a half-humourous suggestion; that the driver didn't think much of it was indicated by the gesture he made in return. The tank man laughed and then withdrew to rejoin his companions, who were cleaning their side-arms by the light of a shrouded lamp in the back of the cab.

'We'll have a go at knocking out that Tiger.'

Ellis's announcement hit the others like the blast wave of a blockbuster. Even Barras looked amazed, and for once had nothing to say. The others had. The moment of stunned silence was broken by a torrent of objections, voiced at a pitch that took no account of the proximity of the enemy.

'Keep the noise down. Keep the noise down.' Ellis's appeal restored some semblance of order.

It was Corporal Morris who summed the matter up. 'You want us, just the bloody six of us, without so much as a bazooka between us, to have a go at a Tiger tank? A squadron of bloody Shermans would think twice before doing that!'

Ellis had made up his mind. He was conscious of the Frenchman watching him, expecting him to reconsider and recant, and getting ready to enjoy Ellis's discomfort when he did. Well, he wasn't going to.

'Take a look down there. It's on a trailer and its crew are in the tractor cab. If we can hit them while they're in there, we can do a demolition job on the Tiger in our own sweet time. We can use the mines.'

'It's you who ought to take another look.' Dicky gestured towards the clearing. 'That big fueller and a couple of the supply trucks are still down there. What about them? Do you expect the Krauts there to just stand by and watch while we creep up on the tank crew and set the charges?'

Barras offered support for the plan. His enthusiasm for killing came as no surprise, but it sounded strange to hear him endorsing any suggestion emanating from the sergeant.

'Three sleepy drivers and their mates. Are you all frightened of the German Transport Corps as well as your own shadows? I say let us hit them now, hard.'

'I don't want to know who's for or against. We're doing it and that's that.' Ellis felt a throbbing sensation behind his eyes, but also the warmth of the alcohol in his stomach. He put off taking another drink; there was little left. He would save it. In passing he regretted the gesture he had made of smashing the bottle of wine. 'Let's see what ammunition we've got.'

Considering the number of men, the weaponry was impressive. Considering their target, it was pitifully inadequate. The final count was one bren gun and four sten guns, plus three pistols; two of them Barras's. There was also the Frenchman's captured machine-pistol. There were eighteen grenades – six incendiary and twelve of the standard fragmentation type. The phosphorus grenades belonged to Barras. Few men would have anything to do with the ghastly things, let alone carry them in their pockets as Barras did.

Ellis risked a quick swig from his flask in an effort to get rid of the buzzing in his head. As the discomfort subsided he examined the layout of the vehicles remaining about the junction.

There were four, spread out in a rough horse-shoe shape, the open end towards the hide. All of them were on the far side of the road running along the bottom of the embankment. The Krupp tank transporter was on the left; the articulated petrol tanker, with its back to them, was on the right. The pair of Opel supply lorries that completed the scene were at the far end of the clearing, stationed either side of the road that formed the third arm of the junction. Cab lights were on in all of them. In the Opels the crews could be seen sleeping, while from the cab of the fueller came occasional snatches of laughter.

The Krupps driver climbed aboard his charge and tried the engine while his mate continued to tamper beneath the raised panel. Again the starter motor whirred, the engine spluttered once, and then stopped.

'All right, but if we're going to have a go it'll have to be soon. That convoy may send back help for them.' Morris elbowed in for a look.

Sergeant Ellis gauged the distances involved, and the risks. The safest way would be to open up a massed fire from where they were. The furthest target, the Opels, were only a hundred yards away. That was point-blank for the bren. The submachine-guns at fifty yards could cut down the two-man crew of the transporter and kill the tank men in the unarmoured cab before they realized what was happening. The fueller was the problem.

92

A single burst might set off its rear compartments, but the two men in the cab up front would be able to get clear before the fire spread.

He mentioned it to Morris. 'It only needs one of those blokes to make it to the trees and start taking pot shots at us with a rifle, and then there's no way we could get to the Tiger and do a thorough job on it.'

A raucous bellow of laughter floated to them from the bowser. A door opened and someone climbed out to relieve himself beside the truck. A narrow spiral of steam rose up.

Across the clearing another attempt was made to start the reluctant motor. It ran raggedly for a few seconds then gave a massive back fire and cut out. Ellis made his decision. He was still determined to go ahead. He would show Barras what he could do, and prove that he didn't need the drink to do it; but even as he formed the thought he was patting his coat pocket to check the flask was there.

'We'll hit all of them at the same time, from close range. Pitt, Church, work your way to the back of those supply trucks. On the signal, give them a grenade apiece. Bird, you go with them to give supporting fire if they need it; they shouldn't. Barras, you take out the pair in the fueller. I'm sure you can manage that on your own. Do it how you like, but don't start a bloody fire. Just to be sure, you can leave those incendiary grenades here, okay?'

'What about me?' Morris asked, as he doled out grenades to Alex and Eric from the pile and moved the remainder out of Barras's reach.

'You stay with me. We'll shoot up the transporter from here, we'll get a better line on it. Down there we couldn't see in. The cab windows must be all of nine feet from the ground. Right, that's it. I'll give you ten minutes to get into position, from . . . now. Don't make a move till you hear the bren, otherwise you'll queer it for someone else.' Ellis felt better now that things were under way.

Barras said nothing, just smiled and melted away into the darkness.

Alex and Eric, with Dicky, paused a moment before going out. It was Alex who spoke.

'Why? Why the hell are we doing this? It was you who said we weren't going to start anything. Just in and out again, you said. Remember?'

'Well, I changed my mind. Look, it's a sitting target. A couple of bursts and we get rid of the opposition. Then we rig something inside the Tiger that'll set its racks off and it's all done. Over in five minutes.' There were doubts in Ellis's mind as well, but they were of himself, not of the job ahead. His doubts were inward expressions of suppressed fear. He understood enough to hide them away, but it nurtured in him an anger, a burning, bitter, frustrated anger that felt as though it could tear him apart. The anger turned outward. 'I've told you what to do. Do it. We're going to get that Tiger.'

He turned away, feeling his face burn. He heard the others depart, and busied himself with the bren. He sensed Morris was looking at him, but pretended not to notice.

Alex and Eric, with Dicky trailing behind as rear guard, crossed the road well out of sight of the junction and plunged into the woods on the far side. They had two minutes in hand when they reached a spot at the edge of the trees close to the rear of the two Opels. After a brief whispered discussion, Alex took out a grenade and crawled to the back of the nearest. Once he was sure no suspicions had been aroused, Eric sneaked across the road and crouched beneath the tailboard of the other. Dicky stayed at the fringe of the undergrowth, sten gun cocked and ready.

Water dripped down from the canvas tilts on to the waiting men. The lumps of metal warmed in their grasp. Their eyes stayed fixed on the distant embankment top, watching for the spark of flame and flash of tracer that would be the bren opening fire on the transporter.

As Barras was about to leave the cover of the trees a door opened in the fueller and the driver's mate got out. The man looked up at the invisible clouds and muttered to himself as he dropped his trousers and squatted. From the vehicle's cab came shouted and, judging by the terse replies, unwanted advice. Even in the deep shadow the white flesh of a large backside showed.

Barras reached down, his hand fastened on the hilt of a knife tucked into the side of his boot. It was his favourite, a nine-inch blade honed to a razor sharpness on one side, the other cut to a saw-like finish by a series of serrations. He felt good. The night had already proved far better than he could have hoped it would, and it was far from over. Slowly, with loving care, he stropped

94

the blade on the sole of his boot.

Seconds ticked by, becoming minutes. Ellis was tempted to open fire; surely the others would be in position by now. He fought down the urge. His eyes began to feel heavy, an almost irresistable compulsion to sleep flowed through him. He thought of the flask and, out of the corner of his eye, took a look at Morris. Only the corporal's profile was dimly visible. His hand came up to check for the tenth time that the sten's magazine was firmly engaged, then reached out to wipe an imagined speck of mud from the weapon's stubby barrel.

Bill Ellis undid the top of the flask while it was still in his pocket to mask the perceptible 'snick' with which it unfastened. Practice had made the single-handed operation easy. He gradually drew it from his pocket and took a surreptitious drink while Morris was still working through the ritual.

'Can't you manage one patrol without that stuff?'

Ellis jumped, though the words had been spoken quietly. His mind raced, seeking something light and offhand to give in answer.

'Is that why you decided to have a go at that thing down there? Because you're stoned again?'

'What do you mean? What are you getting at?' Ellis adopted aggression as his first line of defence.

Morris brushed it aside. 'You know damned well what I mean. You can't leave the drink alone. We all enjoy a drop – but you, you live on the bloody stuff.'

The sergeant's world was crumbling at the edges as he desperately sought an answer to the accusation.

Corporal Morris hadn't finished with him. 'Every time we run into a spot of bother, or whenever Barras has another go at you, you start glugging.' A thought suddenly struck him. 'My God. You're doing this because he needled you into it, and you were too fucking tight to see things straight. That's it, isn't it?'

'I'm not bloody drunk. I make my own decisions.' It was all the sergeant could think to say. He'd been caught off guard.

'Well, you're not sober either. And you, you say you make your own decisions, you've got a committee doing that for you. The chairman's Barras with that bloody flask as secretary. God, you're pitiful.'

'Oh, and you're so bloody clever, aren't you?' Ellis tried to strike back, using words as weapons. 'You couldn't even stay in the Tank Corps, could you? They didn't want you, not in any condition, did they? At least I haven't got slung out of a unit. I may take a drink now and then' – he ignored Morris's snort of derision – 'but no one's had me thrown out for being a bloody coward.'

Morris lunged at him and the two men grappled in the darkness, rolling about in the narrow space, covering themselves in damp earth and pine needles. They fought in silence, save for the occasional rasping exhalation of fist-propelled air as blows found their targets, and grunts as holds were made and broken.

Unseen behind them, dark shapes among the trees stopped, then changed direction. The shapes were men, the men soldiers, and the soldiers, in russet and black autumn camouflage smocks, were a German patrol. The leading NCO signalled his men to fan out, and then from a range of thirty feet emptied the magazine of his machine-pistol at the deep shadow at the base of the cluster of pines from which the sounds came. His timing was perfect. Exactly ten minutes after Ellis had given his men their instructions the tracer, aimed just a fraction high, skimmed the top of the camouflage sheet and flicked out across the clearing.

Action, reaction and result filled the area. A fat German wiping his bottom pitched forward on to his face in the mud as a knife was driven with vicious force into the exposed base of his spine. Two Germans woke and screamed as a grenade clattered in through a window of their cab. A British soldier panicked as a grenade slipped from numbed wet fingers to land at his feet beneath the running board of a truck cab into which he had intended to thrust it. A pair of grimy hands were unlocked from a throat and clenched fists ceased pummelling a bruised and breathless rib cage.

Morris and Ellis broke apart and grabbed for their weapons as a long burst of automatic fire ripped the sheet above them. They whirled round and hosed bullets out into the darkness and were rewarded with screams and the sound of bodies falling and threshing about, before the sten and bren guns emptied.

The doors and cab roof of an Opel were blasted off by an explosion that somersaulted two hideously mutilated corpses into the mud. Slashed and blood-stained seats began to smoulder and blue flame licked out from beneath the steering column.

Across the road another supply lorry lifted on its suspension as a grenade detonated under its front end. Red hot fragments punched up through the thin floor to flay the flesh from the driver's legs. A fleeing figure was lifted by the blast and tossed into the centre of the road to land heavily and lay still.

From his seat in the fueller the driver saw his mate sprawl forward, saw the hilt and two inches of blade sticking out of his back. Two nearby explosions rocked the vehicle on its springs. Hard debris clattered down. The driver dived for the open door, to recoil violently as a wild-eyed face appeared before him. He turned to fumble with the other door catch but the cab rocked again as the figure leapt in. Then the German screamed as something stabbed into his thigh. He half turned to ward off the attack. Instantly the intruder was upon him and he was pinned down by the violence of the assault. A mindless mixture of gibbered French and English and German came from the figure as the driver put every effort he could muster into trying to escape. Darting hands ripped at his clothes and the German was spurred to even greater, but still ineffectual effort, as his trousers were wrenched open.

Doctor Soult's human time-bomb had at last detonated. Barras's fist smashed down repeatedly into the terrified German's face. Then, as frantic resistance slowed, he grabbed the exposed organs and began to hack with his knife.

His terror, the wound to his thigh, his blow-slurred senses . . . nothing could mask the driver's shock as he realized what was happening to him. Unable to move, he howled and screamed his protest, filling the clearing with the noise more completely than the blaring klaxon had a while before.

In the cab of the transporter the tank crew heard the firing from beyond the embankment, had seen the tracer zoom overhead, then felt the twin ripples of air pressure as the grenades blasted the trucks. An instant spent tensing for the momentarily expected impact of bullets gave way to a frantic scramble for the hatches and the sanctuary of the Tiger. They threw open the doors, one of which struck the face of the driver as he turned from securing the engine inspection panel. Even as the man fell back into the arms of his mate, clutching at his ruined face, the panzer crew jumped out, swarmed up the sides of the semi-trailer on to their tank and leapt in through the forward and turret hatches. The thick metal slammed and grated back into place.

The area of the junction was full of people trying to escape from the expected impact of a bullet, from the agony of hideous injury, from the unknown.

With the unexpected success of their opening fire, Ellis whipped round to sight on the clearing, leaving Morris to watch the rear. He was just in time to see the Tiger's hatches slam shut. A burst of fire he was going to throw pointlessly against the inches-thick armour he suddenly switched to the two men by the Krupp. He had an instant to wonder why one was supporting the other before his bullets struck and they collapsed like deflated balloons.

From some distance behind came loud whimperings of distress. Morris sent a single shot in its general direction, but wasted no more when he failed to silence it.

'How many did we get?' Ellis didn't take his eyes off the clearing as he posed the question.

Morris squinted at huddled shapes, trying to determine what they were. 'I can see two out there, and hear another. How many do you reckon there might be?'

'How the hell should I know? At least as many again I should think.'

Morris buried his face in the warm leaf mould as a crackle of shots gouged the tree beside him. 'I just hope that tree-climbing monkey with the sniper rifle isn't among them.'

'Well if he is out there, give him something with my compliments.'

Ellis realized his vision was blurring, shook his head and screwed up his eyes to clear them. He looked out at the junction.

Despite the rain, a fire was building in the cab of one of the Opels. With each puff of smoke came one of steam as water dripped into the flames. From the bowser came terrible screams that went on and on. Ellis turned his mind away from the contemplation of Barras's activities. Two crumpled forms lay in the mud close alongside the burning Opel and another figure was moving sluggishly on the road. From the other supply truck a figure stumbled and reeled, then turned to tug at something attached to the side of the vehicle.

The fire grew suddenly. Morris's sten chattered briefly. From the woods behind came a yell, then the sound of branches being broken by the fall of a heavy object. Something soft hit the ground hard with a sickening crunch of bone.

'I got him. I got him! He was half-way up a tree when that fire flared up. It was as good as a spotlight.' Morris wasn't allowed long to enjoy his small victory. A stream of tracer lanced out at him. He fired back and the incoming tracer jerked up in to the tree tops as the unseen gunner was hit.

Now the flames in the clearing were leaping higher, sending bars of red light in among the trees. At the base of a fir thirty feet away lay an ungainly heap of cloth. The mound moved slightly and Morris sent a single round at it. It convulsed once and was still. The whimpering attracted his attention again. When he located its source he saw the vague outline of a man trying to drag himself off, trailing shattered legs. At the impact of two aimed shots the man toppled on to his side, clutching at his belly, trying to stem the tide of intestines that hung from his gaping stomach and groin.

The corporal quartered the ground time and time again, seeking the body of the German whose tracer had gone wildly astray. He was about to give up the search when, by the light of the burning truck, he saw what at first looked like an irregular lump on the side of a tree. Morris looked harder and saw that it was the elbow of a camouflage smock. The protruding material bucked as a round passed through it; a second shot wasn't needed. Even as he aimed again, from out behind the trunk slid a faceless corpse, nerveless fingers still gripping a sub-machine gun.

'I think that's it, Sarge.'

Morris reloaded. His private fight with Ellis was forgotten, at least for the time being. The action had drained from them their animosity and rechannelled it.

The growing crackle of flame consuming wood was the only noise from the clearing now that the screams and thumping sounds from the cab of the fueller had ceased.

Morris slipped out into the woods to check the bodies. With the exception of one German who died just as he reached him, they were all quite cold, the blood already washed from their visible wounds by the rain. He returned to the hide.

'Okay?' Ellis moved across to make room.

'Looks like we got them all. They were only bloody kids. They couldn't have had a clue. They had us cold and they blew it.'

'We'll have to clear out now, in case they've got any mates who heard. I hope the others have got the sense to come straight back. We'd better get ready to give them cover if they make a dash for it.'

Ellis took out spare magazines and laid them in a row beside

99

the bren. Morris did the same for his sten, and grouped the grenades between them in a hollow he scraped in the soil. Both men laid down and poked the snouts of their guns through the narrow gap between the logs, and waited.

Out of the corner of his eye, Morris thought he saw a movement. He looked at the tank transporter but saw nothing. The two bodies were still where they had fallen, but he was sure there was something different about the scene. Then he realized. The turret of the Tiger was slowly traversing, bringing its cannon muzzle to bear on the bank top.

'Down!' He shoved Ellis's face into the ground as the Tiger's eighty-eight belched white flame.

The tank and the trailer on which it stood rocked crazily with the recoil. The heavy shot flashed the short distance to the embankment and ploughed into it directly beneath the hide. The ground erupted as it exploded.

CORPORAL MORRIS

NORMANDY AMBUSH

The Focke-Wulf 189 sped low over the area of woodland. Paths of cleared land cut through the dense trees like pale green highways.

On the ground the four Shermans churned the soft loam as they raced for cover. They tore through hedges and streams, plastering their flanks with mud, decorating their already heavily camouflaged dark-green hulls with more foliage.

Leutnant Jurgens could see the commander of the last of the file hanging out of the turret and slapping its cast sides, as if urging it on like a horse.

The tanks made it, crushing their way in beneath the thick canopy. From just within its fringe came the twinkling light of heavy-calibre machine-gun fire. Tracer flicked up towards the aircraft.

The armoured glass front of the greenhouse-type cockpit shrugged aside the first half-dozen rounds that struck it. Then, with the closing range, one found a weakness and distorted part of the frame. Glass and bullets flew into the cockpit, striking one weak but vital component of the speeding aircraft.

Leutnant Jurgens knew a moment's surprise, then several moments of pain as something hot and fast moving punched a hole through his stomach and broke his back. His automatic action was to pull hard on the controls. The Focke-Wulf reared up, seeming almost to stop, with the shattered front pointing to the clouds.

Twin engines howled in protest at the load imposed on them. Jurgens forced out a scream of rage and fear against the blast of the slipstream and heard it echoed in his headphones by his crew. Now a second line of tracer joined the first and together they raked the stricken craft.

It hung a second longer, then turned on to its back and plunged nose first into the ground beside a tall oak. Both were consumed by the aircraft's exploding fuel tanks.

The body of Leutnant Jurgens lay a little distance from the wreck, on the fresh soil thrown up by the whirling propellers. He smouldered gently and the remains of his face stared up into the cloud-flecked sky.

Corporal Morris hurriedly secured the post-mounted Browning anti-aircraft machine-gun as his driver whirled their Sherman round to chase after the rest of their troop, already fast disappearing from sight among the close-spaced trees.

The lead tank, a seventeen-pounder-armed Sherman Firefly, smashed a swathe through the undergrowth, saplings snapping off like twigs before the rushing wall of steel. It burst through thick bushes into a clearing and cut twin furrows in the lush grass before plunging back into the cover of the woods on the far side. Like a brood of ugly, oversized fledgelings, the other three tanks followed close in its tracks.

At a radio-transmitted command the group slackened pace, fanned out into line abreast, slowed further and came to a halt within the fringe of the far side of the woods overlooking half a mile of open country. Beneath the deep shadow of the overhanging branches the Shermans were almost invisible, but from each one a man climbed out to make certain their concealment was as near perfect as it could be.

From his spot a yard or two within the trees, Corporal Morris had a clear view of the country before them. From the woods, the land sloped gently down to a stream, some two hundred yards away. Beyond that another seven hundred yards of rich pasture, then the *bocage* began: thousands of tiny fields divided from each other by hedge-topped banks.

Through a narrow gap between those ill-kempt hedges, a thin ribbon of road wound across the meadow, crossed the stream by a single-arch stone bridge and came straight on up the slope towards the woods, turning sharp left a hundred yards from the hidden British tanks to run parallel to their position and away out of their sight.

With the camouflage arrangers back inside, the bird calls lost their note of alarm. Except for the steady, throbbing rumble of the powerful radial engines, the sights and sounds of the woods and fields were as before.

Corporal Raymond Morris, the junior of the four tank commanders, stood half out of his turret, enjoying a change from the devastation and bustling activity of the beach-head. The war had been kind to Corporal Morris so far. A reserved occupation had kept him out of the army until early in 1943, and even then he had been only gently initiated into the realities of military

102

life. Trained as a tank gunner within travelling distance of home, he had been made up to corporal and kept back as an instructor just as most of his intake were being shipped out to Italy and a place called Cassino. Even when posted back to active duties three months later he had been lucky, being sent to a unit that was easy-going.

It had come as a bit of a shock when he had been made up to tank commander. Like many others, he had gone in for the tests and exams, but only to get out of other, more strenuous duties. Then there had been more training, culminating in the journey to France on D+3, when his squadron had been immediately placed in reserve. Apart from joining with a bit of indirect shelling – at what, precisely, no one had bothered to tell them – they had seen no real action in the four days since they had come ashore. They had not suffered any casualties from the sporadic shelling and the whole thing had begun to take on a training-ground air of unreality.

The intercom circuit buzzed in his ear; the voice of Larry Stuart, their driver, came through.

'Not a bad start to our first patrol, eh, Corp? Think we'll be able to stop and pick up a souvenir on the way back?'

'I don't know, we'll have to see.'

'Think you'll get a medal for downing it, Corp?' their bow gunner joined in.

'Are you being funny, Sparks?'

'Who me? Never. It's not in my nature.'

Morris just grunted his disbelief. Still, he did feel a bit cocky about getting the Focke-Wulf. It'd be something to write home about, when he did. Might even make the local paper. That would be something.

'We're overheating a bit. Can I switch off for a moment?'

Morris considered the driver's request. He didn't like the idea of sitting there without power on, but he didn't fancy the engine seizing either. He decided to pass the buck.

'Red Four to Red Two. We have overheating. Permission to switch off.'

He had put it to the troop sergeant-major, but it was the troop commander, Captain Foreman, who answered. Trust him not to miss anything, thought Morris.

'Switch off for two minutes, then on again. If it still rises, give it four minutes next time. Stay alert. You may need power in a hurry.'

The reminder that this was an active patrol, not another exercise, made Morris shudder. Strange to think that he was sitting there, waiting to blow to hell or hospital men who at that moment were unaware of his existence. He had not even seen a body so far. Oh, he'd seen plenty of the little white crosses that sprinkled the fields and roadsides, but not a real body, not a dead one.

He passed the instructions on to his driver. The tank gave a peculiar vibration and then, save for the rapid clicking and ticking of cooling metal, all was quiet. The dense growth blanketed the sounds of the other three engines off to the left.

'Any chance of a quick fag?'

For an instant Morris marvelled over how clear the intercom had suddenly become. Then, with a foolish grin, he realized that the loader was actually talking directly to him.

'Sorry, mate, not a chance.'

He smiled as he heard the lid of a cigarette tin snap back on. Their loader was a chain-smoker and he went through hell on patrol. The Shermans burned too readily to risk a naked flame, even the glowing tip of a cigarette. A shell that penetrated their plate and by some miracle didn't start a fire of its own might still puncture fuel tanks. It took very little to make their high-octane fuel ignite. The Germans hadn't nick-named the Shermans 'Tommy Cookers' for nothing.

'Did you score with that French bird, Corp?'

'Sparks, don't you ever think of anything else?'

The left-hand forward hull-top hatch clanged open and the radio operator stuck his head out and grinned up at Morris. 'What else is there to talk about, apart from that?'

'Anybody want some stupor juice?'

'I told you not to bring that stuff.' Morris ducked down into the gloomy interior of the turret and glared at the driver who had turned round in his seat to offer the bottle to the turret crew. 'What is it this time?'

'Harmless, Corp, that's what it is. Harmless. Just a little brandy, a spot of white wine and just a touch of new cider for flavour. Want some?'

'Put it away. I don't want to buy it just because you're sloshed and end up driving us into a ditch. Leave that muck for the armoured-car crews; those poor buggers have more to worry about. We've got thick plate around us.'

'Thick! You call this bloody thick?' The gunner wrapped his knuckles against the inside of the hull. It rang.

'Just put it away.'

Morris climbed back on his chair to look out. He knew that as soon as his back was turned the bottle would be passed round.

A breeze had sprung up and was rippling the tall grass like an inland green sea. The shadows of fast-moving clouds made dark patches, chasing each other in endless procession. Something made a soundless splash in the stream near the bridge. Morris's tank was furthest to the right of the line, positioned opposite the weathered structure. A thought crossed his mind: what a pity it was to spread the ugliness of war to this piece of unspoilt country.

'. . . and make your first shot count.'

With a panic-stricken feeling of terror, Morris realized he had missed what the captain had said. A file of assorted German vehicles was winding its way out of the *bocage* towards the bridge. The small of his back felt suddenly damp and prickly. He had to arch it to fight off a cramping pain. Think. He had to think quickly.

'Red Four to Red Leader. Your message indistinct. Please say again. Red Four over.'

He said a silent prayer that the captain wouldn't send fitters to check his radio when they got back. When he lifted his hands to wipe them on his overalls he saw that they had left two damp prints on the matt finish of the turret top.

The captain's tone was clipped, icy and precise. 'Red Three to block the head of the column, Red Two to take out the half-track with the anti-tank gun. Red Four to hit the last eight-wheeler when it's on the bridge. I'll take care of the half-track with the flak gun. Did you read me that time, Corporal Morris?'

'Loud and clear, sir.'

In Morris's ear was the faint click of the captain turning to his internal circuit, then another as he turned back to the command channel.

'Prepare to fire on my order.'

Sergeant Harris, commander of Red Three, had a question. 'Do we close down?'

It was the sergeant-major who answered, phrasing his words carefully, in such a way that they sounded like a suggestion. 'Perhaps if we don't, sir. We'll be able to spot the fall of shot better if we keep our heads up, sir. We can always close the lids if they get close.'

'Very good, Sergeant-Major, that's what we'll do. And,

commanders, tell your bow gunners to concentrate their fire on infantry or soft targets. I don't want them wasting ammunition on armour. Right, stand by to fire.'

Morris passed the orders on. The turret traversed slightly and the barrel of the seventy-five depressed to bear on the centre of the bridge. He suddenly noticed that the engine had been restarted. He couldn't recall the moment when the driver had done it, without waiting to be told. He gave himself a mental shake. If he didn't buck his ideas up, it might become his last as well as his first war patrol.

'There's a right assortment coming, Corp.'

His gunner was right. He examined the slowly approaching vehicles through his binoculars. Certainly the column was an assortment. It was led by three motorcycle combinations, then at regular, carefully spaced intervals came a Kubelwagen bristling with machine-guns, an open-topped scout car, two four-wheeled armoured cars, both with light anti-tank guns in their low-sided angular turrets. Behind them was a command vehicle, a complicated selection of aerials folded on its roof, followed by four half-tracks. The first two were basic infantry versions, the other pair were more deadly. One was fitted with a long-barrelled seventy-five-millimetre anti-tank gun, the other with a multiple-barrelled anti-aircraft gun. It was just as capable as hosing its eight-hundred-rounds-a-minute rate of fire over the Shermans as over the aircraft it was designed to engage. Bringing up the rear were two eight-wheeled armoured cars, both with twenty-millimetre cannon.

The motorcyclists sped ahead, crossing the bridge and skidding to a stop on the bend. Morris saw some of them turn to watch the others cross. The noise made by the wide-hulled half-tracks as they scraped the walls on either side was clearly audible above the varied exhaust notes.

'Fire!'

Prepared though he was, the sudden crackle of sound in his ears still made Morris jump. The last eight-wheeler was straddling the bridge. Showers of dust and stone chippings accompanied its progress as its driver misjudged the gap. He had only half-formed the word to pass the command to his gunners when, as one, the four Shermans sat back on their suspensions with the recoil of their main armaments. The crack of the big guns was accompanied by the rapid clacking of the .3 calibre bow machine-guns.

Four glowing dots of tracer arched over the grass, speeding the short distance to their targets, around and above them the stinging hordes of white points from the hull Brownings. Twigs and leaves brought down by the muzzle blasts settled on the hull and turret tops and fell in through the open hatches.

'That's made the buggers jump.'

'Shut up, Guns. Just watch the fall of shot. Reload.'

As Morris spoke, their armour-piercing round struck the target. It hit at an acute angle on the corner of the armoured car's raked bow plate. At short range the shell had lost virtually none of its initial velocity and it plunged straight in through the face-hardened armour. The German vehicle's turret hatch flew open and then clanged shut as it coasted to a stop, demolishing part of the wall and completely blocking the bridge. Smoke began to curl from it and a side door opened as one of the crew groped and crawled his way out.

'What's my next target? What's my next target?'

Morris banged his fists into the hatch cover. He had been so busy watching the results of their first shot he had almost gone into a trance. It was no time for daydreaming. That was something he couldn't afford. 'This is not a bloody exercise!'

'You what, Corp?'

He hadn't realized he was speaking out loud. Morris tore his eyes from the wreck on the bridge and examined the rest of the column. A Kubelwagen lay on its side, wheels still slowly spinning. Two motorcycles burnt fiercely. A hand was draped from the flames leaping from one of the side-cars. Their crews, and that of a third standing nearby, were laid about, unmoving. Fire was spreading from a blazing four-wheeled armoured car to an anti-tank gun-armed half-track that had rammed it. The half-track's gun hung over the side of the superstructure at an odd angle and its shield was holed and buckled.

Infantry were leaping from other vehicles, two half-tracks in particular seemed to be disgorging an endless stream of heavily armed, grey-clad soldiers. Morris sought the flak gun, but failed to locate it and instead laid his gunner on to the other eight-wheeler at the rear of the convoy. It was trying to bulldoze its way past a command vehicle stalled in its path.

'Loader change to armour-piercing. Guns, up fire.'

He had to shout the corrections to be heard, after the first shot missed and hurled chunks of turf into the air five yards short of the target.

The second attempt was perfect, catching the armoured car in its side as it at last managed to manoeuvre clear. The results were spectacular. After an initial puff of white smoke marking the impact, the big car dissolved in a roaring ball of fire. A single large wheel was propelled from the flames by the blast to roll blazing across the meadow and finally topple to rest amid a cloud of steam under the bridge.

'Get that scout car.'

Even as Morris saw it dashing across their front in its bid to reach safety, even as his gunner began frantically to traverse the turret to catch it, the unmistakable crack of the seventeen-pounder on the sergeant-major's Sherman was heard above all the other noises of the conflict. The escape attempt was stopped. A hole appeared in the car's rear armour. It swerved and rolled over twice before coming to rest on its side. Morris could see right into it through its open top, see the jumble of broken men trying to extricate themselves from the mangled metal. Then there was fire and everything was hidden.

Now the Shermans were being fired on. Only small-arms and light automatics so far, aimed blindly into the tree line. But it was growing in volume and the Germans could see at least one of the British tanks as bullets could be heard ricochetting off armour.

The column was in a shambles. Several vehicles were burning and the thick smoke was making the sighting of new targets difficult. It was also giving concealment to those of the enemy plucking up courage to retaliate, and willing to risk drawing fire down on themselves. A thick sapling beside the sergeant-major's tank was felled by a cannon shell. Another round flattened itself against one of the thick ribs of the plate joints on the hull front. Pieces of bough, shreds of bark and leaves rained down. The Shermans' camouflage was fast disintegrating about them.

The ragged fire of assorted light weapons was becoming better directed and more dangerous. A second cannon joined in, probing among the trees for Morris's as yet unlocated tank. Twice bullets struck sparks and paint from the steel beside the corporal's hand. More whistled close overhead, increasing the litter in the turret.

Most of the vehicles on the road were being struck time and time again. Still there was no order to cease fire, and the Shermans kept pounding at the wrecks, sending shot after shot blindly into the smoke.

'Infantry. Swarms of the bastards. About a hundred yards,

at nine o'clock.' As he spoke, the radio operator sent ribbons of solid and tracer bullets from the bow gun at the approaching Germans.

'I see them.'

Morris watched the wakes in the tall grass made by the men crawling towards the trees. He threw himself behind the Browning and sent short bursts at them. The vibration shook the litter from the turret top and his shoulders. As he swivelled back and forth, hardly bothering to aim, he could see the bullets slashing through the grass, cutting the men it hid to pieces. One of the Germans sprang to his feet, shouldered a bulbous-ended tube and sighted straight at the Sherman.

'*Panzerfaust*!'

It was a warning and a scream in one. Morris hurled himself to one side to bring the Browning to bear.

Before the marching line of bullets reached the German, he fired. The result was not what the infantryman had planned, nor what Morris had expected. It exploded in the man's hands, tearing his head from his shoulders and sending it tumbling through the air, trailing strips of ragged pink tissue. The corpse sagged slowly sideways and lay in an untidy heap, burning with a low guttering flame.

Some well-placed support fire from Sergeant Harris's Sherman and the would-be attackers, the few that were left, broke and ran.

The headphones whistled and crackled. Captain Foreman's distinctive nasal tones came over faintly.

'Right, good job so far. One more round apiece of HE at the road, then one of cannister at the bridge. Winkle out any of the squareheads who made it back there under cover of the smoke.'

As the last four explosive shells started fresh fires among the remains of the column, Morris found himself looking into an overturned half-track. He could see every detail of the heaped dead inside it, see their gross burns and disfigurements. The smoke swirled across and hid them from him.

The white puffs of smoke, as the cannister shot burst in the air over the stream, seemed puny by comparison with what had gone before, but the effect of the deadly storm of fragments that they sowed along the edges of the shallow water was incredible. Like giant handfulls of gravel thrown with vicious force, the chunks and slivers of steel mowed down the long rushes and lank weeds, mini-cratered the stream bed and beat a misty plume of spray into the air. It was joined by the upraised arms of a dozen or more men whose hiding places had been found. The butchered bodies collapsed back to blend their blood with the flow of water.

'That's it. Time to be going. Sergeant-Major, take the lead.'

The troop sergeant-major's Sherman belched a cloud of dirty-grey smoke and backed thirty yards into the woods before turning and heading back the way they had come. The precaution of not presenting the tank's thin rear armour to the enemy until the thickness of several trees were between it and their guns, was a prudent one. As the captain's Sherman completed its turn, a panzerfaust bomb blasted a tree behind it. The white-hot jet of plasma generated, punched right through the fifteen inches of timber and splashed molten globules over the tank's engine access doors.

A last defiant bullet hit the back of the turret as Morris's tank turned away from the scene of battle. The sights and sounds of the slaughter were soon lost as the troop crashed back towards their own lines.

Morris listened, without participating, to his crew's chatter. He knew without looking that the last dregs of the driver's bottle of hooch were being consumed in celebration. Still, why not! They had done a bloody good job, knocked out a whole German recce column at no cost to themselves. But it was a hell of a way to go to war, two-thirds drunk. Perhaps it made the pressures more bearable, possibly it even confined them to oblivion for a while.

The fact that the sergeant-major's tank was in the lead was another strange thing about the fighting in this close country. The normal practice of the troop commander's vehicle leading had been dropped when, in the days after the landing, the casualty rate among junior officers had assumed alarming proportions. Rather than have the armoured regiments crippled by a shortage of ranks up to major, the practice had been adopted of having the troops' senior NCOs take the point while on patrol, and the brunt of the risks was now borne by them.

At least the sergeant-major's tank was equipped with one of the new and devastatingly powerful seventeen-pounders. If the Firefly survived the first shot of an enemy surprise attack, it could hit back hard with the only weapon in the Allied armoury capable of doing damage to the Panthers and Tigers now being encountered in ever increasing numbers.

It was being rumoured, though, that having the long-barrelled and very distinctive gun in itself carried risks, as the Germans had already learnt to go for them first, in the knowledge that the standard Sherman offered little danger and could be taken care of at leisure.

Morris wondered what he would do if he was ever promoted that high. Would he pull some stupid stunt to get out of it, even risk losing a stripe? He didn't know, and with luck the war would be over long before he might have to worry about things like that.

The dappled shade of the trees gave way to the bright sun of a wide clearing. Morris looked up at the sky. So close to the safety of their own lines surely only enemy aircraft could pose a threat to them now, and he felt rather smug at being able to take care of them. He was already looking forward to painting a small silhouette emblem on the side of the turret.

They didn't even run the risk of mines, as all four tanks were travelling back in the same track marks they had cut on the way out.

He felt rather than heard the sergeant-major's tank explode. One instant the Firefly was forty yards ahead, its pennant rippling in the breeze, then it was breaking up as it went. The turret went high into the air, a mutilated body cartwheeling behind it. Every piece of externally stowed equipment was blasted off and the hull shuddered to a stop, gouting flame as the tracks broke up. Jagged slabs of metal rained down. The head of an axe bounced on the engine cover of Sergeant Harris's mount. Something that thankfully he didn't see smacked on to the armour behind Morris, and there came the ugly noise of a soft, wet object flopping off the tank. When he looked, it was gone, leaving a broad red smear.

There was hardly time to start to register surprise or form a reaction, when a shout almost burst his eardrums.

'I saw it, in the woods, a muzzle flash. It was off to the right, at three o'clock. I saw it.' The driver's voice was high pitched and loud with fright and excitement.

Morris tumbled down into the tank, pulling the hatch shut behind him. The dull red illumination of the fighting compartment hid details for a moment after the bright daylight outside.

'Sparks, put a burst into the woods. Larry, start backing us out of here. Guns, you watch Sparks fire. If it bounces, he's put it on armour. Give that spot every round of AP we've got left.'

Through his periscope Morris watched the jet of pearl beads flick to, and probe among the trees. The other two Shermans had been faster off the mark. Both fired their seventy-fives at the same instant. The flares at the base of the shells betraying their paths merged as one as they converged on a gap between two stately elms. The first shot shattered against whatever it hit in a great blaze of white sparks. The second bounced upwards, to disappear from sight among the overhanging branches.

'Whatever's in there has got bloody thick armour.'

'Just concentrate on getting us out of here,' Morris shouted at their driver. 'Ease off. You've offered the sod our flank.'

Due to haste, and perhaps the influence of the stupor juice, Larry Stuart was trying too hard, over correcting when the tank slewed one way or the other on hitting a soft patch.

'I see him, it's . . .'

The loader never finished the sentence. The hidden enemy gunner interrupted him. Scabs of metal zipped about the turret as its roof was crushed down several inches by a shell skimming its surface. Lashing down, the round particles of razor-sharp metal took their toll of crew and equipment. Ammunition was dented and gouged, the radio was wrecked, spare prisms were shattered and particles of glass showered everywhere. One of the flakes buried itself in the side of the loader's neck.

Before Morris could stop him, the man had plucked it from his flesh. As he withdrew it a fountain of deep red blood spouted across the confined space, saturating the gunner and Morris. The wounded man panicked and his expression changed from relief to sheer horror. He twisted away from help as he tried vainly to staunch the flow himself. An attempted scream came out as no more than a bleating, gargling sound.

'What's happening? Are we hit?'

For the men in the front section there was the terrible fear of not knowing what was going on behind them – the fear so deep-rooted in all tankmen of leaving a bale-out too late and of being burned alive.

As Morris and the gunner tried to grab the loader to apply a dressing to his wound, they felt the Sherman's speed slacken, sensed the engine revs falling.

'We're all right, just bloody keep going! Get us into the trees. For God's sake keep going!'

Morris's shout came too late. They had already been picked

out for special attention. Thrusting out from the tree line came first the tip of a long, white-ringed cannon barrel, then the gigantic bulk of a Tiger tank.

The great slab front of the Tiger crushed down and swept aside trees that would have defeated the Sherman's efforts. From the comparative safety of the far side of the clearing, from as deep within the woods as they could go while still maintaining some arc of fire the Shermans of Captain Foreman and Sergeant Harris opened up a rapid fire on the advancing panzer. Every shot was a hit, and every one shattered, bursting harmlessly in cascades of molten metal and burning explosive on the frontal armour of the lumbering leviathan.

With slow deliberation the Tiger's turret traversed, and as it came to bear on the damaged Sherman its co-axially mounted machine-gun fired a single round of tracer that flattened itself against the slowly retreating tank, hitting it square on the bow plate.

At so clear an indicator of what was coming, the radio operator, against whose bow machine-gun the round had expended itself, threw open his hatch and began to scramble out.

As he did, the driver, thinking to put the bulky rear of the Sherman between himself and whatever the Germans had in mind to do, slung the tank round in a tight pivoting turn. The immediate effect was to tumble the men in the turret about and cause the dressing that had at last been applied to the rapidly weakening loader to fall off.

The Tiger fired. The eighty-eight-millimetre shell struck the forward right-hand side of the tank where it had been reinforced by the addition of a welded plate. The shell's incredible velocity took it in through the hopefully added protection, through the armour of the hull itself and on into the crew compartment where it passed through the chest of the gunner who had been thrown to the turret floor by the violence of the unexpected turn. But the shell had not finished its brief but full career. Striking the far side of the hull, it was deflected to the back of the turret where it punched through the bulkhead separating the crew from the engine compartment. It smashed the cooling fan, penetrated the radiator and broke up against the engine, severing fuel lines and electrical circuits.

Prevented from completing his escape by first the tank's violent gyrations, and then by the shock of the shell's impact, the radio operator was finally stopped half out of his hatch by a short and accurate burst from his opposite number aboard the Tiger.

Dazed by the noise, cut by slivers of metal and brittle flakes of paint thrown about in the shell's wake. Morris reached for the turret hatch to find it hopelessly buckled and jammed solid. Then his actions became more urgent as the interior filled with fire when spilled fuel was ignited by the spark-spitting exposed ends of wires. Instinct took over and he found himself fighting to get past the loader's thrashing body to one of the forward hatches.

The tank was filled with the stench of petrol and cordite and blood, lit by the orange flare of rolling fire. Morris felt his hair being singed and crisped by the hot air the flame propelled before it as it came like a flame-thrower from the hole the shell had made into the engine compartment.

A spurt of fiery petrol from some twisting fuel line jetted the length of the dying loader's body, bringing to it temporary frantic animation.

Oblivious to every consideration but his sudden terror and fear of death, heedless of his crewman's suffering, the corporal kicked and clawed the burning man aside to reach the escape hatch in the tank's belly plate. He reached it, and as he dived out of the growing inferno he caught for a moment the ghastly expression in the eyes of the tormented creature he left behind.

There was no other thought in his head but to crawl clear before the racks with their remaining ammunition blew up. On elbows rapidly stripped of charred clothing and raw flesh, he dragged himself out from beneath the pyre, to be met with bobbing lines of tracer as the Tiger's bow machine-gunner spared a second from its probing of the far woods to send a vindictive. hail at him.

There was nothing for it but to slide back under the near red-hot armour, painfully turn and crawl out under the back of the hulk. Dribbles of fire found rents and holes in the belly plate through which to inflict more suffering on him.

The crack and detonation of exchanged cannon fire, the rumble and clank of manoeuvring tanks blended with, but couldn't smother, the roar of flame and muffled patter of exploding small-arms ammunition in the Sherman that had so recently been his charge.

114

Morris had reached his limit. Ten yards from the Sherman he could force his body to go no further. It had been drained of its last dregs of will and energy. He became aware of something lying in the cool grass beside him. An unreasoning curiosity made him look, and then recoil, as in the half of a face that remained he recognized his driver. The blood had already ceased to pump from the gaping wound that exposed shattered bone and pulped brain, the dull glint of bullet fragments embedded in portions of the bare skull. Ribs stuck out of the torn chest, and the fingerless hand that had been thrown across the wound at the swift instant of death rested on the bloody shreds of a heart.

A half turn that unrolled a length of scorched tissue from his arm extinguished the last sparks on Morris's clothing. Now he could only lie and wait and hope for help to come, and hope that it would be too late if the only prospect it held out was an extension of the time it would take him to die. Every time he exhaled grey smoke came from his mouth as his lungs fought to clear themselves of the fumes.

He found himself, in a detached way, following the action that still continued. The Tiger, out of sight beyond the hulk of his own tank, was systematically pumping shells into the trees that hid the remaining half of the troop. With a thunder of unleashed power the British tanks broke from cover, tearing and ripping their way across the meadow, racing for the far woods, sending hastily aimed smoke shells at the panzer as they did.

Captain Foreman was gambling literally everything on the Sherman's superior speed to get to safety before the slowly traversing turret of the Tiger could bring its gun to bear.

The German tank commander was just as aware as the British crews of his tank's shortcomings. Even as the great turret began to swivel, so the whole tank began to turn, effectively doubling the speed of traverse. His first shot passed over Morris to tear the turret from Sergeant Harris's Sherman.

Trailing black smoke, shedding burning packs and bits of equipment, it plunged on into the trees, leaving in its wake a series of small fires among the crushed and leaning trunks. Seconds after it disappeared from view there came the report of a violent explosion and a red mushroom soared above the branch tops.

The last tank of the troop, commanded by Captain Foreman, slewed sideways in a wild skid and raced straight for the Tiger.

The panzer stood its ground, shrugging aside the deluge of shell and shot from the Sherman's seventy-five millimetre gun. Then the Tiger tired of the game and loosed a single round at its charging adversary. It was a mortal wound. The Sherman jerked to a halt only a few yards from where Morris lay. None of the hatches opened but, as though there were a smoke generator inside, grey smoke curled from every vision port and imperfectly sealed opening.

Its work of destruction done, the Tiger didn't hang about. It made an ungainly turn, filling the air with the hot aroma of its exhaust, and headed back the way it had come, still closed down. Neither Morris nor anyone else in his troop had seen so much as a glimpse of its crew.

When he found he could no longer close his eyes, Corporal Morris had to force himself to endure the agony of turning on to his side to avoid the glare of the sun. It felt as though his lids had been welded open. Smoke eddied about him, bringing with it unpleasant smells that wrenched at his stomach.

His own tank was already burning out, without having exploded. Captain Foreman's Sherman, however, was beginning to burn in earnest, flames issuing from the engine covers. Through a haze of shock and pain Morris thought he heard a voice, but it stopped and he began to drift into unconsciousness, to be suddenly and frighteningly jarred back to wakeful reality.

'Oh dear Jesus, no! Oh mother, oh Jesus, no, no. Oh mother, no.'

The violent hysterical screams came from Foreman's tank. Morris was aware of renewed sharp pain as the yells made him jump. The screams continued, continued and intensified as the unknown trapped man realized his plight, tried to escape and found it impossible. Morris covered his ears, tried to close his mind to the sound, but it wouldn't be shut out.

'Get me out. Oh please, get me out, get me out. Oh dear God, please get me out. Please get me out. Damn you, I don't want to burn. Oh mother, bloody Tiger. Get me out.'

'Shut up! I can't help you. Shut up!'

'Bloody Tiger. Oh mother, please, get me out.'

The sound of Morris's voice drove the steel-coffined man to even louder pleas and curses.

The fire grew and the trapped man either saw or heard it and he became more violent still in his frantic, hopeless efforts to

116

summon help. Morris shouted back, begging him to be quiet, but the despairing exchange continued. There was a belch of flame from the turret hatch as the fire broke through into the tank's crew compartment. The voice from within became almost unintelligible, soaring higher and higher. Words came out in a mad jumble between animal-like expressions of naked fear.

Morris dared the pain his action brought and pushed his hands tighter against his head but the voice came through. The shared fear became anger at his own frustration.

'Why don't you choke in that bloody smoke?' Don't wait for the fire, use your pistol.'

He forced a burn-stiffened limb to reach down and take out his own Enfield revolver and wave it at the fiery wreck. The screams kept coming, filling the pause between each tormented word.

'Bloody . . . Tiger . . . It . . . hurts . . . oh . . . mother . . . oh . . . Jesus . . . mother . . .'

Tears of rage were forced from him as Morris had to endure and share an agony that far surpassed his own. The screaming went on and on. It didn't seem possible that anyone could or would want to hang on to life in there. In a futile and pathetic attempt to stop the sound he emptied his pistol at the flame-covered Sherman. A hatch clanged open, burst by the pressure of the gasses produced by the raging inferno inside. A pillar of flame jetted twenty feet, the screaming that had gone on for so long stopped, and the ammunition aboard the Sherman detonated.

Morris felt himself being lifted by the blast and thrown. He tumbled through the air and had a brief glimpse, before he landed in it and lost consciousness, of the broad track marks of a Tiger tank.

Corporal Morris regained consciousness nine hours later in a field hospital with no recollection of what had put him there. A severe concussion, combined with the shock of the experience he had been through, had induced a state of partial amnesia.

His other injuries were second- and third-degree burns to three per cent of his body area, mostly on the back of both arms, his right thigh and hip, and his left buttock. He also had extensive minor lacerations of the scalp and shoulders. One pint of whole blood was transfused, but no sutures were considered necessary.

At that time approximately fifteen per cent of all battle casualties were cases of 'exhaustion' or other psychiatric disorders.

Due to the desperate need for surgical beds, and the fact that the 32nd General (Psychiatric) Hospital would not be in Normandy for another three weeks, most men were shipped back to specialist establishments in England.

Morris was sent to a hospital just outside Bath, in Somerset. There he made an excellent recovery and towards the end of July was sent to a relocation unit. From there, after four days' leave, he went to Leyland in Lancashire where, besides the manufacture of trucks and the assembling of Churchill tanks, they were also engaged on the development of prototype half-tracks for the British Army. He joined a small team under the command of Major C. V. Patch, engaged in the evaluation of captured German tracked vehicles.

On the second day Corporal Morris was first asked, then ordered, to drive a Mark 1 Tiger tank from the vehicle park to the trials ground. He initially declined, then refused to do so. Unable to offer any adequate explanation he was placed on a charge and sent under escort to the nearest military establishment with the facilities to convene a court-martial.

The unit was about to move and its officers, to use the adjutant's words, were 'up to their arses in paperwork already'. Morris's arrival was a most unwelcome complication at a difficult time. He was dealt with in an unconventional manner, and with almost indecent haste.

The CO had a brief telephone conversation with Major Patch, then sent for Morris. The commanding officer was a colonel, a soldier of the old school, infantry through and through. He had no time for tank men, believing anything could be achieved by a determined bayonet charge. Behind his back he was referred to as 'Old cold steel'.

He gave Morris a straight choice. Either he could put in for an immediate transfer to the infantry, 'where they'll soon knock some damned sense into you', or he could take his chances with a court-martial. The colonel went to some lengths to point out that the best he could expect from that would be a very long time in Takehill military detention centre near Rochdale, or some similar establishment.

Morris had heard of Takehill. The ex-cotton mill had a grim reputation. He chose the transfer. The colonel saw to it that the red tape was hacked through in no time and the formalities reduced to a minimum.

That was how Morris found himself on a crash conversion

course, along with a lot of other very disgruntled tank men who had been transferred, without the option, to make up the depleted ranks of the infantry in France.

From there it was a short step and a long journey to one of the spearhead battalions of the British Second Army's advance into northern France. To be more precise, the first section of the third platoon, first company. Sergeant Ellis's section.

THE PATROL

23.25 TO 01.20 HOURS

At the instant of firing, the Tiger's twelve-cylinder Maybach engine first stuttered then roared into life. When the echoes of the explosion died away, the clearing and the surrounding woods were blasted by the bellow of its twin exhausts and saturated by the grey fog they spewed out. From its ranging machine-gun a hail of red tracer was hosed over the embankment, lingering for a moment to pay special attention to the area of the fresh crater that decorated its top.

From the centre of the gaping hole rose whisps of steam as white-hot shell fragments were quenched. Some trees about its edge creaked loudly. With so much of their support torn away, the exposed roots strained to hold them upright. For one shattered pine bordering the crater it was too much. Most of its root system destroyed, the stripped and scarred trunk trembled; then slowly but with gathering speed it fell to bridge the yawning gap. It brought down branches from its neighbours and, hitting the ground, flipped into the air the twisted remains of a bren gun.

The Tiger settled back on its suspension and the trailer stopped rocking. From the sides of the turret fell a few flakes of the concrete-like anti-mine paste. Faint metallic noises came from within. A circular hatch in the back of the turret opened and a shining brass shell case was ejected to roll lazily on the engine deck and over the side, to bounce on the edge of the trailer before landing in the mud. The panzer was tidying itself, ready for the next round of the contest.

Private Bird looked at the second-hand of his watch as it jogged towards the moment when Ellis had said the attack was to begin. For the tenth time he checked his sten gun, then looked to where Alex crouched by the nearest Opel. On the other side of the road Eric was just visible. Bird jumped as the sound of a burst of automatic fire and tracer came out from the embankment top.

The two sappers launched themselves forward, wrenching the pins from their grenades as they ran. There was a loud scream from Alex's target as he thrust his hand in through the open cab window and dropped his grenade on to the floor beneath the driver's feet. Something went wrong as Eric went to mete out the same treatment to the other Opel. The metal orb slipped from his grasp to fall under the cab instead of into it.

Eric turned and started to run. He was in the middle of the road when the grenade went off. He was caught, swept off his feet and tumbled through the air to land agonizingly hard on the concrete roadway. Broken ends of bone grated together as his ankle snapped. Slipping mercifully from consciousness, his last impression was of frantic screaming coming from somewhere across the junction.

A German, injured by the fragments that had punched up through the floor of the truck, reeled from the cab. He stood, trying to find his balance, shaking blood from his eyes. Then he saw Eric Church lying in the road and turned to grab at an axe fastened to the side of his truck's engine cover. He wrestled with the straps that held it, freed it, lurched forward a step and raised it above his head. Even as he did Alex was lunging at him with a knife held out stiffly in a rigidly locked arm. The German fell back a pace, recovered and, with blood still streaming into his eyes from a scalp wound, he swung wildly with the ponderous weapon. Alex sidestepped the ill-aimed blow and swept the glinting blade upwards into the German's neck an inch below his ear.

The stricken man froze, his whole body welded in the pose it had adopted at the instant of the blade's penetration. In that stance he died.

Alex didn't waste a second. Before his adversary hit the road, he had grabbed Eric's collar and was towing him back into shelter behind the burning supply truck. A moment to look round, and then he dragged his friend through the mud and puddles to join Dicky at the edge of the clearing. Bird slung his sten and rushed out to help the last few feet.

In the undergrowth, screened from the junction, Alex searched the unconscious Eric for injuries and found the fractured ankle. He sought round for something with which to make a rough splint.

'I bloody knew something like this would happen. The whole show is a fucking shambles, and now this.'

Alex took off his webbing and used it to bind two pieces of stick either side of Eric's ankle.

Firing was still going on beyond the embankment top, but none of it was aimed into the clearing. One stream of tracer soared high above the trees, then abruptly stopped. Sporadic shots continued for a while. The supply truck was now well alight and adding detail to the scene. At last the terrible wailing from the fueller ceased, and at the same moment the unseen battle beyond the bank top ended.

'What do we do now?' Dicky was watching the bank. There was no sign, nothing to give a clue of what had been going on up there.

'We get out of here as fast as we bloody can. That's what we do.'

Alex took Eric's spare magazines and put them in his pockets. The rest of his friend's kit he discarded to save weight.

'What about Morris, and Ellis, and Barras? We can't just bugger off and leave them.'

Alex made ready to lift the unconscious man. 'It sounds like Ellis was pounced on from behind. He must have been followed back from that farmhouse. As for Barras, that mad sod can fend for himself. You heard those screams. If you want to get mixed up with him, then go ahead. Me, I'm getting Eric home.'

Dicky hesitated to help Alex, casting worried glances up to the embankment, then looking back down at Eric. 'I don't know. Maybe we should . . .'

The Tiger fired and a section of the bank was blasted into the air. Red tracer raked the fringe of the woods about the crater. There was a pause, then something shiny rattled on the panzer's hull and fell to the ground.

'That's where the hide is . . . was.' Dicky corrected himself, staring at the shell's point of impact.

'Yeah, now there's no bloody problem, is there? Ellis might have dodged that Jerry patrol a second time, but sure as hell he's had it now. Give me a hand.'

Eric was coming round. He was very pale. What little flesh of his face was visible between the blotches of caked soil was stark white by contrast. He looked down at the bundle swaddling his ankle and attempted a smile.

'I've either got elephantiasis, or I've broken something. Well, help me up then. I'll give it a try.'

Alex and Dicky carefully hoisted him to a standing position, taking his weight while he slowly lowered the bandaged foot and bit his lip in anticipation of the pain to come.

'Just point me in the right direction and I'll hop home.'

He gasped and lifted his foot as the first light contact brought excrutiating pain. A giddy sickness surged through him and he

122

would have fallen if Alex hadn't sensed his distress and steadied him.

'Well, come on then.' The words came haltingly as he gulped the cold air. 'Let's be going. Last one home brews up.'

Dicky and Alex exchanged looks, but said nothing. They struck out for the road below the embankment, taking the shortest route they could, hugging the edge of the clearing, staying barely inside the scant cover of the damaged vegetation about its perimeter. As they started out there was the distant clang of a lorry door being thrown open.

Barras backed from the cab, watching the writhings of the mutilated driver lolling across the seats. The Frenchman drank in the scene. He wiped his left hand across his mouth and, as he did, explored the taste of the blood on it, then held it a little away to watch the rain washing the red stain down over his wrist to be lost in the tunnel of his jacket sleeve. He turned his hand over, opened it to look at what he held. He brought up the knife and held the two side by side. His mind was in a more elated state than drink had ever induced in Sergeant Ellis. Barras laughed silently as the screams from the cab drove from him the last vestiges of sanity.

He was deaf to everything but the frantic agonies and blind to all but the contortions before him. The machine-gun fire, the grenade explosions, the boom and crash of the Tiger's cannon never existed for him. For Barras there was only the ugly trophy in his hand and the screams.

The fueller's far door swung suddenly open and the German was gone from sight before Barras could move to catch him. Undecided what to do, the Frenchman turned from the cab and his eyes lit on the backside of the first German he had attacked. The man was quite dead but his eyes were wide open and still bore the surprised expression with which he had died. Barras squatted down beside the corpse. With elaborate care he washed the chunk of flesh in a muddy puddle and put it in his pocket. He took a hone from his belt and began to sharpen the knife. He worked quietly, humming a tune to himself and occasionally giving the exposed posterior a critical look. Barras paused, tested the keenness of the blade with his thumb, looked again at the dead German; and then, pleased with some calculation he has made, nodded in childlike satisfaction.

The thing that had slithered from the far side of the fueller's cab was a sobbing hulk that a short time before had been a man. Fear, pain and humiliation had combined to reduce the German driver to a state at which even his nervous reactions barely functioned. It crawled, leaving a trail of blood to be washed away by the swirling wind-driven surface water. The last feeble reserves of energy spent, the human wreck came to a halt in the middle of the junction, spasms wracking the body in response to violent messages sent to the brain by shredded nerve endings.

Progress was slow. There were several fallen trees to negotiate and Eric had virtually to be lifted over each one. Every jar to his ankle brought him to the verge of collapse. The Tiger's engine was louder; they were quite close to it. Gusting wind would bring the warmth of its exhaust to them now and again.

'Come on, mate.' Alex twisted his hand in the material of Eric's jacket to pull him up and so take more of his weight. 'We've got to get moving. Those Krauts in the Tiger might have radioed for help. We've got to get back across the road.'

When they paused for a moment after the difficulties of crossing a tangle of fallen trunks, Dicky tried to hide his nervousness and his impatience to be moving again. They were only yards from the Tiger. Above the undergrowth he could see the cupola surmounting its turret. He wondered what it would be like for the crew pinned inside it; how they would be reacting to their situation, stuck up on the trailer with limited vision. They would have no way of knowing if at that very moment someone was creeping up on them with a bazooka or a satchel charge. He jumped as the tank's machine-gun barked a single shot, then gave out a ripping blur of fire at the embankment.

'What's it up to now? It can't be firing at Ellis. He must have been flattened with the hide.'

Alex prompted Eric to start moving again. 'I don't care what it's bloody firing at, just so long as its attention's elsewhere until we get past it.'

The woods behind the Krupp and its dangerously active load were much torn about by shell and rocket damage. Some of the deeper holes, being flooded and linked together, made an impassable barrier, and the three men were forced even closer to the panzer. There was a muffled report, like a small mortar being fired, and a smudge of white smoke showed briefly on the top of the Tiger's turret.

Dicky saw and heard, and remembered an instructor's words.

To shout and act on a warning would have taken too long. He barged into the two sappers and caught them off balance. All three men fell in a heap as the fragmentation mine fired from the Tiger's turret launcher went off over the centre of the clearing. The exploding, ballbearing-packed charge made a compact cloud of off-white smoke twenty feet from the ground, which turned to a boiling, seething mass as the storm of steel hit it. On the road a dying German fell apart like overdone chicken as red-hot shrapnel slashed at him.

Eric had fainted when his ankle twisted on falling. Alex and Dicky grabbed at him and pulled him under the partial cover of a felled tree as a second anti-personnel mine went off. This time it was nearer to the bowser and the sheltering men clearly heard the metallic hail as it rattled against the top and sides of the long fuel tank. Two of the particles punched through the thin metal to produce two jetting streams that made iridescent patterns on the puddles they landed among.

Alex took off his helmet and examined two small dents in the brim. 'The Krauts must be getting jumpy, popping off like that for no bloody reason.'

'Maybe they're doing it as insurance, stop any trouble before it starts.' Dicky had pulled back his sleeve and was trying to pluck from his forearm a broad splinter that protruded from it. He nodded towards Eric. 'We're not going to be able to move very fast carrying him.'

'We're not leaving him,' Alex snapped. 'He goes with us.'

'How the hell can we carry him all the way back? We'd have problems enough if we were travelling light. How we going to manage if we're lugging him about?'

'You won't need to.' Eric's voice was weak, but his determination was clear enough. 'Find me something I can use as a crutch. I'll keep up with you.'

Dicky was about to deride the suggestion, but Alex had already disappeared in search of a suitable piece of wood. With the rumble of the Tiger's V12 as a background, Dicky listened to the sapper thrashing about, breaking down foliage, dragging broken boughs from beneath debris in his quest.

Alex rejoined them. 'Here you are, mate. Try this for size.'

Dicky looked nervously from his watch to the plume of exhaust rising above the junction. 'You took bloody long enough. The ruddy racket you were making, I thought you'd come out with a sedan chair.'

125

He was ignored as Eric tried the crutch and then, watched anxiously by Alex, began to move towards the road.

Dicky shrugged and followed. The side of the Tiger could be seen through the thin screen of trees. It sat there, growling to itself, more gigantic and more menacing than ever, but the three men were forced by Eric's stumbling pace to go still slower as they came level with it.

The explosion beneath them pushed the ground upwards with sledge-hammer force into the face and bodies of the two NCOs. In seemingly slow motion the whole area lifted and they felt themselves being raised on a growing column of soil and roots. The earth pillar broke apart, bursting open and throwing the material in all directions. Ellis and Morris were hurled different ways. The sergeant landed between two trees and was almost buried by a deluge of earth, much of it bound together by intricate root systems. Morris was sent tumbling head-over-heels to a jarring halt against the faceless corpse of a dead German.

Sergeant Ellis spat dirt. It filled his nose, his mouth and his eyes. He knew irrational panic for a moment as his first attempt to move failed. The heap of soil was heavy and he was pinned on his side with one arm trapped behind his back. Before he could try again a figure loomed out of the shadows and began scrabbling with bare hands to pull aside some of the root-woven, clay-like material.

'I thought we'd bought it. What happened to you?'

Mingled with the mud on Morris's face was glistening blood. His hair had snared white, spongy particles. 'I landed on a Kraut who'd had a face lift. There, see if you can move.'

Ellis pushed himself up. He gritted his teeth in expectation of the discovery of a broken or crushed limb. There was none. He had the most appalling headache, but he had at least to admit that it was not as a result of any wound.

'Did you see what happened to the others?'

'How the hell could I? I went up in the air at the same time you did. They must still be down there somewhere.'

While Ellis just stood about, Morris sought round for weapons. He found one German rifle, with two clips of ammunition, and the incendiary grenades. That, with Ellis's pistol, was all they had. Of the mines there was no sign, save for one shredded satchel caught high in a tree. As the corporal returned from his search,

126

Ellis was hurriedly stuffing something into his coat pocket.

Ellis fought the giddiness that threatened to topple him. He clutched at a tree for support, trying to make the action look casual, as though he were merely leaning against it. He waved one hand towards the clearing.

'They must have had it. There's nothing we can do now. We might as well start back.' A nagging doubt at the back of his mind would not be subdued, he sought reassurance. 'They must have bought it, mustn't they?'

'Well, I don't reckon they have, but don't take my word for it. Get a second opinion – ask your flask.'

The sergeant didn't have the will or strength left to argue. All he wanted now was to get back, avoiding any more trouble, and get some sleep. His eyelids felt like cast-iron shutters, suspended by only the thinnest of threads. The drink-induced torpor, compounded by the shock of the explosion, had a grip on his mind. He could only think to take the line of least resistance, even though it meant delaying the start back. Still, he consoled himself, it was worth it if it kept Morris quiet. He didn't succeed, though, in keeping a note of irritation out of his drawl.

'All right, we'll hang around for a bit longer, see if they show. But only for a while . . . just to make sure.'

Morris found a place on the edge of the embankment, not far from the crater. From it they had as good a view as before, but without the advantage of the slight degree of weather-proofing that the hide had provided. They took up position in time to see a man crawl from the cab of the fueller and across the clearing to the middle of the junction.

'He's not one of ours, anyway.'

There was relief in Morris's voice. He felt he had a purpose. He hardly knew the men for whom they waited, but he felt a responsibility towards them, discovered he was enjoying a feeling of importance at being the one to take the initiative, at having virtually taken charge. He had always envied other men their comradeship with their fellows. For the first time he felt he had someone to feel concern towards. There was a great welling up of happiness inside him. It was a glorious sensation.

Ideas flashed before him. He could see himself promoted, could picture himself as the steadfast sergeant, depended on by his officers, begrudgingly admired by his men. The picture grew more ambitious. Perhaps he could make sergeant-major, or even – he

127

held his breath – get a field commission. It could happen; he could make it happen. It wasn't impossible; others had already done it. The speculation ended abruptly.

Part of the piled loose earth at the new crater's rim collapsed into the hole. The slight movement was not missed by the Tiger's crew. Its machine-gun spat fire, three long bursts. The NCOs raised their heads in time to see the first of the aerial mines launched. They buried their faces in the dirt as the stinging balls of steel zipped down, the closest of them striking the ground only inches to their front. When the ringing sensation in their ears began to ease and their hearing once more registered, Ellis and Morris looked up.

The distant supply truck still burned. Two sparkling pale fountains sprang from the fueller's side. The body at the cross-roads appeared different, as if it were somehow suddenly re-arranged, disjointed.

The Tiger's engine revved higher and the giant panzer shud-dered and nudged backwards on its trailer until its tracks were hard against the folded rear loading ramps that jutted up behind it. Again the engine speed rose, the tracks began to turn. Both men watching thought the tank had caught fire as it was half hidden by sparks and smoke. A sound blended of grating metal, and booming exhaust blasted at them. The tracks flailed and scrabbled at the trailer's deck as the driver tried to break out through the retaining folds of reinforced metal slotted into the back of the transporter. Still the ramps held. The engine note dropped, the behemoth ground forward as far as it would, then lunged back again, using the three feet of space it had gained to hurl its fifty-six tons at the buffers that kept it trapped. The ramps still held. The Tiger repeated the trick and this time, when the impact failed, kept its tracks threshing round at top speed.

Trailer and tank together plunged and bucked under the repeated impacts. Sheets of sparks flew wild as rusted steel was worn to a mirror finish. The darting clouds of pin-prick light matched the fiery truck until, without any hint or warning, the Opel's fuel ignited.

Fingers of flame stabbed out, feathering into yellow fronds of fire as the wind caught them. It was as if daylight had been switched on. Gone the madly flickering shadows. In their place a light that filled every corner of the clearing and flooded in among the trees at its edge.

The Tiger's commander and Corporal Morris spotted the three figures at the same moment. But while Morris could do nothing, the tank man was certain what he had to do, and he did it.

Dicky was leading Alex and Eric down the flank of the Tiger to avoid the more difficult going further within the woods, when a pistol port in the tank's turret swung open and the gun-metal snout of a machine-pistol was thrust out. The three men dropped in time and the thirty-two rounds blazed over them: but now they were trapped.

The tank commander couldn't depress his gun far enough to bear on them, but he had other weapons at his disposal.

Caught in the open, the trio were unable to move for fear of coming within the arc of fire of the machine-pistol. Even if Eric had been in any state to make a run for it, when the mine discharger coughed there was only one course of action open to them. On hands and knees, half dragging, half pushing Eric with them, Pitt and Bird managed to scramble under the transporter platform as the aerial mine exploded right over the tank.

Above them the complex bracing of the trailer vibrated in time with the beat of the Tiger's engine. The air was thick with the smell of hot metal, the stench of roasted paint and petrol fumes. The flying fragments from the exploding mine swept over the thick armour of the Tiger, perforated the cab roof of the Krupp tractor unit and butchered the slumped bodies of the crew beside it.

'Screw this for a lark. This is bloody silly.'

Dicky gave up an attempt to support himself above the puddles on his elbows and let his body sag slowly into the freezing water. The cold struck through his already saturated clothes to cramp his limbs. The shock of the contact took his breath and he had to force his lungs to gasp in air.

Eric made no complaint. He lay quiet and still, conserving his strength. He watched as Dicky scraped a miniature drainage channel from the pool in which he lay to a larger one just outside their shelter. Eric observed the water with interest as it flowed from the larger to the smaller puddle, increasing the depth of water in which Dicky lay. Alex had seen it as well.

'Did you mean that to happen?'

He turned to examine the place they had occupied before diving to escape the mine. The bark had been stripped from the larger trees and the others were splintered and broken. The brambles and bushes of the undergrowth had been beaten flat. He couldn't repress a shudder at the thought of what would have happened to them if they'd still been there at the moment of detonation.

Above them the Tiger eased forward again, stopped, and gradually increased its engine speed. Alex gave up trying to calculate the time it would take the three of them to crawl clear and run to the first substantial cover; the deafening racket overhead blotted out all thought. The engine note climbed and climbed until it seemed certain the twenty-three-litre engine must burst under the strain. Flakes of rust fell like heavy snow as, with a crash, the drive was engaged and then almost immediately swamped by the screech of the track links biting into the trailer deck as they threw the mountain of steel at the ramps. The concussion of the impact pushed the trailer down until its suspension bottomed, forcing the girdering to within an inch of Alex's shoulder.

The British soldiers forced their hands hard over their ears and shut their eyes tight to the deluge of sparks that cascaded down through the gaps in the deck. The tank driver kept his throttle wide open. The threshing tracks squealed with nerve-jangling effect on the metalwork, but made no impression on the ramps barring their path. For the men beneath, the noise went on for an eternity. Their throats were rasped by the metal-laden atmosphere, their lungs seared by the acrid grey mist that blew down to them from the twin geysers at the back of the Tiger.

A crack, like a cannon firing, as one of the ramp hinges burst, but the rest held. The engine note died, the tracks slackened their skidding pace and were still. The sparks ceased to dart and flash.

Bird was near the limit of his endurance. Attacked by the wet and cold, assaulted by the noise, he just wanted to lie down and wait for whatever form his end would take – machine-gun fire sprayed under the trailer or a grenade rolled at them. The oily taste of muddy, rainbow-flecked water was in his mouth. Oh, how good it would be just to lie still and not worry any more. Just lie there, and not have to get up again. The cold wasn't so bad, once you were used to it. It was almost soothing, restful. He was glad the tracks had stopped. Now only the purr of the engine, like a lullaby, very peaceful . . . peaceful.

'Come on, Dicky. Dicky! Shake yourself.'

Water was in his face, stinging. His eyes snapped open. 'What? What the hell are you doing? Aren't we bloody wet enough?'

Alex said nothing. It had worked.

A tyre on the burning Opel blew out, scattering blobs of fiery rubber. Some landed on the other supply truck where they spluttered for a while on the wet canvas of the tilt before succumbing to the rain. Others landed on a body in the road. One landed on the shaft of an axe still grasped in dead fingers.

'You've got to leave me and make a break for it.' Eric was building up a shallow mud wall all around himself in an effort to keep out the water. As fast as he completed one section, his twists and turns to reach another would bring the first down. 'There'll be reinforcements along soon. Get going now.'

'That's enough of that. We're all getting out, aren't we Dicky?' Alex took the opportunity to check that Dicky wasn't dozing off again. 'Anyway, that would be the best thing that could happen. When more Krauts come it's going to take them a minute to get sorted out, and while that's going on the tank crew won't be able to use that fucking lethal bomb thrower of theirs. While they're sorting themselves out we'll slip away. Isn't that right, Dicky?' He was using the conversation as an oblique way of checking that Bird stayed alert. 'So all we have to do is hang on a bit longer and wait for some more squareheads to turn up to cover our get-away. Well, we can hang on a bit longer, can't we?'

Eric said nothing, knowing that whatever he said, whatever argument he put forward to the contrary, however soundly reasoned, backed by whatever logic, when the time came, if it came, Alex was going to drag him along with them.

Their chances of escape were slim, wasting further with each minute that passed. Eric felt the pain in his grossly swollen ankle subsiding. The cold puddle in which it lay did at least that much good.

Twice more the Tiger thundered above them and, after each fruitless attempt to break out, the great beast vented its anger and frustration by blasting the corners of the open space with its mine discharger.

Alex watched the last flames amid the melted wreckage of the burnt-out supply truck. The shadows grew longer as the fire sank. The woods once more crowded in on the perimeter of the clearing.

131

'When that goes out we could crawl out under the front of the tractor unit. They might not have such a good field of vision that way.'

Dicky didn't hear. He uttered the thought that had been nagging at him, frightening him. 'Why the hell haven't they dropped a grenade to flush us out? They must have some, and they know we're here.'

As he spoke he curled himself into a ball, clutching his sten tightly, fearful that his words might bring the event. It was Eric who spoke, breaking a silence of ten minutes.

'That's why.' He pointed with the tip of his crutch to the rear of the tractor unit. 'That Krupp must be carrying over a hundred gallons of fuel. If they set it off, well, even a Tiger might get a bit uncomfortable, sat on top of a bonfire like that.'

'I wish you two cheerful buggers would shut up. We've got one or two problems already, about what they are doing, without speculating about what they might get up to next.'

Using the last of the light from the fire, Alex had another go at working out the times and distances involved in making a run for it; trying to figure out the best way of manoeuvring Eric under the trailer, to the front of the cab, across the road up the bank and into the far woods. Unbidden, Eric suggested an alternative.

'Why don't you just leave me? Make a run for it.'

He half hoped, half knew what Alex's reply would be but it still came as a relief to hear the firm, almost aggressive negative.

'Shut up. I told you, we're all getting out, and that's all there is to it. Now shut your gob and save your strength.'

The fire now burned only in the Opel's fuel tank. The explosion had ripped the top from it and the flames flared from the residue of petrol in the container it formed. The wind played with those flames, sometimes driving them down out of sight and plunging the area into total darkness, then drawing them up in corkscrew fashion so that the yellow pillar threw a brilliant circle of light. The men under the trailer watched and waited.

With the return of darkness came a time of danger for the crew of the Tiger. While there was light, they were in charge of the situation, which would change when the illumination was gone. The big beast growled, a deep steady note like the controlled anger of a caged feline. It set about making its position less vulnerable; prepared its defences.

Slowly the turret began to traverse. The long snout of its cannon gradually depressed. It stopped and paused, as if preparing to spring. Violence was unleashed, tank and trailer rocked back until it seemed they must tip over. Mud and water were blasted high above the reeling rig as the barrel spat thunder, flame, smoke and steel.

The blinding light of the muzzle flash was gone, the mud and water showered back down, running in torrents off the panzer and trailer. The transporter and its load see-sawed back to an even keel.

Dicky spat mud, shook his head to rid it of the ringing sensation, blinked to clear his vision of the white fog that obscured it. The junction swam into view. It looked no different from before, except . . . except that a sound he had grown used to was louder. So used to it had he become that for a moment he couldn't place it.

The Tiger's machine-gun clattered. Tracer hosed in a short arc at the bowser. Dicky watched as it broke up on impact, making irregular bright red splashes of colour. The side of the fueller blossomed with the bold gobs of red, was patterned by the vivid strokes they daubed on the metal.

PRIVATE DONALD BIRD

THE INITIATION

The stick swept in broad gestures over the crude map scratched in the dirt as the platoon know-all held forth. The men about him were hunched deep inside their coat collars, not moving, trying to conserve what body heat they had left. A bitingly cold wind whistling down from the Scottish hills. Its numbing effect, their reluctance to move for fear of letting some of the trapped warmth escape, made them an ideal, captive audience.

'So you see it's got to be there. Can't be anywhere else, can it?'

With the tip of the stick he added a few rough details to the ragged outline in the soil that was meant to represent the channel and the British and French coasts. England looked like a pregnant sausage stood on end.

One of the circle of men, more argumentative, or stupid, than the others raised an objection to the know-all's confident prediction as to where an Allied landing would have to be made for the invasion of Europe.

'What about this Atlantic Wall the Germans are always spouting off about? How do you reckon we get past that and off the beaches?'

The barrack-room tactician was not to be put off like that. 'You haven't been listening, have you? Look, the Krauts know that Calais is the shortest route and the most obvious one to use, so they'll figure we'll be crafty and cross elsewhere. You see?'

The blank stare he got by way of answer indicated that his questioner didn't see.

'Look, most of their reserves will be further along the coast in either direction, waiting for a surprise attack. So we'll catch them napping when we sprint straight across.'

'But what about the Atlantic Wall? All those guns and the concrete and the mines and the wire. What about them?' the argumentative one persisted.

'Listen.' The platoon know-all had infinite patience with any man who, by his persistence or dullness, gave him excuse to continue his lecture.

The other men had burrowed further from sight, so as not to get involved.

134

'We've got bombers, haven't we?'

He grew more animated as he developed the idea that had only just that moment occurred to him. From the confidence with which he spoke, though, one might have imagined he had considered the subject from its every angle for weeks.

He went on: 'If we can send a thousand bombers to have a go at German cities, then we can certainly put that many over the French coast. Wouldn't be much left of Haw-Haw's Atlantic Wall after that.'

He looked smugly round at his audience. He was met only by silence, until a voice piped up from the back.

'There is one thing you haven't thought of, something you should have taken into account.'

The man with the mouth and the head to match bent over his dirt diagram and scrutinized it, trying to discover some point he had missed.

'I've thought of everything. What could go wrong that I haven't thought of? Come on, show me.'

'I was hoping you'd say that,' said the voice. 'You forgot the weather. What if it rains?'

With that, an arm came out of the crowd and emptied the contents of a bucket over the know-all, turning him into a gasping, bedraggled scarecrow, and his map into mud

Thirty heads bobbed up from the depths of as many collars to enjoy the spluttering spectacle. The know-all's rapidly growing rage wasn't abated when some unseen wit behind him asked out loud if that was what was known as pouring cold water on an idea. The chilled and water-logged amateur strategist still retained enough dignity to cast about for the rain-maker.

'Who did it? Who bloody did it?'

An apparently contagious bout of laughter was convulsing the men about him as he glared at each in turn, searching for a look of guilt or contrition from the culprit.

'Come on, who did it? I want to know who bloody did it.'

A chorus rose up, above the laughter. Above the howl of the wind it grew to a chant as the know-all pushed his way out of the grinning circle and made off for the truck where the instructor sheltered, to seek permission to return to camp and get changed.

The chant followed him, carried by the wind that caused his teeth to chatter violently. It was a name, repeated over and over again. 'Bird, Bird, Dicky Bird.'

*　　*　　*

135

Private Donald Bird was reclining at his ease on the three planks and wafer-thin mattress that masqueraded as a bed. He was in a happy frame of mind. In fact, since he had arrived at the camp with the rest of the draft just five weeks before, he had rarely been in any other, having made up his mind to make the best he could of a bad deal.

Dicky Bird wasn't one of nature's clowns, but he did have a natural genius for coming up with bright ideas to lighten dull moments. Infantry Basic Training Camp was a succession of dull moments, laced with many uncomfortable ones. At present he was on light duties, following an accident with a wheelbarrow and a deep trench. Fortunately it was a freshly dug one and no one had yet made use of it when he fell in. Although he had suffered only a sprain, until he had been examined, the MO was quite sure that Bird must have received a severe concussion at least. After all, it's not every day you see a man carried in on a stretcher, caked with mud and roaring his head off with laughter.

The rest of the platoon tumbled into the hut, most of them rushing straight to the pot-belly stove that glowed in the middle of the room. A few souls, more hardy or less pushy than the rest, went first to their beds to drop their packs. They would wait for the crush about the stove to thin before attempting to restore their normal body temperatures.

'Ted Williams isn't very happy with you, Dicky.' One of the men at the stove, turning round to warm his nether areas, addressed himself to Bird.

Dicky was not upset by the news. He said so.

'When are you fit again?' someone else asked him.

'I didn't know you'd missed me. If you must know, I'll be back with you full time from tomorrow. Why?'

'Well, I thought you might like to know they've cancelled the film on personal hygiene. Instead we're having an extra session with your favourite sergeant instructor.'

'Not Grimes.'

'That's the one.'

Dicky threw his paper into the air and, without bothering to look where it fell, got up from his bed and strutted the length of the hut with his thumbs tucked into his belt in exact imitation of Grimes. He also assumed the sergeant's voice. All the men turned to watch. It was always a good performance, one they never tired of.

'I am a Tiger tank.'

The first time Grimes had said that, everyone thought he had suddenly gone off his head. Bird continued the impersonation, after allowing a moment for the laughter to subside. He continued to pace up and down, adopting Grimes's swaggering gait.

'I am very big and turn very slowly.'

Dicky did the slow turn on his heels that Grimes always did at that point.

'I can be very deadly, especially to unwary infantry. I have a very long weapon, a very long, powerful, weapon.'

Again Dicky delivered the line in exactly the same dead-pan humourless way that Grimes did.

'My exhaust is noisy so I can't sneak up behind you, but I can give you a nasty surprise if you see me full frontal. I'm at my most dangerous in open country, but you've got problems if you meet me in the woods as well.'

The performance was being hugely enjoyed. Dicky had the sergeant's voice and mannerisms off pat.

'You will have to sneak up behind me if you want to have a go at me, and even then you'll have to give me a big bang before I'll feel anything.'

Dicky peered at the men from beneath beetled brows just as their instructor did. He mirrored perfectly Grimes's intense expression.

'Now, what am I?'

'Big and slow,' came the bellowed response, as Grimes always required of them.

'And what have I got?'

'A great big weapon and a noisy exhaust.' This time the response was partly muffled by several of the audience who had collapsed on to the beds, overcome with laughter. That was one thing they dared not do before the real man, not with Grimes's exaggerated sense of self-importance.

'And what have you got to do?'

'Give you a big bang.'

'And don't forget, creep up behind me. A big bang up the back is no good unless it comes as a complete surprise.' Just like Grimes, Dicky glared at the men. 'And don't forget, you're in for a shock if you see me full frontal.'

The door of the hut slammed open to a howl of protest as a wave of icy air swept in and swirled about them. The man who had burst in ignored the protests.

'Where is he? Where is the little runt? Just wait till I get my fucking hands on him. I'll drown the little bastard.'

Ted Williams was like an enraged bull elephant. The soaking had considerably wounded his dignity. Now he was seeking to extract revenge, if necessary by beating it out of Dicky's hide.

Private Bird made a hurried exit from the hut via a handy window, before the know-all was three paces into it. Williams stood fuming, as hot now as he had been cold a while before. He did one tour of the room, looking under beds, into cupboards, but of course found nothing. He stalked back to the door and stamped out, leaving it wide open.

Dicky, who had been listening outside, vaulted back in.

'He'll get you one day.' The tone of the man who spoke did not convey the impression that his sympathies lay with Williams.

'Oh my God. It's bloody cold.'

That sentiment had been expressed by every single man in the platoon within the space of five frozen minutes, and not without the best of reasons. It really was cold. Not the good honest snap of a frosty morning, not the bracing tingle of a first fall of snow. It was a bone-chilling, toe-numbing cold. A blast of icy wind propelled before it a steady light rain that couldn't make up its mind what to be; rain, hail, sleet or snow. So it took turns at each.

'I can't imagine whatever possessed the Scots when they adopted the kilt as a national costume.'

Andy stamped his feet, showering everyone in mud in the process, in an attempt to restore circulation. Private Bird's mind stirred sluggishly to action.

'I reckon it's because they're so mean.'

Andy's voice floated from the headless spectre his appearance had assumed since he had withdrawn entirely within his greatcoat. A bloodshot runny eye peered out from between the top two buttons of that garment.

'How do you work that one out?'

'Well, you know what they're like with money. With a kilt on in this sort of weather they can keep their assets frozen.'

A corporal instructor came bouncing down the row of huddled humanity, or sub-humanity as he called them. Sergeant Grimes had left fifteen minutes before in the dummy tank. It was an old Hillman saloon on to which had been built a very rough plywood mock-up of a Tiger tank. So that no one should be left in any

138

doubt, the word 'Tiger' was written in foot-high white capitals down both sides.

The purpose of the exercise was to test the platoon's skill at map reading and to develop their initiative. They were split into groups of four or five, given a 'map' of the area and sent off to find the Tiger and plant a mine on it without being detected.

Until recently it had been the practice for the man slapping the simulated mine on the simulated tank to simulate an explosion by shouting 'bang'. This had been stopped after an unfortunate accident. A new instructor had taken the 'tank' out after only the swiftest of briefings. When some poor devil had succeeded in creeping up unobserved and shouted out 'bang', the instructor thought he had shouted 'back', so he did. It rather spoilt the soldier's moment of glory; likewise his face and rib-cage.

The corporal took up a relaxed but alert stance in front of the platoon. He looked disgustingly fit and well turned out. Even his casual posture was in direct contrast to the rigid looks and knocking knees of the men in front of him. The NCO stalked up and down, seeming to draw strength from their misery. The inspection complete, he gave a comprehensive sneer and spat noisily; the impact of the spittle being lost in the downpour that was starting in earnest.

'Now I know we're really scraping the bottom of the barrel.' He craned his neck forward, like a vulture examining a long-dead carcass which even it is wary of touching. 'In fact, by the look of you lot, we've gone through the bottom of the barrel and are scraping up the worms underneath.'

The corporal turned away, as though the sight were too much for him, then reluctantly turned back.

The steadily falling rain and the bitterly cold wind were obviously having an effect on the bladders of some of the platoon. They were the ones constantly shifting weight from one foot to the other and sweating despite the cold. What with that and the others who could no longer avoid being racked by shivers, it appeared as if the whole platoon was gripped by St Vitus's dance.

The corporal handed round maps to each section leader. Although by now every man was fully familiar with every inch of the terrain, the maps were different each time. Prominent features, structures and roads were given different names for each exercise. One week a ruined farmhouse might be a strong-point, the next a power station or an ammunition dump, and so on. The object was to figure out where the Tiger would most likely be and 'destroy' it.

'All right, you miserable bunch of wet hens, on your way. I can't stand the bloody sight of you any longer.'

For some, that was only as far as the nearest clump of bushes. Bird, whose turn it was to lead his group, led his three companions at a fast jog over the brow of the nearest hill, without so much as a glance at the map. His first objective was to get out of the instructor's sight.

It had always been the practice of Private Bird's group to hide close by, allow a decent time to pass for the first of the other sections to return, and then trudge back themselves; having first assumed suitably disappointed expressions. As usual they made straight for their hide beneath an overhung bank were, on previous exercises while others had rambled about in the rain, they had led quite a comfortable existence. It was hardly luxurious, but the thick piled heather kept out the wind, and the tiny space became quite warm after a while.

Once they had crowded in and the ritual arguments finished about who was taking up too much room, Dicky surprised the other three by taking out the map. Normally it stayed in someone's pocket until it was time to hand it back at the end of the day.

'What's up? Have you run out of fag papers?'

Dicky was quite indignant at the surprised looks on the faces about him. 'I can have a look at the map, can't I?'

'Well, you're not thinking of going and looking for Grimes, are you? We spend all our time in camp trying to avoid him.'

'The trouble with you, Andy, is that you've no imagination. Well I have; and I've got something else as well.'

From inside his coat Dicky produced a parcel wrapped in waxed paper. It unfolded to reveal five thunderflashes. Andy's mouth sagged open.

'What are you going to do with them?' he at last summoned up the courage to ask.

'I thought we'd show a bit of initiative and enthusiasm and . . .'

'Cop a court-martial,' added Sandy.

'How would you find Grimes anyway? He could be anywhere out there.'

On the rare occasions Smithy said something, it was usually to offer objection to some plan of Bird's. Dicky was not to be put off.

'Listen, who is it who always finds Grimes first?'

'Ted Williams.' The three voices blended as one.

'Right. And how does he do it?' Three blank stares met him in answer. 'I'll tell you how he does it. He doesn't go charging off. He sits down with his group for five minutes and they work it out. And what's more they're usually right.'

'That bloody arse-licking creep is always right.' Sandy didn't like Ted Williams.

'Is that what we're going to do, sit down and work out where he is?' Andy harboured doubts about their ability to carry out that mental exercise.

'Are we hell? We're going to follow Williams.' Dicky looked at his watch. 'By my reckoning he'll be leading his section out about one minute from now. When he does we'll be following, at a discreet distance of course.'

A few minutes later the quartet were trailing along at a safe distance behind Ted Williams as he led his group on a dead straight course across the sodden country – or sodding country as Sandy described it.

'What are you going to do with those thunderflashes, Dicky?' There was more than a hint of worry in Andy's question.

'Oh, they're just to make Grimes jump a bit, give him a good bang up the back, just like he's always asking for.'

'They won't hurt him, will they? Are you going to use them all?'

'Andy, will you stop bleating? You've seen these things go off on the assault course. Bit of a bang and a cloud of smoke, and it's all over. Besides, I'm not going to use them all. I brought along spares in case some got wet.'

'What about afterwards?' That had clearly been bothering Sandy.

'He's bound to know it was us.' The same point had also been causing Smithy some concern.

'That's the beauty of it. Of course he'll know it was us, but how can he prove it? We'll watch Williams's crowd of clever buggers do the job, and then when they've toddled off and Grimes has settled down again we'll nip in the same way and plant our little surprise.'

'What do we do then?'

'About fifty miles an hour in the opposite direction, I should think.'

Some aspects of the plot caught Andy's imagination – what little of it he had. He spoke with growing enthusiasm. 'He might not even think it was us. After all, we've never managed to find the dummy Tiger yet, have we? And as Dicky says, by the time he recovers we'll be far away.'

The other two remained unconvinced by Andy's optimism. Smithy in particular looked as if he had the utmost forebodings.

They had to dodge quickly into cover as they topped a ridge and saw below them Williams's section commencing a stealthy approach on a small plantation of mature firs. Dicky watched with interest as the others behind him muttered things about damp heather and wet ideas. As he watched, one of Williams's man crept to within twenty feet of the trees, jumped to his feet and dashed in among the stiffly standing trunks. It wasn't until the men leapt in behind a tangle of fallen wood that Dicky realized exactly where the dummy tank lay concealed.

After a brief wait, the rounded form of Grimes appeared. The rest of Williams's men gathered round the sergeant. Then, after a short discussion, they made off back to camp. Grimes turned and surveyed the clump of trees, nodded to himself, stalked back to the pile of lumber that hid the Hillman/Tiger, adjusted a few loose branches, then vanished from sight.

Dicky led the others along the ridge, keeping its crest between them and their sergeant. After they had gone a hundred yards or so he further endeared himself to his companions by insisting that they crawl over the top of the ridge on their bellies. The three coconspiritors muttered rebelliously but did it.

Not only was the ground soggy, but the heather, which in places was eighteen inches high, was loaded with droplets of water. It was like being in a rain storm within a rain storm. A gully gave cover once they were over the top and they were able to use it most of the way to the trees before they had to stop to work out the best way of making the final approach.

It was eventually decided that two men should actually plant the 'mine'. Dicky, of course, had to be one. Andy, to his disgust, was voted to be the other. He perked up a bit when Dicky took out the thunderflashes to find that the crawl through the heather had opened the wrapping and soaked them.

'Slit one open,' was Sandy's suggestion. 'Maybe the powder inside is still dry.'

One of the big fireworks was duly slit open and its contents investigated. The mixture seemed decidedly damp.

'The others will all be the same.' Smithy was no keener on the whole idea now than he had been earlier.

In fact, until Smithy made that remark, Dicky had been about to admit defeat and call the whole thing off, but something in Smithy's tone made him stubborn. He examined the contents of the other fireworks. At first glance they all looked useless, but careful scrutiny revealed that a little of the charge in each had remained dry, and one of the fuses was unaffected.

Sheltering under a ground sheet held over him by the others, Dicky scraped out the dry powder from each thunderflash and repacked it in the one with the usable fuse. Then he bound all the other fireworks about the remade one and stuffed them back inside his coat.

'You're not going to use the whole lot?' Sandy was worried at the prospect.

Dicky hastened to reassure him. 'I don't suppose it'll even go off but if it does, and only that dry powder burns, Grimes will hardly hear it. With a bit of luck, though, it might set off just a bit of the wet stuff and we'll get a decent bang.'

After coming all that way, and with all the work he had put in, he was at least going to try to put his plan into operation.

Accompanied by Andy, he sprinted for the trees. Grimes lay somewhere ahead of them, blissfully unaware of what was coming. With a skill they had never displayed before, the duo worked towards where the 'Tiger' lay hidden. They sidled round the rough trunks, slithered over the fallen ones. So well camouflaged was their objective that they were almost within reach of it before they could make it out through the mass of netting and natural debris with which it was draped.

Whatever else they might think of Grimes, they had to admit, however begrudgingly, that he was certainly good at camouflage. The dappled paint of the mock-up had been generously supplemented with strips of bark, handfuls of pine needles and clumps of heather. Parked amid the jumble of fallen timber the effect was to make the vehicle a part of the landscape.

Dicky studied the rear of the 'Tiger'. The bodywork of the basic saloon car was visible beneath the plywood superstructure. He surveyed it carefully, seeking the best place to position the surprise package.

'That jammy bastard has got the bleeding heater on.'

Andy was right. The vehicle vibrated slightly in time to its running engine, and the sound of rushing air could be heard coming from within.

At the thought of Grimes sitting in the car – dry, warm and

143

comfortable, while they froze, soaking in the cold wind – any vestige of scruple that Private Bird might have had, suddenly evaporated. Without further hesitation he inched forward on his hands and knees, stopped at the back of the vehicle and took out the bundle.

A match flared briefly, then a second. Andy, who was watching, held his breath and listened to the pounding in his chest drowning out all other sounds. Then he saw Dicky push the bulky package up between the metal body of the saloon and the plywood shell.

The two conspirators threw caution to the winds and ran faster than they had ever done before. Branches whipped at their faces as they broke from the trees and raced to where their friends waited. When they reached the gully they didn't jump in, they dived in with all the speed, but none of the grace, of spring-board champions. At seemingly the instant their heels disappeared, their heads reappeared to look in the direction from which they had just come.

When the faintly glowing fuse did at last burn down to the thumb-tamped powder, it produced results that could be described as devastating, terrifying or interesting; depending on whether you were sitting in the middle of it, admiring the results of your handiwork or watching with complete detachment, as were the men of another section who came over the ridge at that moment.

Tattered sheets of plywood flew everywhere, propelled from a growing fireball that engulfed the back of the Hillman as all the thunderflashes ignited. An avalanche of fir cones and needles were brought down and the trees about the spot rocked. The Tiger had ceased to exist.

The four culprits doubled up the gully, pounding down the bracken and through the heather in an unexpressed but perfectly demonstrated example of 'every man for himself' type panic. At the top of the gully each paused for a second to look back at the spreading column of grey smoke rising sluggishly to the low clouds. As they looked it was supplemented, overtaken and overshadowed by a far more dramatic black cloud that thrust skywards from the exploding petrol tank. The trees could be heard spitting, splitting and crackling in the heat. They could see the men of the other section running to the fire, but no sign of Grimes. The four bombers turned and bolted.

To say that the four men who got back to camp wet through and absolutely exhausted were nervous would be rather an under-statement. Their nerves were finely tuned until one hour after they had returned, when stories started to circulate of a somewhat singed and tatty Sergeant Grimes having been seen in the MO's room.

Several wild theories began immediately to do the rounds, most grounded on nothing more than wild speculation. The most interesting, though not the most unlikely, emanated from the vivid imagination of a science fiction fanatic and flying saucer advocate. All these were further fuelled by confirmed sightings of the sergeant making his way back to his quarters with his head swathed in bandages and his battledress in ribbons.

When it became clear that their victim really had survived, the bombers' spirits began to recover swiftly. It wasn't long before the truth was being noised abroad.

Surprisingly, Grimes did not start an immediate witch hunt, as was usually the case when he had some grievance, real or imagined. Worry hung naggingly at the back of Smithy's mind, but was swamped in the others by their enjoyment of the adulation and notoriety they were gathering. The story was being retold for the twentieth time that evening in the barrack hut, when things went wrong.

The room was filled with laughter and Private Bird was at the height of his glory when the door opened and Grimes walked in. He was moving stiffly, the edge of a bandage showed above his collar. His left cheek was an angry red, puckered and glistening where some gel had been applied to it. His eyebrows were gone and his skull was swathed in bandage which, though it didn't quite come down to his ears, admitted no vestige of hair beneath it. He stalked in, his gaze resting briefly on Private Bird and the immediate group about him before flicking to his three especial friends and sweeping over the other inmates.

Dicky and his section found themselves suddenly standing alone as the other men backed from them. Grimes addressed the room generally.

'I am glad you're all here.'

It was impossible from his tone to determine his mood. He was, if anything, just a shade too calm, too subdued. It was like looking into the eye of a hurricane.

He went on: 'I gather you enjoyed the exercise today. I thought that just to make sure you'd learnt the right lessons from it I would come over and cover the main points with you.' His voice hardened, but was still not loud or aggressive. 'Private Bird, with your section, front and centre, now.'

Reluctantly, slowly, the quartet complied and stood in a line in the middle of the room in front of Grimes. He walked up and down before them, looking at each in turn but addressing his remarks to the room generally.

'It would seem that some of you haven't learnt the lessons I've been trying to teach you. On the exercise today one section in particular made some very stupid mistakes. I'll use these four men to illustrate the points I want to draw your attention to.'

This was a new Grimes, a more dangerous Grimes. Gone the usual arrogant lecturing tone. Replacing it, this quieter, far more menacing style. He produced from his pocket a large bottle of tomato sauce and gave it a good shake before unscrewing the cap.

'The four men I'm talking about made stupid mistakes. Stupid because they forgot or ignored the fact that they were supposed to be attacking a Tiger tank.'

He glared about him. The inmates of the room in turn stared back with vacant gaze, each man making every effort to avoid catching the sergeant's eye. As far as the rest of the men were concerned, the four who had been singled out were on their own. With luck they'd stay that way. The platoon waited for the explosion they felt must come.

'Not just any tank mind you, a Tiger tank.' Grimes whirled round to face Private Smith. 'The first mistake was made when one of the men stuck his fat backside in the air as he crawled over a ridge. Now the Tiger could have fired a cannister shot at that big target.' The sergeant jabbed at Smithy with the open bottle. 'Cannister shot is nasty stuff. It opens a man right up.'

Smithy was covered in red blotches. His face was colouring up to match.

'That fool on the ridge would have got fragments all over here, and here, and here.' The sergeant walked round him, dabbing and slashing with the bottle. 'He would have died, but not quickly. He would have screamed the last hour of his miserable life until he had no voice to scream with. Then he would have spewed up the little bit of blood he had left and died.'

Sergeant Grimes was perspiring. His words came out with force, like a burst of machine-gun fire. The lesson was not being lost on the platoon. He stood in front of Sandy.

'Another of the half-wits left his arm over the side when he climbed into a gully.' The instructor used the bottle to draw a ragged red smear down the length of Sandy's arm. 'The machine-guns on a Tiger are MG34s. They fire nine hundred rounds a minute. He would have got fifty in that arm. What would have been left wouldn't have been much use for anything, except mince-meat.'

Sandy stood stiff as a ramrod. Grimes hadn't finished with him yet.

'That wasn't the limit of his stupidity, because the next thing he did was to stick his head up for a look round.'

A vigorous shake of the bottle and a thick dollop of the sauce was dripping down Sandy's face from his forehead. Grimes moved to Andy.

'Mind you, there was one man who showed he was even thicker than that. The one I'm thinking of moved so slowly from tree to tree for cover that the commander of a Tiger would have been spoilt for choice as to which weapon to hit him with and tear him apart. I think, though, the tank man would have chosen the bomb discharger. It's fitted in the Tiger's turret roof. It has an all-round traverse and it's loaded internally. The silly bugger playing peep would have found himself standing right underneath an exploding anti-personnel mine. They're real beauties, an improvement on the original S-mine and, God knows, they were bad enough.'

With slashing strokes Grimes marked off each of Andy's limbs at their junction with his trunk.

'How long would he have lasted without that lot?' He stuck his face into Andy's and elevated his voice to a bellow. 'How long would he have wanted to?'

With great deliberation Sergeant Grimes took a pace to the right to put himself in front of Private Bird. The other three stood staring straight ahead, the red muck running down them. Everyone else in the hut remained stock still and very quiet.

'The last man of that half-wit suicide squad, what about him? Perhaps he's thinking he really would have made it to the Tiger. After all, he managed to avoid being cut to ribbons by cannister shot from the tank's eighty-eight millimetre cannon, missed being ventilated by its machine-gun secondary armament; even dodged being dismembered by an aerial mine. So perhaps he thinks he made it. Would even have made it against the real thing.'

As he catalogued the weapons, Grimes casually flicked more tomato sauce over the three he had already dealt with. He didn't look at the daubed and spotted others. His eyes stayed locked on the face of Private Donald Bird.

Despite his attempts to stand still, Dicky shifted uncomfortably as he tried to tense himself for whatever was coming. Grimes looked him over, tip-toeing to look at the top of his head.

'Funny, I can't see a hole.' The sarcasm was lost as he elevated his volume to a roar, a thundering, full-blast roar that made the platoon and the hut jump. 'But there would have been one in the gut of the clown who tried to plant that mine.'

In a savage underarm blow the bottle was rammed into Bird's crotch. Eyes watering and turning glassy, Dicky fell to his knees, clutching himself. Grimes knelt down beside him, spoke quietly but clearly as he emptied the last of the sauce over Dicky's head.

'In the wall of the Tiger's turret are pistol ports. Inside the turret is an MP38 machine-pistol. It's there for close-quarters defence. With it, the crew of a real Tiger would have blasted the balls from the fool planting the charge and, if he was really lucky, they'd have killed him.'

The sergeant stood up. Dicky didn't. He stayed on the floor, wrapping his arms about himself and rocking back and forth in anguish. For the first time ever in the sight of those present, Grimes gave a smile. A thin and pathetic thing, but definitely a smile. He turned to go, then looked back.

'I do hope you've all learnt something from this little demonstration. For some, it's the only way. Oh, that's not quite true. There is another way, but for that you need a real Tiger tank, all fifty-six tons of it, and you also need five Germans. Some of you are going to learn that way, the hard way.'

He went out, closing the door carefully behind him. No one moved or spoke. The room stayed quiet for a long time.

Private Donald Bird maintained what could be called a very low profile during his last two weeks at Basic Training Camp, managing during that time to curb his ebullience sufficiently to stay out of further trouble.

On completion of his training he was sent to an infantry base depot in the wilds of Yorkshire. While waiting his turn to be posted out to France, he applied for, and was accepted on, a course to be trained as a signaller. That enabled him to while away another four weeks in England, during which time most of the others who had been in his draft were posted to active duty.

When he returned from the course he spent three months with the regiment's base company, in the signals section. In early August of '44, following a thorough combing out of depot personnel, Bird was sent with a batch of others to France. There he was attached to the signals section of the third battalion's first company.

THE PATROL

01.20 TO 02.30 HOURS

'They're under it. They're under the damned thing.'

Morris raised his head as the echoes died away. Ellis lifted his head from the cradle of his arms. His eyes were horribly bloodshot, and he looked drawn and haggard. Comprehension dawned slowly.

'Who are?'

Morris shook him. 'Bird and the other two. They were right beside it when the Opel flared up.'

Screwing up his eyes in an attempt to make them focus, Ellis looked towards the Krupp.

'What the fucking hell were they doing that close to it? They should have circled it. Oh God, why does everything have to go wrong?' He rubbed his face with dirty hands. 'Well, they're on their own now. There's nothing we can do.'

He couldn't cope any more; told himself he had done all he could. It wasn't his fault things had gone wrong.

'It's all your bloody fault.'

The sergeant couldn't open his mouth in answer for a moment, for fear that he would be sick, then he brought up some wind and that made him feel better. He waved his pistol at Morris.

'Well, tell me what we can do then, with these?'

He took hold of the end of the rifle barrel and waggled it. Morris snatched it out of his grasp.

'We could make a diversion of some sort: distract the crew of the Tiger while our blokes make a run for it.'

Bill Ellis would never have asked the question if he hadn't been confident there was no answer. Now he blustered, frantically seeking some way out.

'That's good, make a bloody diversion. If that Kraut gunner sees so much as one little finger he's going to smear us all over France. There's nothing we can do, I've told you. They'll have to take their chances, make a break for it if they can.'

There was pain again in his head, and his stomach was turning over.

Corporal Morris watched the flying sparks as the panzer tried to break out through the ramps, stopped, then tried again. Mines were fired at regular intervals, exploding each time over a

150

different quarter of the clearing. The fire burned lower in the Opel, the illumination became erratic.

'I must have been bloody mad to go along with this crazy idea. You've nearly done for them, what have you got planned for me?'

Ellis heard the sneer but couldn't think of any retort. He was finished. He buried his face in his hands and slumped forward to lie full length in the dirt, hiding from Morris, from the war, from himself.

Ignoring the sergeant, Morris watched the last flickers of flame, willing them to go out altogether, knowing that darkness was the only help the trapped men could hope for. So intent was he on that faint oasis of light that the firing of the Tiger's cannon took him by surprise. He couldn't see what the shot had achieved, then he heard something, a noise he had been conscious of for some time, but now it was louder, like gushing water. The fueller, that was it.

Red tracer bobbed across the clearing, splattered along the bowser's flank and found the stream of leaking petrol. The clearing became as light and bright as day. Without exploding, the eighty-eight-millimetre shell had passed through the thin walls of the fuel compartments, speeding the process two pieces of shrapnel had started earlier. The tracer ignited the pouring fuel and a mushroom of billowing flame flared into the sky. Fire flowed in every direction, carried on the water that filled the ruts lacing the area. Rippling blue fingers flew up the spurting jets from the punctured vessel; a dull explosion came from within, making the whole vehicle lift on its suspension, then the rest of the cargo blasted out the filler caps on top and sent five brilliant spikes of fire a hundred feet above the tree tops.

'What the fucking hell is that? Ellis, here, shake your bloody self, what is it?'

Morris grabbed the sergeant and helped him to shake himself. The sergeant gazed on the scene with vacant eyes.

'What?'

'Look down there, by the fueller. No, there, it's . . . it's gone.'

'What?'

'I don't know. I only caught a glimpse of it. God, it was horrible, like something out of a horror show.' He shuddered. 'It was moving all funny, like nothing I've ever seen.'

Unable to grasp what Morris was on about, Ellis took out the flask. There wasn't much left of the pint he had started with. He had to tip it right up to get some out. He looked at the transporter, now lit as if it were in a search-light beam.

'Are they still there, under it?'

Morris nodded. The flask top was snapped back.

'Well that's it, then. They'll never get out now. We might as well be making a move.' With an effort, Ellis got unsteadily to his feet. 'What are you doing?'

Carefully, Morris was putting the incendiary grenades into his pockets.

'I'm going to give those Krauts in the Tiger something to take their minds off what's going on underneath them, if I can. Maybe it'll give the others a chance to get away.'

'What about me? What do I do?'

Morris was gone before Ellis realized it. He half started to follow, caught his foot in a protruding root and stumbled. When he recovered his balance and looked about him, he was completely alone. The sergeant sat down again and took out his close companion. He held it up until the last dregs had trickled and dripped out. Then he shook it to make sure.

'I was going to do that. It's my patrol. I wanted to have a go at the Tiger, I did. I can't be well, I feel sick.'

He sat slumped, shoulders rounded, and stooped forward. The rain dripped like a bead curtain off the brim of his helmet.

'I've done what I can. They cocked it up, now they won't let me finish it. I could do it if I wasn't sick. Don't need the drink to do my job.'

It took him four attempts to get to his feet, and he only managed it then by leaning against a tree at each stage of the process. He tottered sideways a few steps, then started off between the trees, muttering incoherently.

Time was important now. Help might arrive for the German tank crew any minute. Morris had to hurry. He ran along the top of the embankment, crouching low as his only concession to concealment. He was glad to be doing something, glad to be away from Ellis. From behind a tree opposite the Krupp, he studied the distance he would have to cover before the roof of the cab took him from the field of vision of the Tiger's cupola. Doubtless that was where the tank's commander would be. Morris would have to gamble on his looking elsewhere for the nine seconds or so it would take him to get down to the clearing and cross the frighteningly open ground.

From where he stood it was four strides to the bank top. It

would be a jump or roll down the slope, then it was a case of piling on all the speed he could and dashing straight for the transporter. There was no time for finesse, fancy routes or careful approaches. He would have to stake everything on one bold move.

He looked at the risks. The tank's turret still faced the fueller, so they couldn't traverse that in time to fire at him, even if he was seen the moment he broke cover. The bow machine-gun was masked by the Krupp's cab; that left the pistol ports in the turret side and the bomb thrower. Those he would just have to chance.

Twice he prepared to launch himself, twice he baulked at it. The third time, with eyes closed, he left the tree and threw himself at the bank. At the fifth step there was no ground beneath his feet and he opened his eyes to find he was tumbling through the air. The flight was a short one, the landing heavy. His backside thumped down hard and he slid the last couple of feet. No time to admire his giant shadow cavorting behind him . . . it was up, and on, for the cover of the tractor unit. Some combination of oil and water made him slip and before he realized what was happening he was on his knees, staring up at the huge turret.

The growl of the panzer's engine grew. Like some colossal primevil predator, the monster was elevating its snarl to a roar. Morris felt his mind race, but his legs took no share in the sensation. He couldn't get them to move. They were frozen, refusing to carry out the command his brain screamed down at them. Like a man demented he hammered at them with his fists, ordering his limbs to function.

Stiffly, mechanically, agonizingly slowly, he rose; took one step, then another, but steps only. He was forcing himself to approach the Tiger. It felt as though the noise from the panzer was a wall of treacle into which he had to push to make the slowest progress.

Now he was so close he could have reached out and touched the Krupp's great honeycombed radiator. He experienced a feeling of exaltation as he realised he had made it without being seen. Safely out of the line of sight of the Tiger's vision ports he stood there, reached into his pocket and took out one of the small black objects that nestled among the damp fluff. Pieces of grit lodged under his nails as his fingers closed on the lump of machined metal. Unthinking, he ran his fingertips along the jutting firing arm to clear it of the lodged particles.

Corporal Morris walked round the front of the cab and down its side, stepping over two bodies that barred his path. As he

153

came level with the trailer he looked up at the slab side of the panzer. The teeming rain went unnoticed as he listened to the powerful engine reach its maximum revs, and then felt and heard and saw it unleash its power in another attack on the ramps.

A hand reached out from beneath the trailer and tugged at his trouser leg. He took a step that pulled the material free and walked the length of the rig, through the shower of sparks the skidding tracks created, until he stood beside the simple folded fabrication that was resisting the Tiger's strenuous efforts to flatten it. Waves of heat poured from the platform's metal as the friction raised it to a temperature where it boiled off the rain that fell on it. The steam it formed rose straight up, veiling the Tiger and making a ghostly background for the sheaths of sparks that fanned out from beneath the thrashing tracks.

Above the noise, Morris was dimly conscious of someone shouting. It was the final ingredient needed to forcibly remind him of a burning Sherman he had once seen. Except . . . except that then he had been powerless to act, and now – he looked down at the phosphorus grenade clenched in his hand – now he was far from powerless.

With great care, that had nothing to do with consideration for his own safety, he lodged the grenade firmly between two of the trailer's huge tyres. Carefully, so as not to dislodge it, he pulled out the safety pin. For a moment he just stood there, the hint of a smile on his face as he watched the firing arm spring open. Then he calmly turned and walked back down the side of the vehicle towards the cab.

He was half way there when the device he had set ignited. A harsh white glare bathed the rear of the transporter as the chemical burned rapidly, bright even in the full illumination from the blazing fueller. The Tiger ceased its struggle, as though it had paused to weigh up this new menace.

Fountains of spitting white phosphorus splashed about, even continuing to burn beneath the water of the puddles it landed in. The clearing adopted the appearance of a hellish volcanic region as flame and steam and smoke and stench combined.

'Have you gone off your fucking head?' Alex dragged himself out from beneath the trailer and raved at Morris. 'You knew we were bloody under there.'

He half heard, half saw the turret bomb projector go into action. Another dark cylinder tumbled into the air and blew apart in a twinkle of light, fast drowned by grey smoke from which whistled beads of shrapnel. The two men just made it under cover as the surrounding ground was once more ploughed and gouged to new contours.

Eric and Dicky had crawled under the trailer to lay beneath the back of the cab. Dicky saw Morris as he crawled to join them.

'That bloody trick is the sort of mad-arse stunt I'd expect from Barras. What are you trying to do, fry us?' Acrid fumes were drifting to them, making breathing difficult, causing their eyes to water and their skin to itch. 'Why don't you stick a couple of those bleeding things in the ruddy cab? Go on, do a thorough job. We'll be done both sides then.'

'I was going to.'

Before anyone could stop him, Morris had snaked out from beneath the Krupp, wrenched open the co-driver's door and thrown another of the incendiary grenades inside. White hell boiled from the cab windows as the interior was rapidly consumed.

Dragging Eric after them, Alex and Dicky staggered out from under the truck in time to see the grenade burn through the cab floor and fall to the ground in a shower of fire. Morris joined them and they stood for a moment and watched the Tiger disappear behind the thick smoke clouds given off as every tyre on the multi-wheeled vehicle began to burn.

'I forgot my crutch.'

Alex pulled Eric's arm over his shoulder. 'Forget it. I'm not going back under there for it. Give me a hand, someone. Let's get out of here.'

Dicky supported Eric on the other side and, herded along by Morris at the best speed they could manage, they crossed the clearing and reached the foot of the bank.

The Tiger remained hidden, but not unheard. Its V12 Maybach reached a note indicating revolutions far beyond those set by the manufacturer. The brakes were released, the drive engaged and the main armament fired, adding its recoil to the forces thrown against the near red-hot metal.

The savagely tested construction of the ramps could take no more. Heated to a cherry red by the blazing tyres beneath them, twisted and weakened by previous assaults, they first bent, then cracked, then collapsed before the combined onslaught. Thundering off the back of the trailer with a triumphant bellow, the Tiger's impact starred the thick table of concrete on which it landed.

Its dive to freedom had been witnessed by the men trying to scale the bank, towing their injured companion. Eric struggled to break the grip of the hands that held him. His efforts only served to tumble all of them to the bottom in a confused welter of limbs and weapons. Alex wouldn't give up. He adjusted his grip and started back up again.

'Stop your bloody wiggling, you're coming with us.'

Repeated knocks, redoubled pain, forced Eric to fight against the help he was getting. All he wanted was the agony of his shattered ankle to subside. After that he didn't care what happened. He wasn't capable of thinking that far ahead. For him there was only the terrible present.

As the three men fought the slippery bank, and Eric fought them, the Tiger checked its wild career and braked to a skidding halt among the trees at the far side of the junction, having ridden over and crushed flat the rear of the burned-out Opel in its unexpected, and temporarily uncontrolled charge.

The hatch topping the cupola swung open and a head cautiously rose into view, looked across at the group of men labouriously hauling themselves up the steep bank using clumps of weeds for handholds, and bobbed down out of sight. Tracks slipping at first in the oil-laced mud, the great machine swung ponderously round until it faced the frantically struggling men. The motor was revved briefly, the cannon barrel elevated a fraction, and then with slow deliberation the panzer moved forward.

Morris saw it, and felt his insides turning to cold water. His brain yammered in his head as he tried to steel himself against the impact of shot or shell. But it didn't come.

'Morris, for fuck's sake, help us. We can't get him up on our own.'

Alex's yell ripped the corporal from his terrified trance. Still he couldn't take his eyes from the Tiger as it came straight at them. It wasn't hurrying, wasn't firing, just coming on, looming larger; ever larger.

'It's playing with us, like we were bloody mice. It's playing with us.'

The flame-fed cloud from the transporter swirled in a mass before the advancing tank, absurdly leaving only the tip of its cannon barrel visible, floating in the air.

'I've got a hold, pass him up to me.'

Alex clung to the projecting shred of root, reaching down

156

and grasping for Eric's collar with his free hand.

With all the effort that could be wrung from tired bodies and aching muscles, Morris and Bird hefted Eric up as high as they could. The force they used wrung a scream from the injured man as his ankle was compressed. Alex strained to reach another inch. The root held and his clawing fingers fastened on the rough material. Using Eric as a human ladder the other two swarmed up him, then turned to add their strength to Alex's as he heaved Eric to the top.

'Move! Come on, bloody move, move, move.'

Dicky pushed and pulled at the others as the Tiger came out of the smoke.

The tank came out of the blinding screen to find its intended, and thought to be helpless victims escaping. Twice the bow machine-gun spat briefly, and two bursts of twenty-five rounds sped towards the group. The first fusillade swished over their heads, carving the trees, the second chopped into them, bringing down Morris and wounding Eric a second time. Alex and Dicky dropped with them, to seek the scant shelter of the weeds along the bank top. Each of them was waiting for the crack of the Tiger's eighty-eight that would mark the end for all of them, but it didn't come.

'There's no point in carting me along now, is there?' Eric tucked in his chin and squinted down at the neat black rimmed hole in his shoulder, exposed where Alex had ripped the clothing aside.

'Shut up, and get your ruddy chin out of the way, or I'll stick this dressing over your mouth. It's just a little hole. You haven't lost an arm. Right, you'll do. How's Morris?' This last was addressed to Dicky, who had crawled over to the corporal and was trying to examine his wound.

Morris lay still, very still; one arm rigidly down by his side, the other hugging his clothes tight to him, so that Dicky was unable to check the extent of his injuries. By turning his head as far as was possible, Morris could just see the Tiger. It was still coming on, it hadn't sped up. Presumably it was confident it had done its job. Now it was coming to have a look at the bodies.

The absence of pain surprised the corporal. He had seen the spurt of blood as the bullet passed through his side, felt the hammer impact as it knocked him to the ground, but there wasn't any pain. That couldn't be right.

'It can't be right.' The sound of his own voice startled him.

An idea occurred. 'I must be dying.' It was all very unreal, but there was still no pain, not even discomfort, but there ought to be something besides the growing area of warm stickiness inside his clothing. 'I must be dying, I must.'

'I can't tell you until you move your bloody arm and let me have a look at it.'

He brushed aside Bird's offer of help; and as he moved felt the bulge of hard objects in his pocket. He couldn't remember what they were.

The Tiger had stopped. The turret hatch opened and a head came into view. The cannon barrel elevated slightly.

Corporal Morris found he was watching the scene with a curious sense of detachment, wondering why the German gunner was taking so long to fire. He felt himself being lifted, dragged. His heels scraped twin furrows as hands gripped under his arms and began pulling him into the woods. It's all so silly, he thought. Why do they bother? I'm dying.

'What the bloody hell is that?' Dicky lurched suddenly sideways, shouting out as he was forced by some impact to drop Morris.

A demonic figure capered past to leap and dance on the edge of the bank.

Alex and Eric were knocked down as well. Alex was the first to recover from the shock.

'It's Barras. He's gone off his head. What's that he's holding?'

The Frenchman was naked, smeared with bands of red and brown, festooned with stinking, multi-coloured, blood-dripping garlands that looped about his arms and neck. He leapt down to the clearing in a single bound, landed on his feet and ran straight at the panzer. The tank's bow gunner fired a ragged burst, most of which went wildly astray. The hideous figure half stumbled, recovered and kept moving, screaming, yelling, waving its arms as it ran, gesturing with the lump of flesh it held in an upraised hand.

Dicky scrambled to his feet, grabbed Morris's collar and began to drag him as fast as he could deeper into the woods.

'For God's sake, let's get away from here. Hold on to me.'

Eric made no protest as Alex lifted him and, together, trying ineffectually to synchronize their movements, they staggered away from the clearing, and the Tiger.

ALEX PITT AND ERIC CHURCH

SICILIAN INCIDENT

The two Shermans were locked together, completely blocking the narrow track that clung to the side of the hill. One of them overhung the steep drop to the valley floor, stopped only from falling by the crushed rubble of the stone wall compacted beneath its belly. The other was part buried by the fall of shale its impact had brought down from the bank. It had burned, and from it came wafting the stench of roast flesh.

The breeze blowing up the hillside would occasionally fan a shower of sparks from the still-smouldering wreckage. A body hung from a turret, burnt black with white bone showing in places where the tissue had charred away.

'You took your bloody time getting here.'

A dark figure left the huddle of men crouched at the roadside and walked towards the party of sappers coming up the track. Sergeant Howard leading the group took exception to the man's tone.

'You're not the only ones who want mines lifted. You could always have done it yourselves while you were waiting.'

The corporal in charge of the section of infantry hurriedly altered his manner. He was a tall, thin youngster with an ill-fitting jacket and a helmet so generously dressed with foliage that it looked as if he had a bush on his head. His second stripe was very clean and new. He was nervous of his new-found extra responsibilities.

'Sorry, Sarge, keep your shirt on. It's our captain who wants the road cleared by first light, not me.'

Howard didn't press the point. 'All right, what's the problem?'

With the barrel of his sten gun the corporal indicated the two tanks.

'Those two tried to reach the top this afternoon.' He looked at his watch. 'Yesterday afternoon, rather. The lead tank goes over a mine and sheds a track, so the second one gets a hawser to it and starts to pull it back down. All of a sudden, bang, the second one hits a mine and brews up. The one it was pulling runs back down the hill and clouts it, and they both end up where you see them now. The fire's only just died down. The captain reckons there might be other little surprises buried in the road, so he sent for you lot.'

'Where is your CO?'

'He's gone back down to battalion HQ for a confab. Won't be back till first light.'

Howard scraped a heel in the road surface, gauging its composition and degree of compaction.

'Had any trouble from Jerry?'

'Not a sign, apart from the mines.'

'How far had the armour backed down when the second mine went off.' One of the other sappers joined in the conversation.

The walking shrubbery shrugged. 'Fifteen, twenty yards, maybe. They must have driven over it on the way up.'

A second sapper added his contribution. 'That's just the Krauts getting crafty. They set some of their mines so they won't go off until the fourth or fifth time the springs have been compressed. That way they can knock out vehicles further down a column, get the command wagons.'

The sappers began checking their mine detection equipment while their sergeant sought one last piece of information.

'Has Jerry got a position on this hill? I don't fancy getting sniped at from some artillery observation post they might have on the top.'

'Like I said, we haven't seen a sign of them. Mind you, we haven't patrolled right to the top, but we'd have heard them if they'd been there. I've got a bloke with a bren keeping watch just the other side of the road block. I reckon they've scarpered or they'd have done something by now. Will you want us to cover you?'

The sergeant looked up the hill. About fifty yards beyond the wrecks the track curved from sight round the side of the slope. He gave the question a moment's thought.

'No, we can manage. If we run into trouble we'll come straight down, and they can do the job with flail tanks when it gets light.'

'OK, we'll just hang on here then.' The corporal was relieved that his services were not to be called upon. 'Right then, I'll, er, leave you to it then.'

He took a pace back, hesitantly, then turned and rejoined the men of his section who were taking drinks from a straw-bound bottle in turn. None of them thought to offer any to the sappers who filed past.

Sergeant Howard, Alex Pitt, Eric Church and the other three men of the Royal Engineers who made up the mine-clearing party moved quietly up the track to where their further progress was barred by a wall of steel. On one side was the sheer bank of the hill, rising high above them. On the other, flanked by a low stone wall, a long, long drop to the valley floor. In places the descent was almost vertical. To get past the tanks the men had to climb through the gap in the wall where the Sherman had punched its way through, and then edge cautiously along the hillside beneath the stone-grazed, dust-covered belly of the tank.

The sentry the corporal had mentioned was sprawled amid the debris on the far side. Howard motioned him to silence.

'Heard anything?'

'Not a peep. They must have pulled out. If they were ever up there. Perhaps they didn't think it was worth holding.'

'And perhaps they did. Listen, lad, we're going out to check the road for mines. Now we'll only be in your sight for a while. After we've gone round that bend, if you hear anything, keep your finger off that trigger. Off. Do you hear me? If you see anyone running back this way it'll be us. We've only a bren and a couple of rifles so if we run into trouble we shan't be hanging about. We'll be back in your lap before you know what's happening, so I don't want you blasting away at the first thing you see; chances are it'll be me. Have you got that?'

The sentry nodded. In the sickly pale light of the waning moon he looked very young. He gripped his weapon tighter, as though to demonstrate his determination. His knuckles stood out, startlingly white. Howard climbed back on to the road and stepped out into its middle. 'Come on, you lot, we won't get the bloody thing swept by you hiding down there.'

Scudding puffs of cloud began hiding the moon, but as the sappers gathered by the sergeant they could clearly see the teeth and exposed cheek bones of the charred corpse above them and the scorch marks, where burning fuel had run out into the road, dark stains on the pale compacted stone surface. The gouged ground about a shallow crater's edge showed beneath one of the tanks. There was another some forty yards further up the track.

'So much for the corporal's "fifteen or twenty yards". I hope he's a bugger sight more accurate about there being no Huns about.'

Alex readjusted the straps of the battery and amplifier pack on his back. Eric was gazing up the steep bank, seemingly lost in dreams.

'Come on, Church. Wake yourself.'

'I am awake, Sarge. I was just reckoning how many machine-gun nests you could hide up there.'

'Oh, you cheerful bugger. If you've got any more like that, keep them to yourself.'

Alex passed the head of the detector over his steel toecap to check the set was working; then he settled the headphones more comfortably and was ready.

There were deep ruts at either side of the track, worn into the stone and smoothed over the years by countless wagons bearing their loads of Sicilian grapes and olives. Eric and Alex moved forward, swinging the detectors in a wide overlapping arc, so as to cover every inch of the track. Howard followed a couple of yards behind to make sure they maintained the same rhythmical motion and missed no part of the roadway. It was always the unsurveyed patch of road that turned out to hold the biggest mine.

Eric stopped to reseat his pack. They moved off again together, keeping to the same careful pattern. It was Eric who called a halt, and beckoned the sergeant forward.

'There's something here, Sarge. Pretty big and not too deep.'

Howard got down on his hands and knees and examined the spot indicated. He took from his belt a short piece of wood and with its sharpened end began scraping at the road surface. A minute's careful work revealed the dull grey circular outline of one of the big German Teller mines. Alex whistled softly.

'No bloody wonder that Sherman brewed up. With twelve pound of TNT going off under it, it's a wonder it weren't blown clean over the edge.'

The sergeant stood up, dusting his sleeves and hands. He beckoned one of the other men forward.

'Well, now we know what we're up against. Just lift it for the moment. We'll make them safe later. Put it on the wall for now.' He turned back to Alex and Eric. 'All right, you two, what are you waiting for, Christmas?'

Eric grinned across to his friend, then as one they took a step and began sweeping again.

By the time they reached the crater that marked the spot where the first Sherman had been disabled, there were three more of the 'T' mines embellishing the top of the grey stonework at irregular intervals behind them. They paused a while by a ragged hole to give their arms a rest. Eric sat amid the churned flint and stone flakes, looking back down the track to where the Shermans lay locked together.

'I didn't realize it was so steep.'

Alex glanced back at the series of pot-holes they had created.

'What with the Kraut mines blowing holes, and us digging them, by the time we're finished we'll have levelled the hill completely.'

Howard interrupted the conversation. 'We'll be out of that sentry's line of sight soon, so from now on we'll take it a bit slower. I think if there were any Jerries around we'd have heard from them before now, but we'll go easy, just in case.'

'Yeah, we would have made a sitting target every time we stopped to lift a mine.'

'We're not exactly invisible now.'

The sergeant ignored the two sappers. 'Right, on your feet. Another hundred yards and we'll call it a night. They can finish the last stretch with flails. I don't fancy working these slopes in daylight.'

They restarted, falling immediately into the same rhythm and formation as before. The two with detectors led, followed by the sergeant. Behind him, ready to provide covering fire if it were needed, their bren gunner, and then to his rear the last two members of the group, carrying their rifles slung, ready to come forward to lift any mines that were found.

It was by taking just such care that Howard, Church and Pitt had survived eleven months on that work. First in North Africa, then in Sicily. The composition of the rest of their company had changed constantly as others made mistakes in their hazardous job. Mistakes that were almost invariably fatal.

The track kept following the side of the hill, always climbing higher.

'Hold it.'

Howard pointed to the distant hill tops. A faint yellow tinge was becoming discernable on the highest, and on the base of the cloud bank above them. The dawn was coming.

'We'll do another thirty yards, up to the start of those groves. Then we'll put a marker up for the flail boys and go back.'

There were no more mines. When they reached the first tree the sergeant took out a red and yellow pennant from his pack and pinned it to the rough bark. He took a step back to admire his handiwork. A burst of rapid machine-gun fire crackled out from the depths of the grove and Howard fell. The shooting ended as abruptly as it had begun. So abruptly that Eric, who was nearest to him, heard the sergeant's head crack as if hit the wall.

'Down, down!'

Eric's yell was hardly needed. The others were already seeking whatever cover they could find.

Eric crawled to the wounded man, hesitated a moment, then turned him over. It was obvious there was nothing he could do. The NCO had been hit several times in the face. His jaw had been torn off and the side of his head smashed in. Dark blood jetted from a black hole between his eyes. A froth of pink bubbles came from where the bottom of the face had been; ugly gargling noises came from his chest as fluid filled his lungs and with a last rattling choke he died.

Alex relayed to the others further down the track the thumbs down sign that Eric made to him. The man with the bren started to move towards them.

A frantic shout of warning froze half-formed in Eric's throat as another and longer burst came from the grove. Too late the man saw the line of spurting dust marching down the middle of the track straight at him. He half rose to his feet, intending to dive to one side, but was too slow. With the impact, his body was hurled backwards to turn a complete somersault, then roll to a stop in the rut beneath the wall. He lay quite still, his blood mixing with the dust. The bren lay in the middle of the track, its barrel bent near in half, one side of the magazine ripped off to expose the rounds within.

'Where's it coming from?'

Alex risked drawing fire, and did too, but the enemy gunner couldn't depress his weapon sufficiently to bear. The sapper had to duck as the wall above his head was smashed and powdered by the weight of steel thrown at it. Fragments of stone stung his fingers and the back of his neck. One round carried away a buckle on his pack.

Eric Church took advantage of the unseen gunner's pre-occupation with his friend and raised his head. He withdrew it the moment he recognized the huge outline concealed beneath drapes of camouflage netting among the trees.

'It's coming from a bloody great Tiger dug in up to its eye-balls in the middle of the grove.'

'Let's get out of here. What the hell are we hanging about for?'

164

'Stay where you are. If we raise so much as an eyebrow he'll see us.'

The tank gunner illustrated the accuracy of Eric's statement by filling the air above them with zipping green tracer.

'I'll set up something that'll distract him. Get ready to run when I shout.'

Alex wriggled out of the straps holding his pack and shed the rest of the harness; then he wrapped the whole lot tight around the head of the detector and flung it with every ounce of strength he could muster as far as he could along the top of the wall.

'Now!'

The sustained burst of fire chased after the tumbling pack as the four men leapt up and raced down the hill. Then, almost at once, it flicked back to spatter the road behind them.

Alex passed the body of the bren gunner. He was laid awkwardly and was very clearly dead. Alex knew he would be. The man had seemed to soak up a whole line of tracer before coming to a stop.

The rough flint surface tripped each of them in turn, tearing the material from their elbows and knees, stripping their flesh when the material was gone. The tracer was with them, over, around and behind them until the side of the hill took them from the gunner's sight. Even then they didn't check their pace but kept running. The noise of their pounding boots echoed back to them until it was drowned by the bellow of the Tiger's exhaust as its engine was started.

By the crater they paused for a moment, lungs striving to pump in the cold dawn air. They turned to look back, then stared at each other, as if seeking reassurance that the sound they heard wasn't really the squeal of tank tracks and the crunch and clatter of falling stonework.

'The bastard's coming after us.'

'Don't be mad, the road's mined.'

'Not now it's not.'

'Well they don't know that.'

'Maybe the buggers didn't know it was mined in the first place.'

'Let's get out of here.'

With the sounds of pursuit growing behind them they tore the last forty yards to the road block, racing at breakneck speed over the same ground they had traversed so slowly such a short time before. The sentry saw them, started to level the bren, then raised it and watched their approach.

'What's happening? Where are the other two?'

'They're back there,' Eric gasped, gulping in deep painful breaths. 'We got the mines up, but there was a ruddy Tiger dug in on the top of the hill. Listen for yourself. The damned thing's coming.'

Thunderous in the still morning, the Tiger's engine note roared up and down the scale as its driver juggled to keep the unwieldy beast on course. Metal grated on flint and the crash of falling stone was almost continuous. The corporal came running up.

'What the hell's going on? You go up there to do a simple job and come hurling back down with half a panzer division behind you. Where's your sergeant?'

'Dead, and another of our blokes with him. You'd better get on the radio and call up some help.'

He stared at Alex. 'It's out of action. We're waiting for a replacement.'

'Then send a bloody runner, but for fuck's sake do something.'

Eric kept glancing up the hill, in the direction the Tiger must come.

Having done that the NCO seemed lost. He was out of his depth. He tried to find cause for reassurance, slapped the side of one of the Shermans.

'It'll not get past these.'

Alex snorted. 'You've not seen a Tiger in action, have you? They weigh better than fifty ton. I've seen one ride up over a bren carrier and crush it like it was made of balsa wood. These hulks won't hold it for thirty seconds.'

'We've got a Piat.'

'Right, now find someone who's willing to stand in the middle of the track and fire the bloody thing.'

Even as he said it, Alex knew that someone was going to have to. He could hear the Tiger as it slewed round the bend towards them.

The runner the corporal had sent off for help was still in sight half a mile away. Then a turn in the track took him from sight.

'We'll have to fall back.'

The corporal tried rounding his men up. Without decisive leadership they were milling about, some getting their packs on, others talking nervously or looking up the track.

'Where the hell to?'

The NCO gave a vague wave towards the valley. 'Down there, somewhere.'

A shower of shale torn from the side of the hill where it took the road from view heralded the arrival of the giant panzer. The white ringed snout of its long cannon came first, then the slab front of its massive hull. It completed its ungainly turn in a clumsy series of lurches. The cannon dipped and belched flame.

The armour-piercing round reached the road block before the men behind it heard the sound of its being fired. The shot carved its way in through the side of the burned-out Sherman, further wrecking its interior and pushing the tank several feet sideways down the track.

The British soldiers crouched low behind cover that suddenly appeared desperately inadequate to the task of keeping back the Tiger. Again the panzer fired, the recoil making the big vehicle buck back on its suspension. As it rocked it slid forward a yard on the steep gradient. At the same time its bow machine-gun spat four fast bursts that skimmed the ground to clatter and flatten themselves against the soot-stained flank of the Sherman. This time the round from the main gun was high explosive. It struck just short of the Sherman on the edge, ripping out its suspension, and leaving thirty-three tons of fighting machine teetering precariously. Lumps of shell casing scythed under it to cut down one of the corporal's men.

For another of them it was the last straw. He turned and ran off down the hill, another was about to follow when tracer bobbed over the road block and cut the first man down. He flung his arms in the air and screamed, then the flashing balls of fire flicked back and he tumbled from sight over the wall. The body, near severed by the close-spaced bullets, rolled and bounced down the slope, raising clouds of dust and speckling the hillside with blood.

His would-be companion in flight hurriedly changed his mind and sought shelter behind the burnt-out Sherman. Eric made the most of the opportunity the gruesome demonstration presented.

'You saw what happened to him,' he shouted. 'Do you still want to fall back?' With Alex he tried to rally the others. 'Look, we've got to stop or slow that thing, or we've all had it.'

'We've got a Piat.'

One of the corporal's men stepped forward and put one of the ugly tank-killing weapons on the ground; and with it a case of three rounds.

The Tiger was not prepared to wait for something to be done to it. It did something first. It put a round of high explosive into the hill above the Shermans. An avalanche of stone and dust flooded down, seeded with jagged chunks of shell casing. When it cleared there were three more men down, writhing with broken limbs and massive open wounds.

Eric picked up the Piat, threw all his weight against it to cock the firing spring, then grabbed a round from the case broken open at his feet and slotted it into the firing trough over the thick steel spigot. He hefted the clumsy weapon to his shoulder and took aim at the Tiger over the engine cover of the gutted Sherman.

Again the panzer let loose with its main armament. The explosion against the side of the tank straddling the ruined wall pushed it a fraction further over the drop. The back of the tank lifted into the air as the front swung down more and more. Rock was pummelled to powder beneath it as it see-sawed back and forth, reluctant to take the final plunge. The movement slowed and stopped and the tank remained on the road. Some packs secured to its hull on the far side began to burn.

The effect of the shot was almost as dramatic on the Tiger. It slid forward another ten feet. Sparks and dust flew high as its driver fought to keep the giant straight and check its progress.

At the moment the panzer came to rest, Eric fired. His head jerked back with the recoil as the bomb was sent on its way. It took an age to float the short distance, and finally struck home dead centre on the hull nose plate.

'You got him, you got him!'

The corporal jumped up and down as the panzer was hidden by an expanding orange fireball laced with white and blue sparks, instantly replaced by boiling black smoke.

The NCO's joy was short lived. The cloud drifted clear to reveal the Tiger still intact. There was a large, deep-pitted scorch mark on its front, and spare track links secured to the armour were fused and twisted into fantastic shapes, but the hollow-charge warhead had failed to kill the behemoth.

As though taking exception to such impertinance, the snout of the cannon vomited three shots in rapid succession. All three plunged in through the flanks of the cripples that blocked its path. Sappers and infantrymen alike had to jump for their lives as the hulks were picked up by the impacts and thrown at them. Several of the injured were caught by the moving walls of steel

168

and reduced to bloody bundles as the derelicts ground back.

Sustained bursts of machine-gun fire pinned the men down as they clawed at the bare ground for cover. One of the shells exploding inside a Sherman blasted out its belly armour, scattering its razor fragments over the men sheltering nearby, flaying their skin from their faces and bodies, to leave them writhing in lakes of their own gore.

The sight of the men who were his new responsibility being torn apart about him, galvanized the corporal into action. He ran to where Eric crouched as he fitted another round into the Piat and grabbed the weapon from the astounded sapper.

'I'll get the bugger. Give it here.'

Even as he snatched the loaded bomb thrower, another shell struck the turret of the Sherman embedded in the bank. The gruesome corpse decorating the top was tumbled into the dust from where it grinned up at the lightening sky.

For the Tiger, though, it was one shot too many. As it settled back from the recoil it began to slide again, and this time it couldn't be checked. Against the steep gradient all efforts to halt the slipping monster were useless. With gathering speed, bringing down cascades of shale from the bank and sometimes demolishing long sections of the wall, it hurtled towards the road block. Showers of sparks were struck from the flint road surface as the tank's tracks flailed vainly in reverse.

The moving wall of armour caught one of the mines atop the wall, flicking it high into the air to spin from sight over the edge. Another was caught and a corner of it crushed by the pounding steel, but it failed to go off, though some of the spilled contents were ignited by the sparks and burned fiercely on the track behind the racing Tiger.

For the men in the shelter of the road block there were four choices. They could go over the side, up the bank, back down the road or, an option only and involuntarily adopted by the dead and dying, stay where they were. Most chose to run for it. A couple vaulted the wall and slid down the loose scree of the slope twenty feet before braking themselves to a halt at the expense of their fingernails and the skin of their palms. There they flattened themselves against the hillside beneath the overhanging Sherman. Those who had taken to their heels discarded their equipment as they ran, sacrificing everything to speed.

Eric was about to start after them when Alex grabbed his arm. 'They'll never make it.' He pointed to the embankment.

They had only seconds to act. 'Up there. Up there!'

They flung themselves at the hill, scrabbling for hand holds that disintegrated as they touched them. It was like climbing a mountain of ball-bearings.

'We'll never make it.' Eric's words were drowned by the grinding, thundering scream of the approaching colossus.

The Tiger was only yards from the Shermans when Eric caught a hold of a shred of dried root sticking out of the parched bank and dragged himself up to where the handholds were more plentiful and stable.

'Grab a hold.'

Eric extended his hand to Alex who, at the very moment the panzer struck the road block, leapt to catch the outstretched fingers. He made it. Muscles working at the limit of their endurance as Eric locked an iron grip on his precarious hold.

The corporal still stood with the loaded bomb thrower, seemingly rooted to the spot. He held the clumsy weapon stiff against his shoulder, his eyes on the Tiger now looming above the Shermans it dwarfed.

Alex clung tight to his friend's hand while flailing about in an attempt to secure some hold of his own, to help lift him out of the Tiger's path. As he twisted back and forth he found himself right over the panzer and his ears were nearly burst by the several loud noises that blended in one when the collision occurred.

At thirty miles an hour the Tiger piled into the Shermans, and as it did the corporal fired the Piat. The bang of the bomb's discharge came at the same instant as the blast of its impact and detonation on the turret front of the panzer. The hulls of the British tanks rang as they collapsed with the force of the impact.

Unchecked, the giant tank ploughed on, lifting the precariously balanced Sherman into the air. It fell back and hung on the edge for a split second and then, as the runaway caught it a second time, it toppled forward and bounced end over end down the hill. On the way it churned to pulp the two men who had sought the supposed safety of the slope below it. The turret separated from the hull before it was a third of the way to the valley floor, the hull finishing its journey amid a ball of flame.

The Piat bomb had struck the panzer on the gun mantlet, its thickest frontal armour. Lumps of steel vapourized, leaving deep gouges in the rough finish of the cast steel. Molten metal flew upwards, trailing blue flame. The Tiger brushed aside the

170

burnt-out Sherman, crushing in its hull and suspension.

There was no chance for the corporal to get away. The wreck was tipped over and he disappeared from sight beneath it, to be reduced to a paste as a drive wheel caught in the mangled tracks welded to the panzer's front, causing it to be dragged along on its side.

The added friction of the upturned hulk brought the Tiger to a halt fifty yards further down the road. It came to rest in a great cloud of dust as a section of the wall was demolished. The dust slowly settled to reveal the British tank held above the long drop only by the unintentionally enmeshed metalwork. Except where it was splashed with the corporal's blood, the Sherman's side had been scraped down to bare shining metal.

Casually, almost as an afterthought, the Tiger's turret traversed and from its coaxial machine-gun it sent a series of long bursts after the fleeing infantry. Even as they neared the bend that would take them to safety, the bullets caught them and, in turn, they were struck and knocked to the ground. Some lay twitching for a while but all eventually lay still. The accurate shooting was clear evidence that the corporal's hit had failed to penetrate and cause lethal damage.

Alex let go of Eric's hand and dropped back down, and stayed down, nursing his rapidly swelling ankle that made standing impossible. Eric landed beside him.

'Come on, let's get the hell out of here, before they have a look round to see if they missed anybody. What's up with your foot?'

'The bugger clouted me as it went past. I think it must be broken, it hurts enough.'

The surface of the road about the two sappers was messy with puddles of oil, bits of human tissue, scraps of broken equipment and spilt fuel.

'Come on, let's give it a try. We've got to get out of here.' Eric assisted Alex to his feet.

From the direction of the panzer came the sound of hatches being thrown open. The pair hastily dropped down again, seeking the cover of the shadow of the bank and the confusing litter on the road.

Eric clamped his hand on to his friend's shoulder, forcing him to be still when he tried to reach down to remove his boot to relieve the throbbing pain.

'Leave it. Don't move. Our only hope is to play dead.'

Alex was under no delusions about the chances of his making a quick get-away. 'You'll have to leave me, I'll slow you up too much. Look out for yourself.'

'Shut up trying to be a bloody hero. We're both getting out of here. Just lie still.'

Below them, two black-clad panzer crewmen had dismounted from the tank and were examining the slope through binoculars. Another German pushed an MG34 machine-gun out through the loader's hatch and began to fasten it to an anti-aircraft mount on the turret roof forward of the cupola. The men on the ground, satisfied that they were faced by no immediate enemy interference, went to the front of the Tiger and set about freeing their mount from the hulk that hung from their bow. Alex and Eric, hugging the ground, had escaped notice.

While the Germans were preoccupied at their tasks, Eric snaked back up the road, retrieved a bulky dull grey object and slithered down to rejoin Alex.

'What the hell are you going to do with that?' Alex eyed the 'T' mine.

'They'll be backing that big wagon of theirs up the hill as soon as its free. If I get half a chance I'll stick this under their tracks. That'll make a lovely great bang, then we can stroll back down in our own time.'

'Christ. You're a sweet little optimist aren't you. What do you reckon the Krauts are going to be doing while you're arranging all this? Do you reckon you can get them to hide their eyes while you arrange their cremation?'

'Well you come up with something better.'

'Clear off without me.'

Eric pretended not to hear. They lay still and quiet, watching the border of shadow grow narrower as the sun climbed higher. When that line of light reached them and the shadow disappeared, so too would much of their concealment.

Alex's eyes swam back into focus after a rash move had provoked a particularly severe stab of pain. The sensation washed through his body, threatening to take his consciousness from him.

'What are they up to now?'

'I don't know. They were doing something round the front. Now all of a sudden they've run to the back of it. Perhaps they've . . .'

The sentence didn't need to be completed. From the front of the Tiger came a muted thump and a puff of smoke, followed by the creak and squeal of rending metal. The tank crew were ridding themselves of an encumbrance by the fastest method possible. A small demolition charge had been used to cut the Sherman free. The wreck promptly vanished from sight. For a while there came the sounds of something large and heavy sliding over loose rock. Then, after a final loud crash, nothing.

Casually the Germans strolled back to check the work they had done. While one mounted to the turret, another walked back up the hill. The tank's commander stood half out of the turret and put on his headphones and throat microphone. He spoke briefly and the engine roared into life. The tank lurched through a quarter turn that set it in the middle of the road, then began cautiously to move backwards. The tankman on the ground walked backwards before it, by hand signals indicating minor course corrections to the commander, who in turn passed them on to the driver.

At a snail's pace the Tiger edged back up the path it had slid down out of control not long before. The crewman directing the operation kept glancing over his shoulder up the hill, sometimes stumbling as he did, when his ankle turned on a stone.

Alex fought to hold his rigid pose, drawing only the shallowest of breaths while his pumping heart demanded that he gulp air in. He hissed at Eric beside him.

'The bastard's going right over us. Why don't you run now? I'll never make it.'

'We're getting out together. When I give the word, just hang on tight. We'll have only the one chance.'

The engine noise grew louder as the panzer climbed ever closer. Now the man on foot was level with the two sappers. He didn't spare them a glance, so intent was he on the tricky operation he was directing. His whole attention was on the growling monster that followed him.

The sappers felt the ground vibrate in time to the engine; could smell the unburnt petrol in its exhaust. Brushing both sides of the narrow road at once, the oncoming vehicle was pulling down stones from the dry wall and cutting long gouges in the loose material of the bank. The massive broad rear of the tank was barely two yards from them when Eric at last made his move.

'Now. Hold on tight.'

Alex threw his arm over his friend's shoulder and felt himself hoisted to his feet. The tankman on the road had been looking up the hill and had not seen the two bodies between him and the tank spring suddenly to life, until a shout from the commander shocked him into urgent action. He began to unsling his machine-pistol as the half running, half hobbling pair reached the wall. Eric paused only an instant to thrust the mine under the advancing tracks, then pushed Alex over the top and tumbled from sight after him.

The tank commander's screamed order to his driver came a fraction late. With its last inch of movement the Tiger's right-hand track crushed down the mine's pressure cap.

The explosion pushed the wall down after the two fleeing sappers. Flying track links shredded the machine-gunner even as he squeezed the trigger. Only three wild shots were fired by the automatic action before the weapon was mangled by the impact of a chunk of armour plate.

For the Tiger it was a death blow. The engine was torn from its mounts, fuel lines were fractured and internal bulkheads cracked open. Fire gushed from the gaping hole in the tank's belly and through the rents into the fighting compartments. The commander, still standing out of his turret at the moment of detonation, held his ruined face in his hands; flames licked up the front of his overalls. Ammunition and fuel tanks began to ignite. The pressure of the red-hot gasses generated burst open every port and hatch, and gouted a jet of flame out through the bow machine-gun ball-mounting. Black smoke billowing about it, the stricken machine began to run away for a second time. There was no one and nothing to stop it.

It gathered speed, quickly running off the broken track. The road wheels that side started to dig in, acting as an ill-balanced brake and dragging the Tiger closer towards the edge. One of the interleaved steel discs broke up, pieces flying back to jam others. Yet another section of the wall was destroyed as the panzer slammed into it. Broken stone and clouds of dust joined the black smoke above the tank. The Tiger swept on and out into space before plunging back to earth fifty feet down the hillside, landing on its belly with a force that broke the remaining track and catapulted the engine out through the access doors to fly over the turret and lose itself among the patches of rock littering the slope.

Belching flame, towing plumes of dust and smoke, the Tiger tobogganed on its belly to the valley floor. Half way there the turret was blasted off by an internal explosion that also sent a blazing corpse spinning high in the air, tumbling limply like a rag doll.

The bare flame-covered hull came to rest in a stream, its bulk forming a dam to the clear silver water. As the whispering tide lapped upwards it cooled the red-hot metal and steam rose with the smoke, shrouding the remains and hiding them from view.

'There goes the turret.'

From their vantage point Eric and Alex watched the Tiger's end, saw the huge fountain of mud and water its eventual impact threw up.

It took Eric twenty minutes to drag Alex the thirty feet back to the road. When they made it they sat at the gap in the wall, watching the column of smoke and steam that rose from the pall about the tank. As it drove higher into the warming air the sun reached down between the hills and tipped it with pink.

'Looks like that runner made it.'

Alex pointed down the track to where an open-topped M10 tank-destroyer, followed by two half-tracks packed with infantry, were coming into sight round the bend.

'They're a bit bloody late, but at least we shan't be walking back. I didn't fancy carting you on my back all that way.'

Eric lit a cigarette, offered one to Alex. He took it.

'Thanks mate.' He looked down to the stream. 'That's one I owe you.'

'Forget it. I'm usually scrounging them off you.'

'I didn't mean the fag.'

Alex reached out and picked up a lump of metal. On one side it was deeply scratched. He turned it over thoughtfully in his hand. It was a fragment of track plate, broken from the Tiger by the mine Eric had placed. For a moment he was about to toss it carelessly aside, then he hesitated. He held it up to show his friend.

'That's the one I owe you.' He put the fragment into his pocket.

The approaching vehicles had slowed to a crawl. Their crew and infantry passengers hung over the sides to take a look at the tank debris cluttering the hillside, and at the grey pillar that marked the Tiger's last resting place.

Five days after Alex Pitt rejoined his battalion, fully fit for duty, the regiment embarked for England, where it became part of a Royal Engineers Assault Brigade. They immediately commenced training at Orford for the Allied invasion of Europe.

On D-Day at H+3 as they made their run into the beach at the west end of Le Hamel, their landing craft was hit by direct fire from an emplaced '88' that had been missed by the air bombardment. Out of control, the craft was swept by the incoming tide on to the first line of 'Element C' obstacles where it foundered. Both the Churchill AVRES it carried were lost.

Eric and Alex were among the nine men picked up fifteen minutes later by a rescue launch. They eventually got ashore at 09.00 on D+2, when they rejoined their unit, working on beach clearance for the next ten days.

Other work followed, mainly demolition of German fortifications, and when the breakout from the beach-head came they followed the British Second Army on its push into northern France.

On a cold wet day in the first week of September 1944, they were ordered to draw satchels and mines and, for the fourth time in six days, joined a patrol going out on a road watch behind the German lines, somewhere south-west of Lille.

THE PATROL

02.30 TO 03.19 HOURS

Paul Barras had made a superb job of sharpening the knife. When he rolled the body of the German over and started to slice into the rubbery flesh of the fat man's stomach, the tissue had folded aside easily. He found the blood a nuisance at first but the rain had kept washing it away so he could see what he was doing, and after a while the red flow had stopped. When he stripped, however, and began decorating himself with the intestines and their contents, he regretted not having caught and saved some of the lovely thick red stuff. There was hardly enough left in the body cavities to do a satisfactory job. The madman had taken loving care when he had come to cut out the fat man's groin. He had enjoyed that, savouring the rising sensations in his body as the knife did its work.

'Too much noise, too much noise,' Barras complained to himself at the crack and rattle of gunfire and bomb explosion as the conflict continued on the other side of the fueller. It was a distraction. He was a busy man, had so much to do. He looked down at his own body and grinned. 'I've got one now that will stand up. I'll make mine stand up, up, up, up.' He whispered the word until it became the very essence of his existence.

The work took a long time, but he had to do it properly. At last he stood to take in the full effect, stood looking at the butchered form strewn about him.

Something rocked the fueller beside him. A wave of wind pushed him back a pace and where he had been there was a waterfall; but it didn't smell like water. He stretched out a hand towards it and suddenly flame was all about him. The remains of the pillaged corpse, directly beneath the fiery cascade, jumped back to life as intense heat gripped tissue and muscles, withering and constricting them.

'Perfect. Perfect!'

Barras shouted and clapped his hands, squashing and driving spurts of blood from the chunk of flesh he held. Rivers of flame ran out among the trees. He skipped back and forth among them, then whirled wildly round and dashed into the woods. Behind him the fueller jumped as, with a loud rumble, five pillars of light drove up at the clouds.

Barras laughed and screamed and ran, and kept running, running, running. He howled at the top of his voice. 'I can do anything.' The words were swallowed and lost among the close-set trunks of the trees who were his only audience. Waving the bloody tissue he gibbered and scampered, tearing his feet and his flesh on thorns and rough bark he neither saw nor felt. On he whirled, bellowing and chanting his wild, insane words that no one could hear.

His world was suddenly full of people at funny angles, pulling strange faces; leaning, falling people. He didn't want people, he wanted a machine, a big dark machine with guns and tracks and bombs and bullets and shells. That was what Paul Barras wanted. He saw what he wanted and the dams of his mind burst with the flood of hate that poured out. With a fury and intensity beyond the wrath of hell he knew hatred for the Tiger.

The demoniacal dance took him through the group of men at the edge of the bank. He launched himself without pause towards the focus of his demented emotions. He knew in his mind that he was bad, but he knew the great machine was worse. It took things from you. The Tiger spat little bits of fire at him and he felt something brush past, adding fresh bright living colour to those he had daubed. Balls of flame accelerated by on either side, then one of them hit him. More of the red stuff squirted down one of his legs. It made him stagger, but he kept going.

Another jump and he was on the tank. One bloody hand gripped the cannon barrel. There was pain when he swung his legs up, but it didn't matter. He was where he wanted to be. Straddling the gun he pounced along it towards the turret, while blood from his side and filth dripping from the gruesome necklace spattered down to decorate the hull top. His thighs bumped into the gun mantlet and he reached forward across the broad top of the turret and rammed the chunk of flesh he still held into the aperture of the mine discharger.

As he leant forward, the ranging machine-gun blasted at him and a degree of reality and reason momentarily returned when the bullets, at the moment of leaving the barrel, chewed off one of his feet.

Even as it began its tumble to the ground, the main gun fired. The whiplash recoil scraped skin from between his legs, reopening the thick scar tissue of an old wound, and sent him sprawling on to the turret top. With fist and nails the French-man clawed and battered at the armour, spitting at the vision slits, smearing blood over the periscope lens.

A hatch opened a fraction and the barrel of a Luger showed. Barras saw it, shoved his fingers into the hairline crack. He got a grip on some projection on the hatch's underside and pulled it hard upwards. A single shot grazed past his ear, but he got his other hand to the hold and the hatch flew open, dragging up with it the tank commander, his face stark white with the effort of trying to reclose it. The tankman had dropped his pistol, had both hands clenched about the locking lever as he strove to overcome the maniac force set against him. Barras lunged at the SS Oberleutnant, striving to reach his throat.

The other roof hatch opened. A smoke- and grease-stained face appeared and a machine-pistol was pushed out on to the turret top ahead of it. As the Frenchman's hands fastened on the front of the officer's overalls to haul him within reach, yellow flame tipped the snub snout of the awkwardly held weapon. Blood showered both tankmen as bits of face and blobs of brain burst from Barras under the close-range impact of the heavy bullets.

His body jerked upwards, hands clasped together, then he pitched over the back of the turret on to the engine deck, coming to rest against the armoured exhaust shields.

The dull red glow of the Tiger's internal illumination hid the worst details of the blood and brains that spotted the face and overalls of the loader and commander.

'What sort of men are we fighting?' Oberleutnant Luchs was shocked. Not in eighteen months of fighting on the Russian front had he seen anything to match the demon they had just encountered. 'Where are the rest of them?'

Werner, their dour gunner, answered. Werner saw everything. 'They went into the woods, but they won't get far. Two at least were hit.'

Luchs shuddered, to shake away the last images of the apparition that had materialized and tried to kill him, tried to tear his throat out. The experience of the madman's attack, coming so soon after the nerve-shredding time spent trapped on the transporter, had shaken him far more than he would have admitted to anyone; more than he realized himself. A feeling of tightness in his chest and a nervous flutter in his right eyelid were the first outward signs of a man who had been under pressure for too long. He sought round for something he could get to grips with, something tangible he could do.

'Are we going after them, Herr Oberleutnant.'

Luchs recognized the voice of Lutz, their driver. He didn't answer. Instead he barked an order to Werner. 'Gunner, put four rounds of high explosive into the bank. I want it flattened.'

As the loader sweated at the job of selecting and thrusting each successive round into the breech, Luchs listened to the irregular note of the extractor fan sucking the yellow cordite mist from the compartment. He reminded himself to have a new one fitted as soon as possible. That was if they could get hold of a replacement. The spares problem was getting worse every day. They were still waiting, after a week, for urgently needed parts to repair their radio.

The centre of the embankment broke up beneath the hammer blows and the smoke drifted clear to reveal a rough ramp into the woods.

'Take us up, driver. And remember, Lutz, we've only got the transportation tracks on, so watch for soft spots. Don't bury us.'

There was no murmur of dissent from the crew, not a whisper to convey the misgivings they must have had at the prospect of taking so unwieldy a machine into such perfect ambush country without an infantry escort. The oberleutnant's men knew better than to voice their opinions. With Luchs there were no moments of light relief, no second chance if you crossed him or made a mistake. When the oberleutnant wasn't being a soldier, he wasn't around. His crew had only ever seen him 'on duty'.

The driver eased the fifty-six tons of tank forward. It paused at the foot of the bank, as if summing up the task that confronted it, then gradually it rolled on to the scattered earth, crushing and compacting it as though it would drive straight in and bury itself. Then the tracks found resistance and the Tiger began to climb, canting a little to the left on the irregular slope. It climbed slowly at first. Then, with growing confidence when the tracks sank no further, it increased speed.

As it breasted the top, the wide expanse of the belly armour was exposed for a moment before the point of balance was reached and it swung down on to an even keel, flattening two pines without effort. The oberleutnant settled his throat microphone more comfortably.

'Good, Lutz. Now take us in. We're going hunting.'

Against the background of the rising engine note, the driver's voice came over the headphones.

'We are loosing the light. Shall I put the headlamps on?'

Luchs slid open the forward armoured shutter on the turret cupola and looked for himself. The glare from the fires in the clearing filtered away into the woods, gradually weakening as the shadows of successive trees built up.

'Lutz, we have driven through the dust of a rolling barrage, the smoke and flame of burning towns and the fogs of a Russian thaw. There is enough light here for us to see what we want.'

Timber fell like matchwood before the lumbering bulk of the Tiger as it crushed its own road through the forest. The faceless body of Paul Barras still littered the engine deck, blistering where it lay against the exhausts.

Luchs sat in his chair, stroking the ginger kitten he had recently adopted. The animal, with its built-in ability to adapt to any environment, was prefectly at home in the cramped confines of the tank's turret and hull.

'Bow Gunner, I think the men we are looking for will be heading east. That is the way we are heading. So, if you will, a short burst to the extreme of your traverse, to the left and right, every thirty seconds or so. That should keep them somewhere in front of us.'

Luchs resumed stroking the kitten, his hand firmly upon it as it tensed to the crackle of their bow machine-gun firing. It felt the pressure of the grip on it and relaxed, purring in time to the engine beat.

The giant panzer was fractionally slowed by the stubborn resistance of a stout fir, but the moving wall of steel was irresistible. The Tiger rose in the air as it rode over the uprooted stump, then moved on, crushing lesser conifers without noticing them.

'A little slower, Lutz. We don't want to miss them.' Luchs put the cat in the cardboard box below the signal flare locker and stood to look out. 'Werner, just in case, one round of HE into the large oak to our right.'

The loader hauled the yellow-nosed round from its rack and thrust it into the still warm, shining metal of the breech.

'Ready.'

Werner was already operating the hydraulic turret traverse to bring the main gun to bear. Through habit he stabbed his foot down on the pedal that fired the coaxial MG34. It barked, and the single round of tracer sped the forty yards to bury itself in the base of the tree Luchs had indicated. At the moment of impact Werner pulled the trigger that sent an electrical impulse to the shell in the '88'.

A ball of red flame blossomed on the oak. A thick bough close above the point of impact split away, falling in a shower of sparks while flame played among the tattered bark of the gouged trunk.

'Well, they're not there.'

The oberleutnant was enjoying himself. He would have been very disappointed to have come up on his quarry so soon. The shot wasn't wasted though. Luchs knew that, burdened and slowed by wounded companions, the little group could not be far ahead now. The explosion behind them would throw doubt into their minds, possibly make them panic, make a mistake. Luchs was looking forward to exacting some revenge for the fright he had suffered, and to punishing the men who had thought they could take on him and his crew and their Tiger.

Eric Church felt his world was coming to an end. He half wished it would, and soon. He had to fight continually against the waves of nausea that swept through him. Every moment sent pain shooting up his leg from his smashed ankle, to add to that in his shoulder.

Alex was alternately dragging and half carrying him, and was deaf to his pleas to let go. The constant shifting of position and their jarring, erratic progress over the difficult ground combined to torture the injured man until he was driven to make a violent effort to break free. He had to rest, to simply lie still. Eric succeeded in wriggling from his friend's grasp, only to be immediately hoisted up again.

'Stop your bloody wriggling. You're heavy enough as it is.'

Alex Pitt tightened his hold, forcing himself to ignore his comrade's obvious suffering, in an attempt to put as much distance as possible, as swiftly as possible, between themselves and any pursuit.

'Put me down. For God's sake, put me down.'

Eric broke free again. He knocked aside the arms that came down to lift him. He clenched his teeth against the torment in his shoulder the sudden movement brought; fought the wave of giddy darkness that threatened to engulf his mind.

'How much further do you think you can get with me like this? The whole area will be stiff with foot patrols soon. Leave me and clear out now, while there's chance. Go on, bugger off. I'll be better off in a Jerry hospital anyway.'

'I've told you, we're not going to be bloody bagged, or anything else. We'll put in a bit more distance, then we'll find

182

somewhere to hide up and wait for the ruckus to die down. Ask Dicky. Isn't that right, Dicky?'

Private Bird caught up to them. He reeled to a halt, ashen white with exhaustion, through the effort of supporting and towing Morris. He lowered the corporal to the pine-needle-scattered earth and collapsed down beside him, unable to answer until he had turned his face to the sky and gulped in several mouthfulls of the chill damp air.

'I'll go along with anything, so long as it includes a stop for a rest. I'm knackered.'

Morris watched the exchange from where he lay. He still didn't hurt and he couldn't understand why. He just felt very tired, and weak. Now he lay stretched full length on the wet soil, exploring the curious detachment with which he found he could observe the dangers and discomforts of their situation. It was very strange, being able to float in a trance-like state, and yet be able to hear and see with startling clarity all that went on.

The others tensed and listened as the crack, screech and thunderous detonation of the Tiger's assault on the bank came to them. The rise and fall of its engine note afterwards told its own story.

'Time to be moving again.'

Alex pretended not to hear Eric's faint protests as he took his wrists and prepared to lift him. His cold, cramped muscles ached and had to be forced to respond to his brain's instructions.

Corporal Morris found the strength to push away Bird's half-hearted attempts to get a grip on him.

'Don't waste your bloody time. Give Pitt a hand with his mate. He's in better shape than me. You'll have enough problems trying to get back with one wounded bloke, let alone two. Anyway, I'll never make it.'

The crash and splinter of falling trees could be heard. Pearl beads of tracer dashed away to right and left, glimpsed briefly between the trunks. Bars of orange light surrounded them for a second as the glare of an explosion percolated through the woods. Lengths of bough and strips of bark flew high, towing pennants of flame and steam.

Morris put a restraining hand on Dicky's arm. 'There's a letter I want to go. It's in the usual place, under the seat on the adjutant's truck. See it goes off, won't you? Tell the major what I did. There might be a medal in it for me. Won't do me a lot of good, but me mum and dad would like it. Might even get in the papers, never have yet. Well, what are you waiting for? Go on, piss off, or you'll leave it too late. Get going.'

He was glad to be left alone as Dicky hurried off after the two sappers.

The Tiger was nearer now. Morris could make out the change in its engine beat as its automatic gearbox adjusted to the changes of terrain. The crash of falling trees was closer, sometimes drowning out the engine noises when two or three fell in swift succession. His side was aching, not much, rather like having a stitch. He hadn't had one since he was a kid. There was an occasional pulsing sensation as well. It sort of tickled, but still there was no pain.

He thrust his hand down into the capacious pocket of his coat. As his hand entered he felt the dampness of the material give way further in to cloying stickiness that he didn't let his thoughts dwell on. His fingers closed around a small hard object. He drew it out, then sought the other two he knew were there.

While he rummaged for them he heard the Tiger's progress slowed by a particularly resilient clump of growth that made the panzer pause to summon up extra effort. Then it was coming on again. Tracer continued to spurt at thirty second intervals, and at last he saw the muzzle flash of the bow machine-gun. It wouldn't be long now.

Using his elbows, Morris eased himself back until he could lean against a piece of rotten fallen trunk. The pulsing in his side was made stronger by the effort and he sensed his vision was blurring, felt consciousness slipping away. A shake, that at last brought the first murmurings of pain, forced him back to full awareness.

Two of the grenades rested in his lap, their weight perceptible through the thick layers of his clothing. The third was gripped tight between locked hands.

'Come on, you ugly great bastard, just you keep coming straight on. We'll see how you like a taste of your own bloody medicine.'

With the back of his hand he wiped dripping water from his eyes, striping himself with his own blood. He went to wipe it from his face, stopping when he realized it didn't matter.

The Tiger was still holding a dead-straight course, never wavering in its pursuit, firing its secondary armament intermittently. Morris jumped as the top tip of a pine swished down beside him. Now the panzer was only the length of the felled tree from him. And he could see it. He could see it!

Thirty feet, twenty-five; the broad, flat frontal armour glistened with drops of water trapped among the crevices of zimmerit covering, blotched with the stains of crushed bark. Twenty feet, and the tracer flicked out again, first to right, then to left, zipping overhead to be lost among the trees. Fifteen feet. He was quite calm, pulling the pin from the first grenade and tossing it awkwardly at the approaching tank.

He didn't follow the flight of the small steel-wrapped lump of hell. Immediately it left his hand he snatched up a second, wrenched out the pin and drew back his arm to throw. Ten feet, and there was a vivid white flash beside the Tiger. Spirals of glaring light flared up and out, wreathing the panzer in smoke.

The tip of the bow gun jerked down, firing continuously, but Morris was below its angle of fire. He launched the second grenade even as the tracks loomed over him.

'Burn, you bugger, burn.'

His voice made a scream as the steel links cruched his feet into the soft earth. Straining to hear above his own screams, some tiny portion of his mind retaining reason and purpose, Morris heard the phosphorus grenade land on the hull, and the clang of a hatch being thrown open; knew a moment's exaltation aś the whole top of the Tiger was bathed in sight-searing flame. Then the tracks were on his body, and he died.

Of course it was Werner who first saw that the dark patch on the forest floor was more than just a rotting length of timber. Luchs was overjoyed.

'That's one of them. That's one of them. Go right over the top of him, Lutz. Right over the top.'

The oberleutnant watched through the thick prisms of a periscope as the body on the ground grew more distinct. Perhaps the man was dead already; but Luchs could wring as much satisfaction from pulping a dead body as a live one. He had a lot to gain revenge for. He still couldn't control the twitching in his eye, and an itching rash had come up on the back of his neck. He watched for any vestige of remaining life. They were almost on top of it before there was movement.

A small dark object flew towards the tank from the upraised arm. The commander was beside himself with rage.

'Bow Gunner, fire, fire, fire! Now! Fire!'

Brilliant light streamed in through every vision slit and periscope as an incendiary grenade ignited and rolled down their armour. Mercifully it didn't stick. The loader hit the extractor fan switch an instant before the first choking fumes seeped in. From the front compartment came the non-stop chatter of the bow gun.

There was a tinge of panic in a voice that came through over their headphones. 'I can't reach him, he's . . .'

The sentence wasn't half finished before Luchs was throwing open his hatch, pushing the machine-pistol out before him. The oberleutnant heard the terrible scream and sensed, rather than felt, the great mass of the Tiger ride up slightly as it crawled on to the body. Then another of the little black things was rolling in lazy circles on the hull top in front of the turret.

There was no time for a half-formed curse that never passed his lips; no time to duck or even shield his eyes. The glare of the exploding grenade was the last thing Luchs saw, but not the last he felt. As the skin of his hands and face peeled off he tumbled back down, his sleeves brushing pools of the burning chemical that had splashed on to the turret and dragging some of it back inside with him.

'Get the extinguisher!'

'He's on fire.'

'What's happening? What's happening?'

A lot of noise, sounds of violent movement, shouted orders and contradictions. Luchs registered the confusion, realized how thin was the veneer of self-control his firm hand imposed on his crew. They're like headless chickens, he thought. Then he was occupied in fighting for his own control as he tried to open his eyes, found they were open, and it came to him that he was blind. It took an effort to stop from screaming. It had nothing to do with his burns.

They had stopped. The crewmen up front kept calling over the intercom, trying to find out what was happening, fearful of being left behind, and of making a bale-out too late.

Someone tore Luchs's jacket from him, and the pin pricks of fire burning his body and arms ceased. The air was foul and scorching hot.

'Keep going, keep going. We're all right. I'm ordering you to keep going.' The oberleutnant pushed aside hands that tried to tend him. 'I'm ordering you to keep going.'

The burns hurt, but he had known worse. It was the darkness that frightened him. He kept blinking, trying to restore his vision.

Hesitantly, the Tiger began to move, and the movement brought an improvement to the atmosphere in the tank. Breathing became less painful.

'Report damage.'

Until the roughly administered injection that Werner had pumped unbidden into his arm began to work, he had to have a distraction to counter the pain. His duty was his life, that would do.

There was no damage apart from what Luchs had suffered personally. The twenty-six millimetres of armour above their heads, plus the concrete-like paste applied to it, had kept out all but the smoke of the short-lived chemical fire. The Tiger was still fighting fit. It had just suffered a little brain damage; and that had only made it more dangerous.

'How much further?' Dicky was gasping for breath as he stumbled along, tripping in the dark over every projecting root and stump. He was trying hard not to, as every harsh movement wrenched a groan from Eric.

'The stream's just ahead. What the hell's that? Has he got it?'

Rippling, waving shadows pulsed past them, coming from an intense source of white light back along the route they had come. A long burst of automatic fire stopped abruptly as a second wave washed past, brighter than the first.

Without breaking pace, Pitt and Bird snatched glances back over their shoulders to try to see what was going on. Then the stream was in front of them and they had to stop. Now it was more swollen than before, an occasional surge making it lap over the banks. It carried along with it uprooted saplings and rafts of molding leaves that broke up and sank, to be churned over by the tumbling brown water even as they came into sight.

'Where's the bridge? It should be there.'

'There it is.'

Alex pointed out the partially submerged structure just in time for them both to see one of its components carried away by the flood, leaving only the two outer logs precariously maintaining their hold on the fast-disintegrating bank.

As they carried Eric towards it, neither of them noticed a mud-plastered figure huddled beneath a holly bush. Nor did that sodden heap acknowledge or even see the bedraggled group of tired and wounded men who shuffled past him. The pathetic thing that Sergeant Ellis had become just sat, hugging something beneath his coat, trying to ignore the world and put off the moment when he would be able to hide from it no longer. He cocked his head on one side, catching the distant drone of the Tiger's approach.

The small group passed from his sight further along the stream, beyond some bushes. The sergeant shoved a hand into his pocket and drew out the familiar object on which it fastened. Without so much as a glance he threw it into the swirling torrent. He grinned; not the grin of a happy man, or a man pleased with something done, or thought or remembered. It was the only outward expression of a single fixed idea, adopted part out of some half-understood determination and half out of desperation.

Alex sat with his legs dangling in the fast moving water, straddling the log he had picked as the most secure. He inched along it until he was within reach of the far bank. He steadied himself, wrapped his legs as tightly as he could about his uncertain perch, and reached out to get a grip on Eric.

Dicky leaned out as far as possible, pushing the sapper before him towards the outstretched arms of his friend. Eric was too weak to offer more than feeble, token assistance.

'Push him further. Further, damn you. I can't reach him.'

'If I push any more we'll both be in.'

'Push, damn you, push.'

Alex succeeded in hooking a finger through Eric's top buttonhole and started to pull. Some large pieces of debris, unseen beneath the dark agitated surface, brushed against the log, and it moved.

Dicky hurled himself forward to land on Eric as he started to slip off, pinning him to the rough wood. Alex lost his grip on the log and disappeared beneath the turbulence. He kept just that one fingertip hold on Eric's coat. It was enough. He lunged forward against the current, putting everything into the attempt. He managed to get one arm about the trunk. The log sagged lower, but held.

Most of the bridge's length was under water now. Dicky had to risk letting go with one hand to support Eric's chin above the flow.

The Tiger was very close. As the three men struggled to cross the swollen stream, its engine note came to them above the slap and splash of the water that battered at them. Mud-caked, numbed to immobility, the exhausted soldiers could only lie

188

on the far bank and wait for the arrival of the persistent panzer crew. There could be no more running now. The hunt was nearly over.

'There they are. Shall I finish them?'

Luchs began to stand, to look through the periscope, before he remembered there was no point. He groped for the machine-pistol.

'Where are they, and how many of them?'

'There are three of them. They're on the far side of a stream, and they're not moving.'

Luch considered Werner's answer. 'Weapons?'

'I can't see any, Herr Oberleutnant. They look exhausted, like they don't have any fight left in them.'

The oberleutnant's questing hand found the machine-pistol. It felt rough, crusted and pitted by the burning chemical spat from the grenade. He didn't need to be able to see it to check it. It was still in good order. He groped for a spare magazine and put it in his pocket. His eyes registered nothing, not even degrees of darkness, just the pitch black of total blindness. He had such a lot to exact revenge for.

'Drive up to the edge of the stream, directly opposite them.'

As the Tiger lurched forward, Luchs felt the tracks slip, noticed the fractional course correction the driver applied to compensate and bring them into position. He released the MP 38's magazine, ran his thumb along the top of it to check it was full, replaced it and cocked the weapon. The mechanism worked smoothly. With a slight jerk, the Tiger stopped and the engine note died to a whisper.

'We are in position, Oberleutnant.'

'Thank you, Lutz. Werner, open the hatch. I have some business to attend to. Now!' He had sensed a moment's hesitation. He wondered if he would have if he had still had his sight.

The surge of cool clean air felt good. There was rain in it but it was untainted. Feeling for his holds, pushing away a helping hand, he eased himself up until he was standing half out of the turret, orientating himself by feeling for familiar projections. His fingers dipped into the opening of the mine thrower, and quickly withdrew. The short barrel set into the roof was filled with something pulpy and unpleasant. Luchs spoke quietly into his microphone.

'What are they doing now?'

It was Lutz who spoke. 'They are still in front of us on the ground, a tank length away, dead ahead.'

'A very good choice of phrase, Lutz.'

Oberleutnant Luchs brought the machine-pistol to the firing position at his hip. He hesitated before his finger sought the trigger, savouring the moment.

There was a sound behind him. There was an instant's confusion in his mind, then there was no mind at all.

Eric opened his eyes, woken by the cold that brought a merciful, if temporary, relief from the throbbing in his leg. The first thing that met his eyes was the Tiger, only the width of the stream away. A hatch swung open and a figure rose into view. He watched uncomprehending as it seemed to grope about the turret roof, recoiling for a moment from some contact, then turned to face them, bringing a submachine-gun to bear. Either side of him, Alex and Dicky were trying to rise, to drag themselves and him to cover. They hadn't the strength, collapsing back into the mud. Alex reached out to his friend.

'This is it, mate. I don't think the buggers are taking prisoners.'

He gripped Eric's arm, closing his eyes to await the impacts that would bring an end to the nightmare they were living. He opened them again at an exclamation from Dicky.

Another figure stood on the engine deck behind the Tiger's turret, its arms were upraised, holding something above its head. The man at the hatch half turned, and the standing figure whiplashed down and smashed its load on to the armoured hull.

Ellis was torn to shreds by the explosion. The mine he pounded on to the tank's thinnest armour blasted a hole right through it to break open the engine cylinders, exposing the hot metal and puncturing a fuel tank.

Luchs was slashed in half and gobs of raw meat swept forward across the stream. Flame spouted from the open turret and boiled from the gaping hole in the engine covers.

Dicky looked at the gruesome mess that adhered to him, scraped the worst of it off with a handful of wet grass. Alex raised himself to a sitting position, felt in his jacket for a sliver of dull metal. As he got ready to lift Eric again, he flipped it towards the pyre.

'All square now, mate.'

Getting to their feet took time and effort, but they made it.

They moved off, very slowly. There was a long way to go, but there was a chance, just a chance, that they might make it.

Red tongues pushed thick black smoke from every opening in the Tiger. Part hidden by the mass of fire playing across the engine deck lay a mutilated body. Still visible on it were garish daubs of red and garnishes of discoloured tissue.

The fire grew hotter and flares began to ignite inside the turret. The driver's hatch clanged open and something was flung out. As it left the blistered hand, the tank's main ammunition detonated and the Tiger was gutted by an explosion that made the huge machine jump forward to overhang the stream. Burning fuel danced on the water, dribbling from cracks in the distorted plates. They caught up to a bobbing object snared by some exposed roots and flared about it until the flames were drowned and the scorched flask swept from sight.

The kitten sat at a puddle's edge. It rose unsteadily, shook itself, sat, and began to lick its singed flanks. The light played over its orange stripes, casting a huge shadow behind it.